ÂF489877

BOOKS BY COLLIN R. SKOCIK

DREAMS OF THE STARS
THE FUTURE LIVES!
THE SUNBURST FIRE
VOYAGE INTO THE UNKNOWN: VOLUME ONE
VOYAGE INTO THE UNKNOWN: VOLUME TWO
VOYAGE INTO THE UNKNOWN: VOLUME THREE
VOYAGE INTO THE UNKNOWN: VOLUME FOUR
VOYAGE INTO THE UNKNOWN: VOLUME FIVE
VOYAGE INTO THE UNKNOWN: VOLUME SIX
VOYAGE INTO THE UNKNOWN
VOYAGE INTO THE UNKNOWN 2: THE VICTORY OF MORDRAX
VOYAGE INTO THE UNKNOWN 3: BACK FROM THE FUTURE
VOYAGE INTO THE UNKNOWN 4: A FOND FAREWELL
VOYAGE INTO THE UNKNOWN 5: THE NEW BEGINNING
VOYAGE INTO THE UNKNOWN 6: THE MIND MACHINE
VOYAGE INTO THE UNKNOWN 7: PASSAGE TO HYRON
VOYAGE INTO THE UNKNOWN 8: THE REIGN OF EDMONDS
VOYAGE INTO THE UNKNOWN 9: THE KROTUS HORROR
VOYAGE INTO THE UNKNOWN 10: THE THERMIAN MENACE
THE PRIEST MONSTER
UNEASY ALLIANCE
"THAT'S WHAT THEY WANT YOU TO BELIEVE"
COUNTDOWN TO WAR
VOYAGE INTO THE UNKNOWN 11: THE ARMAGEDDON STRATEGY
A GALAXY IN RUIN
LOVED AND LOST
TO CONQUER THE DREB
VOYAGE INTO THE UNKNOWN 12: RESURRECTION
REPERCUSSIONS
A STATION DIVIDED
THE THERMIAN DESTINY
VOYAGE INTO THE UNKNOWN 13: REVELATION
THE LAST OF ZACH MORTIMER
THE FLAMES OF REBELLION

VOYAGE INTO THE UNKNOWN

STATION POST ONE
THE FLAMES OF REBELLION

Collin R. Skocik

Cover art: Jonathan R. Skocik

Visit the author's website at
https://www.deviantart.com/voyageintotheunknown/gallery/51355952/bookstore

VOYAGE INTO THE UNKNOWN
STATION POST ONE

THE FLAMES OF REBELLION

CONTENTS

Prologue: Zach Mortimer's Parting Message

It was not easy to usher the Sev in a group from the brig. They shouted and shook fists and some tried to make a break for it. Additional security was on hand to keep them from escaping. Butch McCrae resisted firing his sidearm at the ceiling; he didn't want to do any damage, and firing on stun wouldn't make a satisfactory noise.

"Listen up! Everybody, I want you all to calm down. I'm going to take you down to Dock Deck One, transfer you over to the *Phoenix*, and you're going to be taken back to Fantasia!"

Someone shouted, "We don't want help from you!"

"Well, I don't care! I've got my orders! You're going to get our help whether you want it or not! Now all of you calm down or we're going to have to start stunning people, okay?"

"Excuse me, Butch?"

Butch turned at the unexpected voice of Dr. Ebor DuBois.

"Can I have a word with them?"

"We're a little busy right now, Ebor!"

"I think I can calm them down."

"*I'm* the Chief of Civilian Security, I—"

"Please. Can I just have a private word with Arnold Livingston?"

"All right, all right..." Butch raised his hands to the mob and bellowed, "Okay! Can we have Arnold Livingston here? Ebor DuBois wants a private word with you, okay?"

Livingston stepped from the crowd, a tall, big-nosed man with unnaturally pallid skin.

Butch stepped aside, shaking his head. "Aw, Jesus."

"Okay, everyone, please," DuBois said.

"Calm down, everyone," Livingston said. "Let me just have a word with Dr. DuBois."

His words worked magic. The shouting and threatening stopped, and the group stood—their expressions angry but their manners calm.

"What is it?" Livingston asked.

"In the corner please." DuBois pulled the pale man into the corner, out of Butch's earshot. "I have a message for you from Zach Mortimer."

Livingston cocked his head. "Excuse me?" It was impossible; Zach Mortimer had been executed.

"Yes." DuBois held up a digifile and pressed "Play."

The voice of Zach Mortimer sounded. "My people, this is Fweery. I'm alive and well and on Zelnor on one of the Sev life ships. I'm looking forward to many happy years with my family, just as I'm looking forward to your fulfillment and happiness. What happened on Station Post One should be a learning experience for everyone, humans and Sev. Do not be angry. No one has died. But even had I died, it would have been for a good cause. You must carry on now. You have the knowledge you need. Some of you carry the Sev gene. The gene will endure. The Sev will survive. Oneness is the future of all life. Have faith in that and prosper. You have my best wishes. Good luck."

DuBois lowered the digifile and said, "Go to Fantasia. All's well now."

"How is this possible?" Livingston asked.

"Let's just say that Zach Mortimer found a way."

Livingston returned to his followers and announced, "My people, we will go to Fantasia and we will cooperate with the humans."

DuBois tapped Butch on the shoulder. "I don't think you'll have any more trouble, Butch."

To Whom the President Bows

The worst part of being a prisoner was usually the boredom. Elmer Tepper remembered that well enough from his incarceration on Finneus Prime.

Now he was once again in the hands of the Darians, but this wasn't an old school converted into a military base, like the Darian outpost where he had been confined before. No, now he was on board the Darian Central Space Station, the fairest approximation of Tepper's own personal hell that he could imagine.

It wasn't that he was being tortured—physically, at least—or that the Darians were even conscious of the torment through which they were putting him. And their casual indifference was as infuriating as any other aspect of his incarceration.

The problem was that this space station was so *organic*. He felt as though he had been swallowed by some impossible space monster from Butch McCrae's collection of classic twentieth century space opera.

The walls, the floor, the ceiling, they rippled and moved with hissing, breathy sounds. The station itself seemed alive—as alive as the Darians themselves were becoming.

No longer a soulless army of killer robots with bronze bodies and vent faces, the Darians had now mimicked human bodies—specifically *his* body—and enhanced themselves through the use of nanotechnology.

This station itself was made of billions of tiny robots, each of them a Darian in its own right. His impression that he was inside a giant organism was almost literally true.

On the plus side, since he had no toilet and had no choice but just to go in the corner, the station somehow cleaned up for him, leaving no trace of urine or feces—or of their odor.

He tried to lie in his bunk and to ignore it. He had been taught many tricks to avoid losing emotional control in high-stress situations, and those tricks worked for a while. But no matter how long he practiced those techniques—doing sit-ups, closing his eyes and reciting regulations, singing—in the end he was always here, in this dark and fluid cell. And he had no idea how long he would be here, and was losing track of how long he had already been here.

He tried to pray, all his pent-up emotion pouring out in a burst of tears. "Dear God…What did I do wrong? Why have You made such a mess of my life? It's not enough for You that the entire Darian Empire has to be made over in my image, but now I have to be their prisoner here in this…in this *thing!* And I have no idea if they're going to put those nanites in me again to turn me into one of them. I've always tried to be a good person. Maybe I don't always know what I'm doing, but I've always tried. Why are You doing everything in Your power to turn me into a *bad* person?!"

The heartfelt burst of sheer emotion left him numb for a time.

Sometimes he tried to engage the Darians directly—usually with a heavy dose of sarcasm.

"Good morning, Tepper. Good morning, Tepper. Where are the Teppers? Come on, let's all keep each other company!"

But as isolated and alone as he was here, he might as well be the only man in the universe. That being the case, why *shouldn't* there be a thousand of him out there?

At last, he was wrenched from a deep sleep by a slap across the face.

"Wake up," his own voice said.

He looked up and saw his own face staring down at him. It was *him*, Elmer Tepper…the thick, black, curly hair, the light brown skin, the well-trimmed mustache—but no soul in the eyes. It had his face and his voice, but none of his depth. It was one of the Darian human styrotypes. A being modeled on the data they had extracted back on Finneus Prime—from *him*.

"Well, well, well," Tepper said, blinking away his grogginess. "What a pretty face you've got."

"H.S. #2001 wishes to see you. Come with me."

Well, anything to get out of his cell. Tepper got up, self-conscious of his body odor and bad breath, and followed. It was nice to stretch his legs again, even if he was walking through the phantasmagorical, living environment of this undulating, convulsing station.

H.S. #2001's office was stable and well-lit, looking like one of the old Darian control centers— which it very well might be. Tepper had wondered several times if he could shut this whole place down by destroying the control center, or if the Darians had evolved beyond that Achilles heel. It didn't matter, since they had taken his sidearm.

H.S. #2001 was another Tepper twin. Behind him stood two other Teppers. All stared at Tepper with cold, lifeless eyes.

"Presenting Elmer Tepper," said the Tepper who had come for him.

"Hey, ol' buddy," Tepper said with a broad grin, "there's another familiar face! What's shakin', man?"

The Tepper at the desk folded his hands under his chin and regarded Tepper with a stony expression. "H.S. #898 has not reported any change in his mental processes."

"That is correct," said one of the Teppers behind him. "I remain delinked. I mated with Brandi Taylor, yet I am not aware of any influence by this gene that you spoke so highly of."

Tepper wondered how long he had been confined—how long it had been since H.S. #898 had slept with Brandi Taylor.

"For that reason," H.S. #2001 said, "I must assume that you did lie to us and I must go through on my threat to infect you with our nanites and send you back to Station Post One as a spy."

Tepper's breathing quickened, his heart pounded. "Wait, wait, listen! It takes a while for the gene to take! I remember when Zach Mortimer first mated with Fweery, he didn't start reporting telepathic contact until almost a year later! You've got to give it time."

"You wish to wait almost a year and remain in captivity here?"

"God, no! But—no, look, I'd do anything rather than get infected by those nanites again. All right—you just—you just give it time. Give it time. I don't know how long it's going to take."

"I remain unconvinced of your sincerity; nevertheless, as no adverse effects have been reported, H.S. #898 will remain delinked for one more week, at the end of which time we will observe whether there are indeed deleterious effects or telepathic contact with the being you call Fweery. You will remain in isolation until then. Take him away."

Two Teppers appeared from behind him and gripped his arms. "Wait!" he objected. "Wait, now, look, can't we just—"

"Calm, Elmer Tepper."

"Just let me go! I'm not doing you any harm!" But H.S. #2001 was finished with him and would hear no more objections. It was back to that cell, and this never-ending nightmare, while the Darians pursued their quest for that intangible thing they called "meaning."

———

Cranius steered the TSR *Saviour* rather clumsily into its berth at Dock Deck One, slip two. He wasn't used to this big, unwieldy ship with its controls designed for the crablike Valdor. His rough-skinned, jet-black hands were bigger than human hands, with fatter fingers, and so he had more trouble with the sensitive controls than did humans. He was used to the total automation of the ships of his home planet, Vron, and he was puzzled that the Valdor had designed vessels requiring so much manual control.

But he managed to dock, and with considerable help from the flight crews, attached the mooring lines, power umbilicals, and pressure snake. He powered down, opened the outer hatch, and stepped through the pressure snake into Station Post One.

His conscience bothered him as he made his way from Dock Deck One to the Civilian Hab where President Damon Kramer awaited him. Kramer was his friend, and he'd lied to him.

He took a deep breath—a breath that never seemed quite enough in the oxygen-poor human environment—and buzzed the doorchime on the Presidential Pod's door.

The door hissed open to admit him,

Damon Kramer was at his desk, as usual, reviewing agenda items on his realscreen. "Cranius. Good to see you. How did things go on Vron?"

In fact, Cranius had not been to Vron; he had been illicitely transporting Zach Mortimer to Zelnor—Zach Mortimer, who had been condemned to death for treason and secretly saved by Dr. Ebor DuBois. Cranius was not a good liar.

"The meeting with President Lyskia is arranged," Cranius said. "You're expected to arrive at Growron Spaceport at planet dawn on Krad second—that would be a week from today."

"Yes, I confirmed that with President Lyskia," Kramer said. "I also confirmed that you were never on Vron."

Cranius felt his skin go cold.

"Want to tell me what's going on?" Kramer said.

"Sprog," Cranius swore. "Mr. President, all right, I didn't return to Vron. I was on a mission of a personal nature."

"I authorized you to take one of our two scoutships on a special mission on my behalf. Now, I have no problem if you want to go on any kind of a personal mission, but it has to be arranged so as not to conflict with any of the activities of the *Frontier*, the *Saviour*, or the *Phoenix*."

"All right, I understand."

Kramer relaxed and said conversationally, "So, what kind of personal business was this anyway?"

"Well, it was personal," Cranius said defensively.

"All right, all right. That'll be all."

Cranius left, his right eye twitching as it always did when he felt guilty.

———

"No incidents during the trip," Captain Andrei Petrov said, "except that the people are convinced that Mortimer has risen from the dead."

Commander Tobey Dingell stared in disbelief at the realscreen image of Captain Petrov, who sat on the bridge of the Space Star *Phoenix*, freshly back from his mission to take the Sev prisoners back to their colony world of Fantasia.

"All right, thanks, Andrei." Tobey clicked off the transmitter, his mind haunted by the strange coincidence that Zach Mortimer's body had gone missing. "Ebor, you have any luck locating that body?"

Dr. Ebor DuBois looked pale. "No, no, I…"

"Any chance the Sev might have taken it?"

DuBois shrugged. "Possible, I suppose. Hard to see how."

———

Every day, Burt Kaisman transmitted his three-hour news and talk flatscreen show from the SSBC studios in Station Post One's Civilian Hab, and his ratings were soaring. The people loved his suave British accent and his biting wit, and his opinions had begun to sway public discourse, which delighted him immensely.

"Good afternoon," he said as his thundering theme music died away. "Welcome to *Kaisman and Friends*. I'm Burt Kaisman, here with Derek Winchester and Shellie Hurlburt. And today we look at the aftermath of the execution of state traitor Zach Mortimer. And his Sev followers believe," Kaisman chuckled condescendingly, "that he has risen from the dead."

Derek Winchester and Shellie Hurlburt laughed along with him, rolling their eyes.

Winchester spoke in the Jamaican accent that female viewers found adorable. "The real danger here, Burt, is that now Mortimer is a martyr to the Sev Army. They rally around this belief that he has risen from the dead and use that—"

"I understand what you're saying," Kaisman interrupted, "but it's absurd. This claim can have no validity unless Mortimer actually takes the lead of their army."

"Burt, the fact that they have a martyr may make them even more dangerous."

"More fanatical, you mean," Kaisman said.

Shellie Hurlburt said in her high-pitched, screeching voice, "Yeah! Yes! More fanatical, and now they have the ability to put whatever words they want into Mortimer's mouth because he's not around anymore to deny it!"

"And he did deny a lot of their activities—"

"Some of them," Winchester said.

"He pretended to preach a message of peace."

"Well, to a certain extent, although he came out in his trial and admitted that he wanted to spread the Sev gene throughout the entire human race."

"Yes, but now his followers could claim, 'Zach Mortimer ordered us to destroy Station Post One,' for example."

"Or to take and kill hostages!" Shellie screeched. "Which Arnold Livingston has already done! And now he's in charge of the Sev Army!"

"Well, changing subjects," Kaisman said, "'President' Kramer is planning on making a visit to Vron in order to meet personally with President Lyskia. Once again we see him allying himself with those who are determined to *prevent* the Valdor from fighting the Thermians."

"Yes! Yes!" Shellie squealed. "It's outrageous! It's just another example of Damon Kramer's aliens first policy!"

"This is not a big surprise," Winchester said with a chuckle. "Damon Kramer has had a close relationship with the Vron ever since we first encountered them. This probably goes back to the fact that he was rescued by a Vron back on the planet Chiana after that first disastrous attempt to make contact with a Thermian."

"One would have thought that that disastrous attempt would convince him that there is no reasoning with the Thermians," Kaisman said with a smug smile, "but an ideologue never allows reality to trump his beliefs. So what kind of an agreement will he make with President Lyskia?"

"I think we're going to see him making a show of condemning Vron activities against the Valdor," Winchester said in a reasonable tone, "but in the long run, he will seek to get the Centralized Committee to recognize the legitimacy of Vron's complaints."

"Derek, you and I are in agreement."

———

"We have word from President Frodax of Hyron," Chief Engineer Jerome Flynn said.

Commander Dingell had no desire to speak to the psychotic President of the Hyron Supreme Council, but he kept his moaning to himself and asked, "All right, what's he got to say?"

"It's just a written warning that the human race and all other Republic members who stand against Drayonne's readmission into the Hyron Empire are frozen out of Hyron affairs."

As Flynn spoke, the doors to the Prime Hab Center opened and admitted Butch McCrae, the Chief of Civilian Security. "Uh, Commander?"

"What do you want, Butch?"

"How long has it been since we've heard from Tepper?"

"It's been a week and two days now," Tobey said with a sigh.

"How long before we do something about it?"

"Let's just hold off and wait."

"There's no telling what's going on in that station—"

"I don't have time for this right now!" Tobey snapped.

———

On the bridge of the Space Star *Phoenix*, Captain Andrei Petrov stood over the helm console, watching the data on Reve Ruchinsky's screen. Behind him, the President and his Vron chief of staff stood next to the command chair. He hated when his passengers loitered on the bridge, but he couldn't very well order the President of the Unified Republic away.

"All right, get me to Vron," President Kramer ordered.

"Yes, sir," Pretrov said. To Ruchinsky, he ordered, "Set course for Vron."

"Yes, sir." Ruchinsky played his fingers across the screen, the curving lines moving and numbers flicking by while he sought the optimal course. "Course plotted, laid in. It is a four-day course at light speed factor eight."

Petrov sat in his command chair. "Very well. Ahead light speed factor eight."

"Yes, sir. Factor eight."

Petrov heard the engines roaring to life, felt the vibration through the ship's structure. Then the main screen shifted from a camera view of the space outside Station Post One to a computer-simulated view of the stars.

"We have light speed factor eight," Ruchinsky said. "Engines operating full capacity. Gravity propulsion system under control. Drive field seven-one-four-zero-six. Reactors two-six-zero-one. Coolant systems full power. Manual Generator System operational, deviation two-six-one. EGI rate three-four-seven. G-32 monitors fourteen. Course shows no impediments. ETA is three days, eighteen hours, fourteen minutes."

"Thank you," Petrov said.

"We're on course, Mr. President," said First Officer Elizabeth Chapman.

"Thank you," Kramer said.

Petrov hoped that would be their signal to get off the bridge, but Kramer remained standing there, his arms crossed over his chest, staring at the main screen, while Cranius drummed his fingers on the back of Petrov's chair, driving him crazy.

———

Tobey found Dr. Ebor DuBois in his cubicle in the Wheel, the huge ring around the Prime Hab which was used as the science section.

"Butch tells me that *you* delivered the recording to Arnold Livingston that convinced the Sev that Mortimer had risen from the dead."

DuBois did not look up from his terminal. "Well, that's ridiculous," he mumbled. DuBois was not a very good liar.

"Is it?" Tobey pressed. "You've been so goddamned evasive every time I ask you about the whereabouts of Mortimer's body."

DuBois looked up from his work with a sigh. "Look, I don't know the whereabouts of Mortimer's goddamned body."

"What exactly did you say to Arnold Livingston? What was in that message that you delivered?"

"Look, it was just an old message from Mortimer reminding them to be peaceful and stuff like that."

"Do you mind if I listen to the recording?"

DuBois's attention returned to his work. "Well, I don't have it anymore."

"What do you mean you don't have it anymore?"

"Once I delivered it, I deleted it."

Tobey did not believe him. "You didn't think it would be a little bit important for us to listen to it? It's got to be in the computer bank somewhere."

"It was just a last message he wanted conveyed to his people. I didn't think it was that important."

"Well, Ebor, I'd like to believe you, but this whole matter of the missing body—"

"Either charge me with something or leave me alone."

"Ebor!"

DuBois swallowed, cleared his throat, and said, "I'm just tired of hearing about it."

Tobey stared at him aghast. "Go to your privacy pod. You're relieved of all duties."

DuBois stared at him. He appeared to be about to argue, but he saved his data, shut off his terminal, and left.

Tobey left the Wheel, headed for the Prime Hab Center, then changed his mind. He rode the elevator to level five, headed around the winding corridor and went through the Manway into the Civilian Hab. He crossed through the maze-like corridors to the security section, where Butch McCrae sat at his desk.

"Ebor DuBois is under suspicion of treason."

Butch gaped at him. "You've got to be kidding me!"

"You yourself heard him deliver that message to Arnold Livingston."

"Yeah, but isn't *treason* a little bit much?"

"I hope he's not guilty, but I'm opening an investigation as to his complicity in perhaps aiding and abetting Zach Mortimer's escape."

Butch scoffed. "Come on! We all witnessed Mortimer being put to death."

"Ebor has the scientific and biological knowledge to counteract the lethal injection."

"All right, but look…I'm going to ask permission to take the *Saviour* out to go to the Darian Central Space Station and rescue Tepper."

"No."

"It's been a week! It's *way* past time—"

"You fucking hear me?!" Tobey raged. "My answer was *no!* We've got too much going on here! My chief scientist is under suspicion of treason, the Hyron fleet might be amassing to attack us as soon as they're done with Drayonne, and I'm *not* provoking a confrontation with the Darian Empire! We wait for news on Tepper. I need you here."

Butch's face had turned to stone. He didn't offer a "yes, sir," and Tobey was afraid to demand one, considering Butch's tendency to go rogue. Tobey could only pray that Butch obeyed orders, did his job, and stayed on the Station. He turned and left.

———

The *Phoenix* emerged from light speed. Right on cue, President Kramer and Cranius arrived on the bridge. Reve Ruchinsky and Strom Gielgud grinned at each other, since Petrov had predicted their arrival.

"Secure from light speed," Ruchinsky said. "Vron dead ahead."

"Registering several space stations," Elizabeth Chapman said. "I've got a code two-oh-one."

That meant the ship was being scanned. The Vron knew they were here.

"I have space traffic control in the city of Growron," Gielgud said.

Kramer stepped forward. "I'll talk to them."

Petrov gritted his teeth; damn it, the *Captain* was supposed to speak for the ship. But he relented. "Patch him through."

"Transmitting," Gielgud said.

Kramer announced, "Vron space traffic control, this is President Damon Kramer aboard the Space Star *Phoenix.*"

"Greetings, *Phoenix*," replied a voice similar to Cranius's. "We have you on our outer monitors now. Please assume orbit around the planet and stand by for escort to Growron Spaceport."

"Thank you. President Kramer out."

As Ruchinsky burped the slip pods to adjust the orbit, a light blinked on the command intelligence station. Chapman examined the data and said, "Picking up escort ships now. They were standing by in synchronous orbit. They're breaking orbit for plane change."

"We'll reach rendezvous position in half an orbit," Ruchinsky said.

"Let's go, Cranius," Kramer said.

"Right."

Petrov breathed a sigh of relief as they left. The bridge was too small for too many people, and he didn't like a higher-up's eyes scrutinizing him too closely when he was at work. It made him nervous, and when he was nervous he made mistakes.

———

Dock Deck One was darkened for the nocturnal shift. Butch McCrae found only one flight engineer working alone on a QV Fighter. Butch walked casually up to him and asked, "Everything okay in here?"

"Yeah. Why?"

"Somebody said something about a drunk vagrant down here."

"No, not here."

"Okay, maybe it was a prank. Let me know if you need help." He wandered off in the general direction of the elevator, waited for the tech's attention to return to the fighter.

When he was sure the tech was no longer interested in him, he ducked into the shadows and ran for the pressure snake. Luckily the tech neither saw nor heard him, and he ducked into the pressure snake without attracting attention.

Nevertheless he was cautious as he entered the *Saviour*. It was possible someone was in here doing maintenance. There was no one in the lounge, and no sign of activity; that was encouraging. He went aft, down a short corridor, and peered down into the engine room. Empty. Good; if there was maintenance being done, it would most certainly be in there. He went forward, through the lounge, and into the cockpit. He switched to internal power and listened for the hum of the reactors. Then he reached for the tab that would detach the power umbilicals, when a voice stopped him.

"Hold it there!" A panel under the console opened. "You're not taking off while I'm still aboard."

It was Jerome Flynn, decked out in engineering overalls, a maintenance kit slung over his shoulder, and a sidearm in his hand.

Butch dropped his hands from the console. "Aren't you here a little after shift?"

"A little problem with the navigation computer."

"Uh-huh. Well, get the sidearm out of my face. I'll go quietly."

———

Tobey Dingell was always in an ugly mood nowadays. Being pulled out of bed in the middle of the night to learn of yet another dereliction by Butch McCrae was bound to blacken his mood still further.

"He was powering up the *Saviour*," Flynn said, "apparently to take it out without clearance."

"All right, thank you, Flynn. That's all."

"Yes, sir." Flynn turned and left, thankful he wasn't the one Tobey was mad at.

Tobey stood and faced Butch, his eyes aflame. "Butch—"

"You can't expect me to stand by while my friend is missing, possibly being tortured, executed, or who knows what."

"I'm very disappointed that you're falling back into the erratic behavior you displayed last year. If I can't trust you, I can't use you. Now, you have a choice: you can be a team player, obey my orders, and abide by Station Post One policy, or you can go off chasing after Tepper. You can take a refugee ship to Fantasia and pick up your ship, the *Beethoven*. But if you leave this time, you're not coming back. Say the word."

Butch stood, stewing, mulling over two unpalatable choices. Finally he snarled, "What are we going to do about Tepper? How long are we going to wait?"

Tobey sat down, stared at his desk for a moment, then said, "All right. This is classified information. We have a secret agreement with the Throrb to extract Tepper."

"The *Throrb?!*" Butch was appalled.

"They've got no fondness for the Darians. That's our backup plan. As for how long we're going to wait, the Throrb asteroid Laroob will be in striking range of the Darian Central Space Station in three days. If we haven't heard from Tepper by then, we'll activate plan B. You happy now?"

"Yeah," Butch said, chagrined. "Yeah, I'm happy now."

"Staying or going?"

"Staying." Butch paused, then added, "Sorry."

———

President Lyskia was the lightest-colored Vron that Kramer had ever seen. Cranius was as black as deep space, and all other Vron he had seen were just as jet-black. Some of the lighter-skinned ones were about the shade of Earth's ancient Aborigines. Lyskia was so light he was merely a dark gray. Cranius had explained that Lyskia had an unusual cellular condition called *zephillibret,* which caused light skin tone and hermaphroditic sexual organs.

In Lyskia's case, the dominant sexual organs were male, and so he was considered male. But his voice, and his attitude, were decidedly effeminate. He rose on their arrival, clothed in resplendent purple and gold robes. On his head he wore a gold headdress which Cranius had told him honored the Vron gods Wushno and Deemu; although official policy was required to be secular, the Vron did not have strict separation of church and state.

"Welcome to Vron, President Kramer," Lyskia said in a velvety, feminine voice.

"President Lyskia, it's good to meet you in person at last."

"I trust your trip was comfortable."

"Very nice indeed."

"Cranius, welcome back."

Cranius bowed his head. "Thank you, Mr. President."

They stood in the President's office, located at the top of a skyscraper in the capital city of Growron. Despite all the ceremony of Lyskia's clothing, the position was even less glorified than Kramer's; the President of what Cranius always translated as "the Democratic Republic of Vron" was more like the CEO of a company—and indeed, from Cranius's confusing explanations, it was unclear to Kramer whether the government was run by the corporations or if the corporations were run by the government; it seemed a little of both.

The President returned to his seat. "So. What brings you here?"

Kramer and Cranius sat in two of the three chairs facing Lyskia's desk. Kramer said, "The Republic has deep concerns about Vron's activities against the Valdor. We're concerned this could be destabilizing the situation. As a Republic member, Vron's actions could be viewed as an extension of Republic policy. The Republic desires no hostilities with the Valdor."

"Yet the Valdor are blatantly defying Republic policy in regards to the Thermians," Lyskia said. "I would like to reiterate Vron's zero-tolerance policy regarding the use of the Thermian Destroyer."

"I understand that policy, but your actions against the Valdor are not only alienating you from the Republic and casting a negative light on the Republic itself, but your actions result in intrusions in other worlds' sovereign space."

"You speak for the Congressional Council. Are you sure you speak for the Centralized Committee or the Hyron government?"

Kramer almost smiled. "Well, I don't speak for the Hyron government."

"No, of course not. You're at odds with the Hyrons right now, aren't you?"

"Well…as a Republic member, you too are at odds with the Hyrons; at least that's according to your terms of membership. Now, you're a sovereign world; I have no authority over you. I can only express to you the Republic's desires. If my word isn't enough for you, we'll arrange a conference with the Triumvirate Council."

"I appreciate that very much."

―――

"Well, Derek," Burt Kaisman said, "you were right as usual." He spared a wink for the camera. "'President' Kramer has decided to take President Lyskia's arguments before the Triumvirate Council— no doubt to argue on the Vron's behalf."

Derek Winchester chuckled. "Well, he may find that the Centralized Committee is not as receptive to the Vron as he might have thought. After all, the Centralized Committee was originally organized by the Valdor, and they may prove to still have Valdor sympathies."

"Yet they did vote to censure the Valdor."

"Well, that's true. They have to walk a narrow political line between appeasing the various other Republic members and maintaining their own agenda, which has always been fighting the Thermians."

"And! And! And!" Shellie Hurlburt shrieked, "the Centralized Committee is just one-third of the Triumvirate Council, and I don't think the Hyron Supreme Council will be too sympathetic!"

"Good point, Shellie," Kaisman said. "Meanwhile, the investigation into Ebor DuBois' treason. The search continues for the missing message from Zach

Mortimer—*and* Zach Mortimer's body is still missing. Will Dr. DuBois be convicted?"

"This may not even go to trial," Winchester said dismissively. "The trail is ice-cold. Commander Dingell is making a show of investigating one of his own most trusted people in an attempt to prove that he is not a part of Damon Kramer's tyrannical regime."

"Is Commander Dingell trying to distance himself from 'President' Kramer?" Kaisman asked.

"You don't stay with a sinking ship!" Shellie Hurlburt shrieked.

"Yet *could* Commander Dingell be complicit in the disappearance of the final message from Zach Mortimer?"

"Well," Winchester said with a laugh, "I think that's very likely. *If* Zach Mortimer is still alive and has been spirited away—"

"But *not* risen from the dead!" Shellie shrieked. "Only one man in history has ever done that, and it was *not* Zach Mortimer!"

Winchester continued, "—I don't think it's very likely Dr. DuBois could have pulled that off on his own. I think it started at the top, with either Commander Dingell or Damon Kramer or both."

Burt gave a charming grin to the camera before returning his attention to Winchester and Shellie. "If that can be proven, is that the end of the Kramer presidency?"

"Absolutely!" Shellie shrieked. "That would be obstruction of justice! And that is grounds for impeachment!"

———

When two Teppers came to rouse Tepper, his spirits rose; perhaps the Sev gene had finally taken. But then his heart sank; it was apparent from their stoic, cold demeanor that they did not hold the genetic memories of the placid, peaceful Sev.

He allowed himself to be conveyed to H.S. #2001's office.

"There's as yet no evidence that H.S. #898 has benefited in any way from the copulation with Brandi Taylor," H.S. #2001 said in a flat tone.

"Look, I told you!" Tepper's voice shook with frustration. "You've got to give it time!"

"We've given it time. We have been more than patient. We have determined that this was either an attempt to infect us with some sort of nanotech weapon or a stalling technique to lull us into a sense of security while your people mount an attack on us. Therefore a new offensive will begin against the Unified Republic."

"Now, wait!"

"And *you* will be infected with nanites."

Tepper felt his heart stop for a moment; he honestly wondered, for a split second, if he was going to drop dead. "Now, wait!"

"Proceed," the commandant ordered.

One of the Teppers pointed a device at him.

Though he knew it would do no good, he kept pleading, "Now, wait, wait!" He didn't know how, or even exactly when, the tiny robots entered his body. He supposed he must have breathed them in. Or maybe they entered through his eyes, or his ears, or his pores. But quickly they took effect. His will was subsumed by the all-consuming Darian directives, and the ever-present link to their control center.

"Put him back on the *Frontier*," H.S. #2001 ordered, "and program it for a course to Station Post One."

"As you wish," two Teppers said in unison.

Tepper accompanied them without protest— without *physical* protest, that is.

———

The *Phoenix* was under way again, Vron receding into the all-consuming blackness of space.

The rec room intercom chirped. Kramer wasn't much enjoying his dinner anyway, so he seized on the excuse to push his plate aside and get up. "Excuse me, Cranius."

"Sure, sure," Cranius said as he continued to shovel his black and gray spaghetti-like Vron stuff into his mouth.

"Kramer here."

"This is Petrov. Two Darian warships approaching."

"Damn!"

"Gielgud picked up the bogey five minutes ago. I stepped up to level two, we ran all the proper checks, manned fighters and gun turrets, and then auto-det-id confirmed the warships' identity. I am launching fighters now."

"Thank you. Give me updates when and only when you have the time. Kramer out."

He returned to the table.

"What's going on?" Cranius asked with his mouth full.

"We're under attack. Darians. That means Vron will probably be attacked too."

"I'm sure space traffic control has picked it up and notified the President."

Kramer looked up at the ceiling as though he could see the battle out there. "As if that'll do any good."

Unappetizing though it was, Kramer went back to his meal. There was no better way of taking his mind off the battle raging outside. The ship shuddered. Alarms sounded. Bootsteps thumped outside the door and above. Several times there were shattering crashes that sounded like the whole ship was ripping apart.

As much to make conversation as anything, Kramer asked, "When I assigned you to take the *Saviour* to Vron to arrange this visit with President Lyskia...where did you go? Really?"

Cranius looked uncomfortable. "Look...I was helping out a friend...and...I'm trying to keep a friend's secret. I felt bad about deceiving you—"

"Don't misunderstand me, Cranius. I'm not angry with you. It's just that I've always felt I could trust you. And I'm not sure I can trust you anymore."

"You can," Cranius moaned. "I'm sorry."

"You're an important contact with the Vron—and more than that, you're my friend. That's the reason I sent you on that mission. Couldn't you confide in me?"

Cranius shook his head. "I just couldn't. And I still can't. Would you trust me if you knew I was the kind of person who would betray another friend's secret?"

Kramer accepted that answer. He was about to say so when the intercom chirped.

"Kramer here."

"This is Petrov. The Darians made several kamikaze attacks on the *Phoenix*; most were shot down, but one made impact on deck seven. The outer hull was breached, but the inner held. Fire in chem lab. Toxic atmosphere warning in upper level of landing bay. But then something fired on the Darians, a beam of energy, lots of x-rays and hard radiation. A fusion beam, I think. Both warships were quickly disabled and then destroyed. We're trying to determine what kind of beam it was."

Kramer raised his eyebrows, impressed. "Thank you, Captain Petrov." He turned from the intercom and looked at Cranius. "Any idea what came to the rescue?"

Cranius beamed. "The Larinax Defense Station!"

"And what's that?"

"The Larinax Defense Station is a military base on Larinax, one of the moons of Gongan, a gas giant in our outer system. The base there is top secret and requires a top secret code given by the President in order for it to open fire."

Kramer laughed with relief. "The cavalry arrives!"

"Mr. President," Petrov's voice said over the intercom.

"Yes. Yes, Andrei?"

"There are still a lot of Darian fighters out there. Should we offer them the chance to surrender?"

Kramer thought it over. A lifetime of ethics told him to give the enemy a chance to surrender…but these were Darians. He had to be practical no matter how much it bothered his conscience. "No. We can't allow any of those nanotech devices on board. Just get us out of here."

———

Tobey could barely believe his eyes when he saw the shape of the vessel that emerged from light speed off the Station. It was the *Frontier*.

A familiar voice sounded: "Station Post One, this is Elmer Tepper requesting docking instructions."

"*Frontier* returning," Flynn said, "it's Tepper! He's requesting permission to dock."

"Tepper, this is Commander Dingell. How'd things go? Did you drop off Brandi Taylor?"

"I did," Tepper replied. "Copulation went off as planned."

"Any change in the Darians?"

"Well, as you know, it takes time, so it's really too early to say."

"Grant docking clearance?" Flynn asked.

"Tepper, stand by." Tobey silenced the transmitter. "Hold on landing clearance, Flynn." He hit the intercom tab. "Butch McCrae to PHC."

Butch's reply was immediate: "On my way."

A few minutes of silence followed, broken by Tepper's voice: "Station Post One, this is Elmer Tepper. I'm still standing by. Do I have docking clearance?"

"Stand by, Tepper," Tobey said, "just gotta work something out here."

"Marked."

It took Butch McCrae ten minutes to walk the winding corridors and staircases from his office in the Civlian Hab to the Prime Hab Center. "Commander," he said as he entered.

"Tepper's back," Tobey told him.

Butch's expression lit up. "Oh! Great!"

"*Frontier*'s asking for permission to dock, but Butch, listen—he was out there on the Darian Central Space Station, he sounds a little strange to me; I just want to—I want you to hear the sound of him. I want you to let me know if you think he's infected with Darian nanites."

Butch's expression of glee had turned to a more typical scowl. "All right." He stepped up to the command desk and hit the transmit tab. "Hey, Tepper, it's Butch. How's it going?"

"Butch!" Tepper's voice answered. "How's she flying?"

Butch shrugged and said to Tobey, "Sounds okay to me." Returning to the transmitter, he asked, "How'd everything go out there?"

"The operation was a success. Brandi Taylor was delivered. Copulation was completed as scheduled."

Butch muttered, "Now *that* doesn't sound so okay." He thought for the moment, then asked, "So, were the Darians infected with the killer robots?"

"Come on, Butch, quit kidding around."

Tobey pulled Butch aside. "Butch, Butch…if he is infected with Darian nanites, then he's linked with the rest of the Darian Empire and they know everything he knows about his mission. So it's not like he or any other Darian would be ignorant of it."

Butch shoved his hands in his pockets, looked down at his feet, and nodded, feeling stupid. "Yeah."

"So what do you think, just from listening to him?"

"He does sound awfully strange. I mean, it could be strain; you know, he's been gone two weeks— maybe he went through a rough time. But yeah, he does sound a little off. And he does sound a little like some of the Darian human styrotypes we've encountered."

Tobey sat at the command desk and hit the intercom tab. "Tepper, please stand by."

"Standing by."

"Flynn, order up an intercept squadron."

"Yes, sir."

Butch was alarmed. "Ho, now, you're not going to blow him up or anything, are you?"

"We've got to be prepared for every contingency."

"Remember what happened last time you blew up some of your own men," Butch said tactlessly. "Besides, we can't afford to lose the *Frontier*."

Tobey blew up. "What we can't afford is to let Darian nanites aboard this space station!"

The Station vibrated with the reverberations of fighters bursting from the Dock Decks. The main screen showed the incandescent plumes of plasma engines as the small craft swept toward the incoming *Frontier*.

"Fighters scrambled," Flynn said, "Dock Decks One and Two."

Tepper's voice sounded again. "Station Post One, *Frontier*. Why are you launching fighters?"

"Standard precaution, Tepper," Tobey said. "Please continue to stand by."

"Butch, this is Tepper. Can you read me?"

Butch glanced at Tobey, who indicated the transmitter. Butch stepped up to it and said, "Yeah, Tepper, this is Butch."

"What's going on over there? Don't you trust me?"

Butch glanced at Tobey, who simply shrugged. Taking a deep breath, Butch decided to level with Tepper. "We've just got to take certain precautions. You were in the Darian Empire."

Tobey shoved him aside. "Tepper, this is Commander Dingell. Just continue to stand by."

The alert klaxon sounded. Flynn said, "Two Q-splashes registering. One-eight-four mark seven and minus ninety-four point three. Two Darian warships just emerged from light speed. One four points abaft of the Civilian Hab, the other off the Electronics Hab— now a third, closing from the other side. We're surrounded."

"Set level one!"

"Set level one."

"Scramble all fighters!"

"Scramble all fighters."

"All gunners to gun turrets!"

"All gunners to gun turrets."

"Is there anything I can do?" Butch asked. "I know I haven't got a fighter anymore—"

"Make sure civilians are out of the corridors," Tobey said, "locked in their privacy pods. Seal your grapple shaft and Manways and be prepared to detach from the Station if necessary."

"Right."

As Butch left, Flynn said, "All fighters launched. Darian ships are launching their fighters."

"Order all squadron commanders engage," Tobey ordered.

"All squadron commanders engage."

"Send a high-priority distress signal to all nearby Republic worlds and space stations."

Communications Officer Clio Steele said, "Sending distress signal."

Tobey got up, walked forward and leaned against the rail, looking down at the rows of consoles in the Trench. "Listen, everybody!" He clapped his hands. "Attention, everybody!"

Everyone stopped what they were doing and turned to face him.

"I'm not going to lie to you. Our chances are not too good here. These odds are…incredible. I need you all here and I need you at your best, but if any of you feel like pausing to pray or whatever you want to do to prepare, you might as well do it."

From the looks of it, a number of the techs did exactly that. Others went back to relaying reports, entering or retrieving information, coordinating between different pods, or communicating with the fighters. The atmosphere was one of calm urgency. Tobey was glad there was no panic, no sobbing or screaming.

"Squadron one green team just made primary engagement," Flynn said.

Tobey nodded. There was nothing more he could do. It was in the pilots' hands now.

Outside, men and women were fighting for their lives, fighters flying in and among the Darian squadrons, firing and eluding energy beams of pure death. The pilots were skilled, but it was still a dangerous environment out there, and inevitably some unlucky pilot would intersect an antiproton beam and flash into vapor.

"Marked, Battlehab, thank you," Flynn said. "Commander, all three warships are charging up their big antiproton cannons."

"Reinforce external shielding." Tobey knew that would be useless against the Darians' huge artillery mounts, but he had to do *something*. Even if only a few pods survived, that would be something.

"External shielding on maximum," Flynn said.

"It won't be enough, sir," Station Coordinator Lorne Michaels said, "they'll blast right through it."

Flynn said, "Estimate they'll fire in… five…four…three…two…one."

Tobey gripped the edge of the command desk and braced himself. "Hang on, everybody, hang on….It's been a privilege serving with you all."

Nothing happened.

After several seconds, Flynn said in a puzzled tone, "They've not fired. What are they waiting for?"

"Did the fighters take out the artillery weapons?"

"Negative. Fighters are still engaged against the enemy fighters. The warships are pulling back now. Signal from *Frontier*."

Tobey hit the transmitter tab. "*Frontier*, this is Station Post One."

The tone of Tepper's voice had changed. No longer the stoic, robotic voice of a man infected with Darian nanites, no longer the cheerful goof who listened to NeoChi music and needled Butch McCrae, Tepper now sounded peaceful, benevolent, and wise. "Station Post One, this is Fweery. I'm sorry about the delay, but the genes have finally taken hold. I've countermanded all the attack orders. The ships will be pulling back. I request permission to dock."

Sighs of relief swept through PHC.

"Could be a trick," Tobey said.

Flynn shook his head. "Darian fighters are returning to the warships."

"This could all have been orchestrated just to get Tepper on board." Tobey hit the intercom tab. "Dr. Lazarev."

"Dr. Lazarev here."

"Get a medical team and isolation equipment to Dock Deck One. The *Frontier* is going to be docking. I want Elmer Tepper put into isolation immediately, full medical examination. Scan for Darian nanites and the Sev gene."

"Yes, Commander."

———

"What has come aboard our Station?" Burt Kaisman said to the camera. "A Darian? A Sev? Both? And with word that the Triumvirate Council has now endorsed Vron's activities against the Valdor, clearly we are now in the hands of aliens. We will have much more as continuing medical examinations of this being who looks like Elmer Tepper is fully examined."

Shades of Treason

The halls were filled with civilians chanting "Kill Ebor DuBois!"

Butch McCrae was having considerable difficulty keeping the angry mob out of the security section. "Taylor! Carpetta! Get those crowds back and make sure they don't get past the main intersection!"

As his two guards ushered the crowd back, someone shouted, "That filthy traiter sold us out!"

"Now, nothing's proven yet," Butch tried to reason.

Tobey rounded the corridor, leading DuBois, Attorney Mary Roebuck, and two command security guards. "Okay, move it along."

"Okay, people, hold it!" Butch ordered.

As DuBois passed before the chanting mob, their shouts grew angrier, and the chants were peppered with shouts of "There he is!" "There's the traitor!" "Get him!"

Butch placed himself between DuBois and the advancing mob. "Now, hold it right there! None of you's going—*ahh!*" A large object hit him across the head and he lost his balance.

Tobey rushed to the intercom. "Medical team to Prime Hab corridor two. We need extra security here." He turned and saw DuBois bending over Butch's sprawled body. "Ebor, hurry!"

"Is Butch going to be all right?"

"Come on! Hurry along!" Tobey grabbed DuBois by the arm and shoved him violently ahead.

At a safe distance, Burt Kaisman caught every detail with his linkpad which transmitted live to the SSBC studios. "There has been a great deal of protest here from the crowds as Dr. Ebor DuBois is led from the brig into the hearing pod where preliminary charges will be read, and where Senator Ramsay will decide whether or not an indictment is in order. Civilian Security is holding off the crowds. So far no deadly force has been used, but of course we will cover it should that happen."

Dr. Marfida Lazarev rounded the corridor ahead of two EMTs pushing a gurney and two nurses. She knelt next to Butch. "You all right, Butch? Oh, my God, look at you. Let's get you to the Infirmary quick."

The EMTs lifted him onto the gurney and Lazarev scanned his head with her APT. As she and the others sped the gurney away, Kaisman stepped into the angry mob and stuck is linkpad in a random person's face.

"And what are you hoping to see from today's proceedings?"

"I just hope that bastard gets what's coming to him. This Station's got a whole lot of trouble on its hands, and the last thing we need is somebody up in the command staff selling us out to these aliens."

Tobey Dingell, Ebor DuBois, Mary Roebuck, and the rest of their entourage disappeared into the hearing pod. The door closed, but Kaisman was able to monitor the goings-on with an earpiece tuned to Senator Ramsay's desk transmitter.

For the next hour, Kaisman waited at the hearing pod door, providing a running commentary peppered with speculation, opinion, and conversations with members of the mob. He listened to his earpiece.

"And we have word from the hearing room—yes, Senator Ramsay decided not to indict on the charge of treason. Commander Dingell agreed to lower the charge to aiding and abetting the escape of a criminal. And the indictment is being pursued on that charge. The crowd is getting a little out of hand now as the word leaks out. Obviously they wanted the higher charge to be prosecuted."

———

A different mob with different gripes had gathered on Dock Deck One for the arrival of the Space Star

Phoenix. Their chants of "No more aliens!" echoed through the Dock Deck. A shuttlecraft taxied into slip two. The flight crew moved aside while Secret Service agents laid down generators for force field barricades to keep the shuttle—and Kramer and Cranius—separated from the crowd.

Looking out on the chanting crowd, Cranius remarked ruefully, "Well, I see nothing's changed."

"What is the *matter* with all you people?" Kramer shouted. "Don't any of you have jobs?"

"Yeah!" someone replied. "Don't *you* have a job?!"

Walking close beside him, Cranius said, "I sure hope they aren't armed."

"Don't worry about it. Secret Service has the force field barricades up. They can't get anything through them." And although there was plenty of angry shouting, no one even tried to shoot or throw anything as Kramer and Cranius passed the mob and entered the elevator.

———

Tobey's heart was pounding when he arrived in the Prime Hab Center. The shouts of "Kill Ebor DuBois!" were still with him. Although PHC was silent except for the hum of equipment and the occasional sound of someone talking to another station, Tobey could still hear those chants.

"I want all the civilians confined to the Civilian Hab!" Tobey shouted. "How fucking difficult is that?"

Lorne Michaels said, "The President promised the civilians full access to the Station. Besides, it's not just civilians. We've got crew—we've even got security personnel involved in that mob."

The intercom on the second-in-command's desk chirped. Jerome Flynn, still feeling uneasy with his new position, hit the tab. "Flynn here."

The voice of Don Sikuru, the acting BHC chief, said, "Yeah, we've got a warning here from Drayonne that the Dreadnought *Kinetic* is on his way here."

"All right, thanks, Don." Flynn turned to Tobey. "Did you hear?"

"Yep," Tobey said. "Fuck. Out of the frying pan, into the fire."

"Well, I'd rather deal with one Dreadnought than the entire Darian Empire. Between Station Post One and the *Phoenix*, we can handle one Dreadnought."

———

The Secret Service kept the crowds back as Kramer and Cranius made their way to the Presidential Pod. Once the door was closed behind them, and the chants largely muffled, Kramer grumbled, "God." He sat at his desk, leaned back, and rubbed his eyes.

Cranius sat across from him. "So. Do we go right to work or have a drink first?"

"Go grab drinks for both of us." He touched the intercom tab. "PHC, this is the President."

"Tobey here."

"Just letting you know we're back, we ran the gauntlet, and we're in the Presidential Pod."

"Good to know!"

"Why don't you come down here. Looks like there's a lot for you to catch me up on."

"Be right there."

It took twenty minutes for Tobey to navigate the chanting mobs and arrive in the Presidential Pod. Kramer and Cranius took the time to have their drinks and review the latest Congressional transcripts. During the trip here aboard the *Phoenix*, Kramer had been more consumed with the reports on the civil unrest on the Station than in the Congressional record.

The doorchime sounded.

"Come in!" Kramer called.

Tobey entered. "Hi, Damon. Sure is good to have you back on board."

"Back, but not in command."

Cranius got up. "Care for a drink?"

"Wouldn't turn it down, but I'm on duty." Tobey sat across from Kramer. "Been a hell of a week."

"Turn my back for five minutes and the Station goes to hell," Kramer said.

"Would you mind not leaving ever again, ever?"

"When did Tepper get back?"

"Right about the same time you and the *Phoenix* were fighting off the Darians."

"Thanks. I'll want to see him as soon as possible."

"Righto."

"So. I've been keeping up with what's been happening here, and I must say I'm…well, speechless. Charging Dr. DuBois with treason—"

"We still haven't located Zach Mortimer's body," Tobey said defensively, "and Butch said that he saw Dr. DuBois deliver Mortimer's last message to Arnold Livingston in the brig. That's when the rumors started spreading that Mortimer had risen from the dead."

"So, what are you suggesting? That Dr. DuBois—"

"And that's another thing. That message is missing. I asked Dr. DuBois to let me listen to it, and he said he deleted it."

Kramer was growing tired of being interrupted. "Perfectly reasonable to delete an old message."

"Everything ought to be in the computer somewhere! You know that!"

Kramer sighed. "Dr. DuBois was very upset about Mortimer being sentenced to death, and he actually asked me to allow him to be the executioner."

————

Butch was nearly knocked over when Ophelia ran into his arms. "You all right are?"

He held her lovely, blue-skinned body, looked into her dark eyes. "Yeah, fine, just a scratch."

"What happened?"

"Oh, just some Human Power animals throwing stuff."

"Do I understand not," the former Etuknip ambassador said, "how one people so divided could be."

Butch slouched into his easy chair and rubbed his head. Lazarev had given him a queasinol for the pain, but his head still ached. "I seem to remember your own people were a little divided."

"*Klay*, but that saw you did. That destructive could be saw you how. Have not learned you stop to violence such?"

Butch loved Ophelia with an all-consuming passion, but deciphering her word salad was not the best remedy for a headache. Deciding he had the gist of her sentence, he said, "If I could I would. Those guys haven't seen it. Or even if they had, I mean, God, most of them are old enough to remember the destruction of the Earth. You'd think that would learn 'em."

"Butch, must this stop. Destroy this Station will it not if stopped."

"I know it. Just…everything we do makes it worse."

————

The sounds of the clamoring mob were distinctly audible outside Tobey's privacy pod. Security was trying—without much luck—to usher them back to the Civilian Hab, and Tobey wondered how long it would be before someone opened fire.

Tepper sat across from him, a gentle smile on his face.

"Do we have any guarantee the Darians won't return?" Tobey asked.

"I'm in communication with all of them now." Tepper's tone was exultant. "There will be no more attacks. I want to thank you. You've given the Darian Empire what they've been searching for: meaning. And you also secured the survival of the Sev."

The doorchime sounded. "Come in," he called.

Dr. Lazarev entered, linkpad in hand. She sat next to Tepper.

"Well?" Tobey asked.

She placed the linkpad in front of her. "An exhaustive analysis of the blood sample shows the presence of Darian messenger molecules."

"Well, I don't think any of us doubted he's been infected with the Darian nanites, but surely *he* didn't sleep with Brandi Taylor."

"No," Tepper said, "Brandi Taylor slept with H.S. #898, one of the Darian human styrotypes. He was de-linked from the rest of them in order to test whether or not I was telling the truth that sleeping with her would infect him with the gene that would provide the Darians with meaning. That's the reason for the long delay in the gene taking hold of the rest of the Darians. Once H.S. #898 was re-linked, the Darian Empire became One with Fweery."

Tobey winced that the phrase; now that Mortimer was gone, it seemed Tepper had stepped in to replace him. "Well...Battlehab Center confirms that Darian warships have been retreating from all targets."

———

It was the day of Dr. Ebor DuBois' trial.

Burt Kaisman loved catching major news events on camera, but even he was worn out by the shouting and protesting—not that he would admit that out loud.

"Not much going on here. The protests have been peaceful so far despite some attempts by Civilian Security to forcibly herd civilians back to the Civilian Hab in direct violation of Station Post One policy that civilians have free access to the entire Station. Nevertheless, most of the civilian protesters have returned to the Civilian Hab. What you see behind me now are actually members of the Station Post One command crew protesting the lowering of the charges against Ebor DuBois. Right now we are waiting for Dr. DuBois to be escorted to the hearing pod where the trial will commence—although rumor has it that 'President' Kramer will declare a mistrial due to lack of evidence. This, of course, is no surprise, since Dr. DuBois is a good friend of our dear president, and the two of them have no doubt been in on the conspiracy all along. One must wonder if the missing message from Zach Mortimer to his followers might tie in to 'President' Kramer's audit of Human Power-affiliated groups, the evidence of which he has tried to suppress. How much evidence has this government tried to keep from us?"

Commotion caught Kaisman's eye. "And here! Now! Here comes Dr. Ebor DuBois. He is being escorted by his attorney, Mary Roebuck, and Civilian Security, towards the hearing pod. We'll try to get close enough to ask Dr. DuBois some questions…"

The shouting of the protesters threatened to drown Kaisman's voice out, and to his irritation reporters from other news networks were also trying to pin the scientist down. But Kaisman was nothing if not persistent. He shoved his way through the crowd, even shoved aside a fellow journalist into the hands of the protesters.

"Dr. DuBois! Dr. DuBois! Is the missing message affiliated in any way with the illegal audit—"

A security guard got in his way. "Stay back."

"My client has no comment," Mary Roebuck said.

"All press stay back," the guard said, spreading his burly arms to shield DuBois.

"Ah, press is not being allowed access to Dr. DuBois," Kaisman said in a smug tone. "No surprise there."

There was more commotion. The shouting drowned out even Kaisman's abrasive voice, and he saw erratic movement of people beyond the security guards. He raised his linkpad in hopes of catching something he couldn't see at eye level—

Then came the flash of a sidearm.

"And something has happened here," Kaisman said, straining to see past the moving bodies. "Dr. DuBois has collapsed, I thought I saw a sidearm burst. We can't confirm yet what happened. A medical team is now bending over Dr. DuBois. Presumably he will be taken to the Infirmary and we will have some answers for you later. Dr. DuBois has collapsed, it appears he might have been shot, it's not clear yet. We'll get back to you soon. I'm Burt Kaisman, this is SSBC Morning News."

———

Dr. Ebor DuBois lay on the gurney with his clothes torn open. Lazarev ran to him as the EMTs rushed him into the Infirmary. She bent low over his chest, then said, "I need an airway. I need an airway! Scissors!"

The EMTs scrambled while Nurse Jarrod Parker rushed over to assist. Nurse Larry Arroway had escorted DuBois part of the way here and had done the preliminaries.

"We got a pressure?" Lazarev asked.

"Seventy over forty," Arroway said. "Pulse weak and thready at one fifty."

"Do we have a cross match?"

"A-negative," Nurse Alan Searls said. "We have three point seven liters."

"Get it. Tell Morgan to prep. –Not you! Larry, you. Alan, I need you to hold this. Mike, get the rapid infuser over here. Start dopamine. Ten mics per kilo per minute."

———

Kramer paced the Presidential Pod, agitated and worried. "This played right into their hands."

Tobey agreed. "Only reason this happened is because that jack-ass Burt Kaisman was reporting that you were going to declare a mistrial."

Kramer nodded. "You were right. I should have recused myself. I just didn't want a repeat of Zach Mortimer's trial, with the judge already prejudiced against him. Tobey, you never should have charged DuBois with treason."

"I know, I know. It should have been a lesser charge from the start. I'm—I admit it, I was intimidated by Kaisman and Human Power and all this crap going on."

Kramer sat at his desk. "Their ideology is so extreme that the rest of us are being pushed closer and closer to their side, otherwise the rest of us appear to be extreme to the other side, and any attempt to report the objective truth is seen as bias."

The intercom chirped. Kramer glanced at Tobey, wondering what the latest bad news was, and hit the intercom tab. "Kramer here."

"This is Flynn in PHC. We have a message for you from the Hyron Dreadnought *Kinetic*, Commander Zoran."

"Put him on."

"Yes, sir. Transferring."

Kramer kept his tone carefully neutral. "Commander Zoran, this is President Kramer."

The gravelly voice of the insane Hyron commander who had sworn an arbitrary Vengeance Quest against Kramer said, "President Kramer, how good to hear your voice. You may be interested to know that my assignment on Drayonne is now complete. I am on my way to you now. My *dutimortis* is lifted; my Vengeance Quest is reaffirmed. I suggest you prepare for battle."

"Very courteous of you to warn me, Commander Zoran."

"It's the least I can do."

The icon went red, indicating Zoran had terminated the connection. Kramer swiveled his chair to look up at Tobey, who did his best to remain impassive. "What is the situation on Drayonne?"

"Not much news gets out of there," Tobey said, "but from what we have heard, public sentiment on Drayonne has turned against the separatists ever since Bykroff Island acceded to Hyron annexation. The Drayonni culture has come to lean a lot more in the direction of the Unified Republic."

"That doesn't mean the Drayonni government exerts more power than it did before."

"No, but the encouraging news is some high-ranking military leaders in the Hyron Star Navy have been turning over to the Monarch's side."

"Well, is that confirmed or is it a rumor?"

Tobey grimaced. "Well, it's a rumor."

———

The crowds continued their angry chants of "No more aliens!" in the corridors of the Prime Hab, and now they had almost reached the door of the Prime Hab Center.

"What in the name of God is going on here?!" Butch McCrae demanded. "I thought all the civilians were supposed to stay confined to the Civilian Hab!"

"They broke through the Manway," said Civilian Security Assistant Chief Pereira. "What could we do? Cut the Manway off and depressurize?"

"What is the *matter* with you people?!" Butch demanded, throwing his hands in the air.

"The people have spoken!" a man in the lead said. "We want control of Station Post One and our destiny!"

The others shouted a chorus of "Yeah!"

Butch turned to Pereira. "Go get some Dock Deck security guys and get them up here as fast as you can."

"Right."

As Pereira hurried off, Butch put his hands on his hips and said, "You people listen to me! This Station is controlled by capable people!"

"Didn't you get enough of this before?" asked a man Butch recognized from his last beating.

"Yeah," someone agreed, "we're taking over!"

The crowd surged, and Butch, finding himself alone against a mob, backed up. The intercom next to his head chirped. "Now, just a minute!" He turned to the intercom and turned it on. "McCrae here."

"Just what is going on out there?" came Tobey Dingell's voice. "Do you have the mob under control?"

Butch looked doubtfully at the angry, shouting faces. "Uh, barely."

"Pick somebody to speak for them and send him in to talk to me."

"Right." He turned back to the crowd. "Okay, okay, the commander wants to speak to one of you! Now, who wants to speak for the group?"

———

Kramer tried to get in touch with the Hyron Monarch, but the best he could manage was to leave a message with the chief of staff and former regent. When Session was over for the day, Cranius joined Kramer in the Presidential Pod, and Kramer played Eilonwy's message.

"Station Post One, this is Eilonwy speaking on behalf of the Monarch Keilah. President Frodax has been arrested. Drayonni forces have suppressed the separatists and the Monarch has called off Zoran and his followers. Zoran is acting on his own. At the moment there is a lot of confusion in the Star Navy and it will be a while before the chain of command is restored, so I can't send you aid right now. Zoran will reach you in two days. Good luck."

Kramer looked across the desk at Cranius. "What do you think? I can't tell whether she's speaking under duress or not."

Cranius's expression was, as always, inscrutable—black eyes in a black, lumpy face, no nuance of human emotion. "Well, it's hard to tell. But what she says backs up intelligence reports."

"Well, whether she was speaking under duress or not, obviously we can't expect any support from the Hyron Empire. We're going to have to fight Zoran."

———

Butch escorted the group's spokesperson into the Prime Hab Center. "Commander, this is Ti-Hua Chin. He's speaking for the group."

Tobey extended his hand. "Mr. Chin, Commander Tobey Dingell."

Chin shook Tobey's hand. He was a short man with a friendly smile, but carried himself with the self-assured demeanor of a natural leader. He was a civilian, and Tobey wondered what kind of job he held—and how he had ended up with this mob.

"What can we do for you?" Tobey asked.

Chin sat at the auxiliary systems desk, facing Tobey. "The people of Station Post One have decided we no longer trust your leadership or that of President Kramer."

Tobey cocked his head toward the door, through which the chants of "No more aliens!" were still audible. "Well, that seems to be pretty obvious. We've made every effort to address your grievances."

"Except that clearly President Kramer plans on declaring a mistrial at that traitor Ebor DuBois' trial."

"President Kramer would have decided everything in accordance with the evidence. Lest you forget, I'm the one who originally charged DuBois with treason."

"To make it look good, yes."

"I let you in here in good faith, to talk. What is it you want?"

Chin counted off items on his fingers as he spoke. "First, we want all aliens off the Station. Second, we want an ample supply of food and water to sustain our lives. Third, we want total transparency from the government leadership of Station Post One."

"Your third condition is already met. What will it take to convince you that that's true?"

"Full disclosure of your conspiracy to aid and comfort aliens, to target Human Power groups, and to hasten the escape and survival of Zach Mortimer."

Tobey could no longer keep the frustration out of his voice. "I cannot give you confirmation of events that people like Burt Kaisman simply made up. Now, as for food and water, I promise you we are doing everything in our power to provide for everybody on board this Station. And now that the Darians *appear* to have backed off of their invasion of the galaxy, there will be no more alien refugees coming through the Station. Does this satisfy you?"

Chin rose. "No, sir, it does not. We cannot function under leadership we do not trust, and we do not trust you or President Kramer."

The heated goings-on on Station Post One had turned Burt Kaisman into a field reporter; for the past two days Tyrone Raimi had filled in for him on *Kaisman and Friends*. The show's ratings might suffer, but he was not about to miss all this excitement.

"I am standing here in corridor one in the Prime Hab, and behind me is the entrance to the Prime Hab Center, or PHC, the control center of the Station. The crowd here has calmed down considerably since Ti-Hua Chin was elected spokesperson and entered PHC to talk to Commander Dingell. And we are told that the demands the crowd has put forward toward Commander Dingell are, firstly, no more aliens are permitted on Station Post One; secondly, the command crew is to provide the Civilian Hab with adequate food and water and shelter for all; and thirdly, that the Command Section as well as the Congressional Council are to disclose all materials regarding their preferential treatment of aliens and the illegal targeting of Human Power groups. There's no word yet on how the talks are going, but the fact that Commander Dingell opened the doors to a spokesperson from the group is a hopeful sign—Actually, here is Ti-Hua Chin emerging from PHC now...Mr. Chin, I'm Burt Kaisman, SSBC. How did things go in there?"

Chin looked at Kaisman, then at the linkpad, and fumbled nervously. "The Commander promised adequate, uh, food and water for all civilians, the Civilian Hab, and that no more aliens will be passing through Station Post One, but he refused to disclose information regarding the conspiracy to harbor aliens and let Zach Mortimer get away and to target Human Power groups."

Kaisman looked into the linkpad, aware that the group around him was now growing volatile with Chin's pronouncement. "Well, there you have it. What began optimistically as what appeared to be an open-minded talk between Commander Dingell and Ti-Hua Chin has failed."

Butch McCrae arrived with a group of Civilian Security personnel. "All right, let's break this up now! Everybody get back to the Civilian Hab! The talk's over! Everything's over now! Move on! Move back!"

Kaisman made sure to catch as much of the crowd's angry reaction in his lens as possible.

———

Tobey could hear the raised voices; for a few moments things had settled down, but now people were pummeling the door, kicking it, and shouting obscenities that were distracting and intimidating the crew. He hit the intercom tab. "Damon, this is PHC."

"Kramer here."

"It's getting ugly up here with this crowd. I'd like to recommend a state of emergency be declared."

"That's granted."

A moment later, Kramer's voice boomed throughout the Station's PA system. "Attention all personnel. This is President Damon Kramer. I'm declaring a state of emergency Stationwide. All security personnel throughout the Station are to report to Prime Hab corridor one, disperse crowd. All civilians are to be forced back to Civilian Hab. Sidearms are to be set on stun, but the use of force is authorized."

———

Kramer's announcement was met by an outpouring of jeers. Butch drew his sidearm. "All right, you heard the announcement! This demonstration is over! Everybody back to the Civilian Hab! Come on, move it! Anybody cause any more trouble's going to get stunned! Okay? Who wants a stun blast? Nobody? I didn't think so! Let's go! All right, move it!"

The shouts increased, though many of the crowd obeyed. There was some jostling, however, some words of protest, and a man came at Butch. There was no time to tell whether he was attacking or if he had been shoved; Butch fired. The man stiffened, his face contorted in pain, and fell.

"All right, that's a demonstration for everybody! Now, move back to the Civilian Hab!"

A group of Dock Deck security guards tromped down the corridor, their leader calling out a cadence, "Move it! One, two, three, four, one, two, three, four," with the practiced skill of an MTI. "All right, Butch, the cavalry's here!"

Butch was more relieved than he let on. "All right, let's get these guys out of here!"

"Let's go, people!"

Rather than being intimidated, the crowd got even more resistant. One squeaky-voiced guy in particular got into the MTI's face and shouted, "You can't force us to the Civilian Hab! We're not prisoners here!"

Sidearms fired. Three of them. Three people fell. Others retreated, but some continued to press forward.

Butch signaled to his men, "All right, ready… fire!"

They fired. More people fell.

Burt Kaisman materialized at Butch's side like a genie from a bottle. "And now, for the first time, deadly force is being used. Civilian Security is opening fire on unarmed civilians…"

Ignoring the "news"man, Butch marched after the now cowed crowd, brandishing his sidearm. "Come on, let's move it!"

There was no more trouble forcing the protesters back to the Civilian Hab.

———

Kramer appeared in the press pod that evening to make a statement.

"Good evening.

"This has been a sad day on Station Post One. As you all know, violent protests erupted throughout the Station in response to the pretrial hearing of Dr. Ebor DuBois. It has been my standing policy to hear the complaints of the people, to weigh their concerns, and to act in as open and fair a manner as I can.

"Unfortunately, there are those on the Station who are not willing to be as fair and even-handed as I have always tried to be. This afternoon, protesters attempted to gain admittance to the Prime Hab Center, the nerve center of Station Post One, urged on by lies and propaganda, forwarded by certain media pundits. Some civilians and crew on board Station Post One, belaboring under the misapprehension that we're lying to you, attempted to forcibly take over our Station.

"For this reason, I declared a state of emergency and authorized the use of force. Sidearms were set on stun. No one has been hurt. Civilians are to be confined to the Civilian Hab for the time being. Due to the clear and present threat to the structural integrity of our Station which supports our lives, I'm declaring a temporary state of martial law. Civilian Security will enforce the confinement of civilians in the Civilian Hab. Manways will be sealed. And to minimize confusion, it is with the deepest regret that I'm shutting down all news services and disseminating all information to you personally.

"I repeat this is a temporary measure. You have my assurance that I will tell you the truth. These steps are being taken for your safety. If these steps seem severe, they are. But please remember, this is not a world, this is a space station. This is a confined, pressurized environment. We must all work together to continue to sustain our lives. Be assured, your complaints and grievances have been heard, and steps are being taken to immediately address them.

"Thank you and good night."

Kramer turned and left without taking questions.

———

Overriding the door lock with his APT, Butch McCrae forced his way into Burt Kaisman's privacy pod. Kaisman was working at his desk and nearly tumbled out of his chair in astonishment.

Butch pointed his sidearm. "Burt Kaisman?"

"How dare you come into my privacy pod without my permission?!"

"By presidential order, you are under arrest for fomenting mutiny."

"I don't recognize the authority of Civilian Security to arrest me!"

"Well, whether you recognize it or not, I got it. You have the right to remain silent. Anything you say can be held against you. You have the right to legal representation. You have the right to challenge this arrest through Civilian Security or through the Command Section. You have the right to a supervised communication with anyone on the outside whom you wish. Do you understand these rights?"

"I do! I *wrote* half of them!"

"All right, let's move it!" Butch grinned. "I've been waiting for this for a long time!"

Butch wondered about Kaisman's daughter, Meyer, but she must be at school. Satisfied that there was no one else in the pod, he marched Kaisman out the door.

"Would that I were so easily silenced," Kaisman said.

Butch simply shoved him in reply.

At the security office, Kaisman used his communiqué to contact Commander Dingell and demand to see him. Butch took great pleasure in shoving him into a cell and shutting the plasma bars, but he was also aware that it would be politically impossible to hold him for long.

If only he could wipe that smug expression off his face.

Tobey arrived fifteen minutes later.

"Well," Kaisman said with a cocky smile, "what brings the commander of the Station to my humble abode?"

"I'm responding to your appeal of your arrest," Tobey said.

"I have a right to free speech. You cannot imprison me for that."

"You have a right to free speech if you don't cry 'air leak' in a crowded spaceship. Your editorials coerced the people of this Station into violent acts of rebellion."

"Violent?" Kaisman cocked his head. "A peaceful protest?"

"Dr. DuBois was shot. Cranius has been assaulted twice. And don't forget the armed conflict between Human Power and the Sev Army."

Kaisman chuckled. "Oh, please. You're going to hold *me* responsible for *that?*"

"Responsible, no. Complicit, yes."

"So now we see the nationalization of the news media!"

"Don't give me that propagandistic bullshit!" Tobey cried. "No matter what Damon does, you're going to accuse him of overreach or incompetence or tyranny or whatever. *You* drew the line in the sand. Damon and I wanted this whole Station to work together."

Kaisman laughed derisively at that.

Tobey gritted his teeth. "We're here for all of your protection!"

"We don't need you to baby-sit us!"

"You created a situation where action was necessary. You wanted an emperor, you've got one." Tobey whirled and left.

———

Butch sat across from Tepper in the Rec Pod, looked into his eyes. "You in there, Tepper?"

"Of course I am, Butch. It's still me." Gone was the dead intonation of a Darian, but there was little trace of the Elmer Tepper that Butch knew. Like Zach Mortimer, Tepper spoke in a serene calm with a beatific expression and constant gentle smile. It didn't suit him and Butch didn't like it.

"I feel like I'm talking to Zach Mortimer," Butch said.

Tepper pointed at his temple. "Tepper is in here. Fweery is in here. The Darian Empire is in here."

Butch shook his head. "Oh, Tepper, Tepper, Tepper."

Tepper regarded Butch with pity. Gently he explained, "I never understood the appeal of Oneness. I was as creeped out by Zach Mortimer as anybody else on the Station. But I understand now. There's an enormous peace and fulfillment that comes from Oneness. I understand so much about the universe now."

"And if we took the nanites away? You think you still would?"

"This isn't demonic possession, Butch. I'm still me."

"You're not talking like you."

"I've gained something I lost a long time ago: peace of mind."

"But it's *false!*"

"No, it's real."

"It's *induced* by this outside—*thing!*"

"You only say that because you haven't experienced it."

"Well…" Butch got up. "We'll see what you say if we can get this out of you." No longer desiring his old friend's company, Butch left.

———

Tobey and Flynn looked up in surprise when Kramer entered the Prime Hab Center.

"Mr. President!" Flynn exclaimed.

Tobey rose and shook Kramer's hand. "Damon! What are you doing here?"

"Tobey," Kramer said softly, "during the period of martial law, I am assuming operational control of Station Post One. I'm sorry."

"Sorry?! Jesus, all yours!"

Kramer sat at the command desk. "How long before Zoran's Dreadnought gets to us?"

"Estimating seven hours now."

"Have you any updates on Dr. DuBois' condition?"

"Well, he's recovering."

"I'm dropping all charges."

Tobey shifted his weight. "Dropping all charges?" he asked uneasily. "The people aren't going to take to that too well."

"Well, I don't have to give a damn now that we're under martial law."

————

Cranius entered the Infirmary, looked around for Dr. Lazarev, spotted her leaving one of the examining rooms. "Dr. Lazarev?" he called.

"What is it, Cranius?" she asked with concern, stepping over to him.

"Oh, no, no, I'm fine, I'm fine. I was wondering if I can talk to Dr. DuBois."

"Oh." She gestured to the room she had just left. "Go on in. You can talk to him briefly, but let him rest."

"Thanks."

Cranius went into the examining room and sat down. DuBois lay on his back, his chest bare, his heart monitor *beep beep beep*ing away.

"Hi, Ebor. Cranius here."

DuBois' eyes opened. "Oh. Hi, Cranius." He mumbled, his voice hoarse, but he was alert.

"How are you feeling?"

"Oh, a little groggy, I guess, but otherwise okay." DuBois sounded so sleepy and comfortable that Cranius now felt like going to sleep.

"Well, I wanted to let you know that the President has declared martial law. The civilians will no longer be able to do something like this."

"Oh, God. Under martial law over me?"

"Well, he's also dropped all the charges—which is good news for me, because now there's no way they can trace down the fact that I was complicit in Mortimer's revival and escape."

"I wouldn't have thrown you under the shuttle."

"I guess you wouldn't have. I don't know how much word reaches you since your arrest, but I wanted to let you know that Tepper is back from the Darian Empire, and the plan worked. The Darians have been implanted with the Sev gene. But Tepper has been implanted with Darian nanites, so—so now he's a Sev too."

DuBois did not reply; Cranius thought he had fallen asleep until he stirred and said. "Well…um… well, as soon as I get out of here, I'll…um…I have nanites that can cure him."

———

"I don't want to be cured," Tepper said.

DuBois, healed and discharged from the Infirmary, sat at his console in his cubicle in the Wheel, a display of his nanotech antibody on his realscreen.

Tobey stood just inside the entry to the cubicle. Butch paced around the small area of the Wheel that surrounded DuBois' cubicle, annoyed and concerned and frustrated. "Oh, come on, Tepper, of course you want to be cured!"

"No, I *don't* want to be cured." Even as tranquil as Tepper's manner was, he injected real firmness into the statement. "I know what I want, Butch. This is a whole new life for me, and for all humankind."

DuBois said, "You don't carry the Sev gene. You are merely in contact with other beings who are tied in to one person who carries the Sev gene.

"I know that."

Butch stopped pacing and said, "Well, that means that you can't go sleeping around and implanting other people with the Sev gene."

Tepper turned to DuBois. "What do you say to that, Dr. DuBois? Are the nanites sexually transmitted?"

DuBois considered. "They could be."

"Cure him," Tobey ordered.

Tepper raised his voice. "I have no desire to be cured!"

"Well, we're talking about the safety of the Station now," Butch said, "so you don't get a say in it."

"Send me to Fantasia."

"Absolutely not!" Tobey said.

Butch squeezed past Tobey and knelt in front of Tepper. "Look, Tepper, how about we make a deal? We cure you now, and if you want to go back, you can always go to Fantasia and sleep with a Sev and get reinfected. How's that sound?"

Tepper mulled the suggestion over. "The thought of being without Fweery even for a brief time—"

"Don't go all creepy on me, Tepper—"

The conversation was interrupted by the alert klaxon. Flynn's voice echoed, "This is a level one alert. All pilots to fighters, all gunners to gun turrets. Level one alert. Level one alert."

Tobey had leapt to his feet and scurried to the exit. Butch instinctively bolted toward the door before he remembered he was no longer a pilot, and so redirected himself to go to the Civilian Hab and see to people's safety.

———

When Tobey entered the Prime Hab Center, Jerry Flynn was barking data out to Kramer.

"Q-splash at one-oh-four mark five," Flynn said, "quantum ping at one hundred seventy-six kilometers, one-eighth blueshift. Negative contact acquisition beacon, negative response to hail. Auto det-id confirms Hyron Dreadnought. All QV Fighters manned, all gun turrets manned. *Phoenix* in position, ready to launch fighters."

"Damon," Tobey asked, "is it Zoran?"

"It sure is," Kramer said. "Well, keep trying to hail him."

"Still trying," Clio Steele said. "He's receiving, but not replying."

"Station Post One calling Hyron Dreadnought. Come in please." There was only silence. No one in PHC spoke. Kramer tried again, "Station Post One calling incoming Hyron Dreadnought. Come in please."

"Jump in the QH factor," Flynn said. "Looks like their Zargeron Field is up."

"Incoming Hyron Dreadnought, this is Station Post One. Respond please."

Silence reigned in PHC. The tension was palpable. There was sweat on every forehead.

Kramer repeated, "Incoming Hyron Dreadnought, this is Station Post One. Respond please."

"Multiple plasma streams," Flynn said. "Looks like they've launched their fighters."

"Launch fighters."

Tobey hit the intercom tab. "All fighters launch."

The Station vibrated as the fighters burst from their cribs, hurtled through the launch tubes, and into space.

"Fighters are off the Agrihab," Flynn said. "Dreadnought and fighters both closing. Range eleven million and closing, speed approximately fourteen thousand kilometers an hour, dropping off as they approach."

Kramer hit the icon connecting him directly to the bridge of the *Phoenix*. "*Phoenix*, Station Post One. Intercept incoming Hyron Dreadnought, launch fighters, attack."

"Yes, sir," Captain Petrov replied, "we are moving in."

"*Phoenix* is under Electronics Hab," Flynn said, "attitude point seven-eight yaw, rotation half-degree plus one, engaging fusion drive."

Kramer leaned forward over his desk, stroking his chin as he watched the tactical display on the big screen.

"Hyron fighters now pulling ahead of Dreadnought," Flynn said, "ROTs are closing in, fourteen point seven, range now two million kilometers, closing fast."

All eyes were fixed on the big screen except for Communications Officer Clio Steele and Station Coordinator Lorne Michaels, who were busy with a multitude of communications.

"*Phoenix* moving in behind," Flynn said. "Relative speed twenty-eight million kilometers per hour."

"PHC, BHC," the intercom said, "squadron commander Team One reports primary engagement."

"Squadron Commander Squadron One reports primary engagement," Flynn repeated.

There was little to do now but wait for it to be over. For the Hyrons to be defeated or for the Station to be destroyed. It was in the hands of the fighter pilots.

Flynn's voice trembled as he said, "*Kinetic* is moving on by."

"Those fighters are just distracting our fighters from attacking the Dreadnought," Tobey guessed.

"Well, but if the fighters turn their backs, the Hyrons will destroy them," Kramer said.

"*Phoenix* coming in to intercept Dreadnought," Flynn said. "Opening fire with main batteries."

Kramer saw the image of the *Phoenix* on the visual display on the right-hand screen, a triangular arrangement of white windows and red running lights shining in blackness. The flashes of weapons fire lit up its shadowed surface. The Hyron Dreadnought returned fire.

"Telemetry shows severe damage to *Phoenix*," Flynn said. "Lock joints two and seven destroyed, half the starboard launch tubes have been hit, looks like a fire in the engine room."

"*Kinetic*'s going to walk right through the *Phoenix* and hit us," Tobey said.

Kramer couldn't argue with that. His eyes shifted from the tactical screen, showing the moving blips of fighters, Dreadnought, and *Phoenix*, plus the green X of Station Post One, to the visual display, showing the incandescent plasma streams of the fighters and the flashes of weapons being fired—and, occasionally, the burst of brief flame and shower of ice crystals as a ship exploded.

Abruptly, unexpectedly, there were three brilliant flashes. Kramer recognized the telltale light booms that accompanied spaceships emerging from or entering light speed.

A puzzled Flynn said, "Three ships just emerged from light speed. Big ships…um…Darian warships!"

"Oh, Jesus," Tobey said.

The Darian warships opened fire—not on Station Post One or the *Phoenix*, but on the Dreadnought and its fighters.

"Darians are opening fire on the Dreadnought," Flynn said.

Kramer watched in amazement as the three box-like, silver warships blasted away at the Hyron vessel.

The command center of the Hyron Dreadnought *Kinetic* was a scene of intense concentration. Zoran sat in his chair on the command platform, looking over his console at the row of stations encircling the command center. Today, at last, was the day he would avenge himself on Damon Kramer, the man who had humiliated him four years ago, whose petty attack had crippled his engines and stopped him from going after the Thermians.

But the arrival of the Darian warships surprised him. He knew the Darians had been occupying Republic worlds, but hadn't realized they were so close to Station Post One. Well, no matter; he would destroy

Station Post One and leave the drifting debris for the Darians.

But he was in for another surprise.

"Incoming Darian warships opening fire on us," First Officer Melkon said.

"There are three of them!" Zoran shouted in rage. "Why would the Darians be defending Station Post One?!"

There was barely time to reorient the *Kinetic*'s weapons or to pass new orders to the fighters; the Darians' antiproton beams were too much for the mighty Dreadnought to handle. The designers had anticipated almost every contingency, but any spacecraft had its weaknesses. The problem with an Axis Dreadnought was simply that it was too big, and a defensive system that tried to protect that much hull from that much power was bound to fail.

"Blackhaven!" Zoran shouted in fury. His ship was in flames. The Darians' antiproton weapons had caused a feedback in the Zargeron Field and shorted out portions of it, and the alien machines were now blasting right through the ship's defense screens.

Melkon ventured to say, "One Dreadnought can't stand up to three Darian warships, a Space Star, and a space station."

Zoran did not want to admit that; he *never* wanted to admit defeat. But the evidence was all around him in the red lights all over the command center, the alarms screeching, and the crashes of thunder from all over the ship. "Recall all fighters and retreat."

"Yes, sir," Melkon said gratefully.

Zoran stared hatefully at the image of Station Post One on his screen. This was one more humiliation, and as good an excuse as any to renew his Vengeance Quest.

———

"*Kinetic* is retreating!" The relief in Tobey's voice was palpable.

"Fighters have broken off their assault," Flynn said, "returning to *Kinetic*. BHC reports squadron commanders asking permission to pursue."

"Negative, negative," Kramer said. "Return to Station."

"That's a negative, BHC. Have them return to Station."

Clio Steele turned from her console and said, "Incoming message from Darian ship."

"Let's hear it," Kramer ordered.

"Station Post One," came the voice of Elmer Tepper, "this is H.S. #117."

"Station Post One. President Damon Kramer of the Unified Republic speaking."

"We've protected you against the Hyron attack as a gesture of thanks for the help you've given us. Thanks to you, the Darian Empire has found *meaning*. And the Sev will survive, as they now not only permeate the Darian Empire, but Structure Prime in the Andromeda Galaxy."

Tobey giggled. "That's right! I'd forgotten we'd linked a Darian with Structure Prime!"

Kramer marveled at the enormity of this moment. "Does this mean that the Darian Empire is now on our side?"

"Yes," H.S. #117 replied, "we are allies of all life. Call upon us when you need us. Thank you again. H.S. #117 out."

After a pause, Tobey said, "You know, I know this is wonderful news, but for some reason I just find this creepy."

The situation was too new for Kramer to feel anything but relief. "Well, we've survived another day. That's what counts."

The Powerless and the Powerful

The little boy was nervous as he stood in the doorway of his family's privacy pod. "Dad, be careful."

"It's okay, son," his father said. "We'll get the drink dispenser fixed in the morning. I'll just run down to the Rec Pod and get you a drink. I'll be right back."

The door closed on the little boy, and the father went down the hall. But before he could reach the Rec Pod he was frozen in place by the call of *"Halt! Halt!"*

Two Civilian Security guards ran after him and threw him against the wall, face-first. "You're out after curfew! Do you have your identification?"

"No," the father gasped, "I was just going to get a drink. I was going to head right back."

The guard spun him around and frisked him. "Haul him to the security office."

The father grunted as the guard hit him in the back with his night stick; he needed no further prodding to cooperate fully.

———

At that moment, President Kramer was delivering his nightly address.

"Good evening, Station Post One. We're now one hour past curfew and there have been no incidents of violence. I regret to inform that some civilians have been taken into custody due to violation of curfew, but the investigation will be quick, and those civilians are likely to be released shortly.

"I continue to assure you that the current state of affairs will be brief. Those who have asked that no more aliens be permitted to go through Station Post

One will be pleased to know that the last refugee ship departs tomorrow.

"I anticipate that very shortly, life can go back to normal. There have been no further hostilities from the Darian Empire, all of the Sev have removed themselves from our Station, intelligence reports indicate the situation on Drayonne has been settled, and the Republic remains united against the Valdor.

"Our priority now is on tripling food manufacturing so that all civilians can live healthy and comfortable lives."

———

Butch was working on arrest reports when a shadow fell over him. He looked up at the hulking form of Derek Winchester, one of Burt Kaisman's co-hosts on *Kaisman and Friends*.

"Ah," Butch said, "I guess you want to see Mr. Kaisman."

"Yes, I do." The Jamaican accent that Wichester's viewers found so charming was barely discernible.

"Okay, right in here." Butch led the way to the cell block. "Okay, you've got five minutes."

"Thank you; I won't even need that long."

Butch went back to his desk.

"Burt," Winchester whispered.

Kaisman walked casually to the bars.

"You got it?" Winchester asked.

"Yes." Carefully Kaisman reached between the plasma bars and dropped a digifile into Winchester's massive hand. "Here it is. Be careful and don't get caught."

Winchester grinned. "I'm very good at not getting caught."

———

At noon, Winchester crouched in a secluded cubicle with some other SSBC alums and, via a special hookup, went on the air. "Good afternoon, Station Post One. This is Derek Winchester, and you are listening to

Free Speech Galaxy, and I have a message here for you from Burt Kaisman."

There was nothing here fancy enough to plug the digifile directly into the transmitter, so he simply held the device up to the mic and played Kaisman's message.

"Hello, Station Post One, this is Burt Kaisman. I am alive and well and still reporting the facts, all the facts, and nothing but the facts. I was detained by the command staff of Station Post One and I'm being held in the brig. Why? For speaking dissent against our 'president' and his policies. Yes, the 'president' wants to be the sole voice that reaches your ears. He wants to spread only his own propaganda and to stifle all those who speak against him, or who reveal the facts that he is uncomfortable revealing.

"But here are the facts: The 'president' has declared martial law and we are now living in a police state. Voices of dissent have not only been silenced, but arrested and imprisoned.

"It is important that all of you know this, for this does not only affect those like myself, who have consistently spoken against him; it speaks to *all of you*. There is no one who is not endangered by a regime which exercises power to silence its own citizens. I urge you, therefore, to rise up against this tyranny and to show the leadership of Station Post One that we the people are the voice that cannot be silenced."

———

Tepper, restrained in a chair in the Wheel, struggled and argued. "Look, I told you—"

"Hold still, Tepper," Butch said, tightening the straps around Tepper's wrists.

"I don't want to be cured! This is not a disease. This is a way of life that I have chosen freely."

DuBois emerged from his cubicle holding an injector. "This is *not* a life you have chosen freely. This is a way of life that was forced on you. You'll be given the free choice once you're cured, and then you can choose to go back *if you wish.*"

"That not what I want! I want—"

"Stop wasting time," Butch said, "just inject him!"

DuBois knelt by Tepper, pressed the injector against his arm, and pushed the trigger. There was a click, and millions of tiny robot antibodies swarmed into Tepper's bloodstream. "It's injected," DuBois said. He ducked into his cubicle. "Computer shows the nanites are seeking out their equivalents. You'll start feeling better almost immediately."

Tears streamed down Tepper's face. "She's going. I can feel her drifting away."

Butch patted his shoulder. "It's for the best, Tepper, it's for the best."

"She's drifting away," Tepper sobbed.

———

Tobey was uncharacteristically happy when he arrived at the Presidential Pod.

Kramer had just come out of the bathroom and was preparing to meet with Cranius before going to the hearing pod for Burt Kaisman's brief and perfunctory trial. "How is everything, Tobey?" he asked brusquely.

Tobey smiled. "Everything is calm, quiet, there've been no incidents during the night, nothing this morning, no protests in the halls, no terrorism, that jack-ass Burt Kaisman has finally shut up—this is a step we should have taken a long time ago."

"This was a devasting step," Kramer snapped, "an appalling bit of overreach on our part, and it will come back and bite us. The calm that we're experiencing now is temporary and it's forced."

———

Flynn ordered up a breakfast of eggs and sausage and sat in a corner of the Rec Pod, preferring to eat alone and read the Republic newsfeeds. But he couldn't help overhearing the conversations around him.

"It was so nice to lie in my privacy pod last night without being woken up by chanting mobs in the hall all night."

"Boy, you're telling me. I left my privacy pod this morning and I was able to walk down here without being punched in the face."

"Yeah, nobody wants to live under martial law, but President Kramer made the right choice. What else could he do?"

"That's for sure. People backed him into a corner."

————

Burt Kaisman stood before President Kramer in the hearing room, hands locked behind his back, his expression defiant.

It had been a quick trial. There were no lawyers, no tribunal, no witnesses. Butch played several exerpts from *Kaisman and Friends* along with sound clips from various protesters—including those who had gunned down the helpless Sev prisoners in the brig—and Kaisman had spoken on his own behalf with a plea of freedom of speech.

Kramer rendered his verdict without deliberation. That was martial law.

"Burt Kaisman," Kramer said, "I find you guilty of incitement to mutiny and rabble-rousing. I sentence you to two years in the brig. This court is adjourned."

————

"Two years?" Cranius was usually mild-mannered and friendly, but now he was clearly angry, or at least deeply concerned. "For expressing an opinion that you disagree with?"

"Two years for inciting a rebellion that nearly tore the Station apart." Kramer sounded more unrepentant than he felt. He knew he was on very shaky legal and moral ground, but he also knew his strict policy was working.

"You've told me on numerous occasions that you will not forcibly silence people's speech no matter how much you disagree with them."

"And I still stand by that," Kramer said in a tired voice. "I just can't afford to be lenient right now. Besides, Kaisman's not going to serve that whole sentence; martial law won't last that long. It was all about making a gesture."

"A gesture that's more likely to turn more people against you than keep the Station under control."

"There's no choice right now, Cranius. There are two types of people on the Station: those who support me and those who are against me. Whatever I do will inflame those who are against me into hating me even more. Those who are for me are ideologically committed. No matter what I do, they'll stick with me."

"You're giving me the impression your species isn't very intelligent."

Kramer smirked. "I'm afraid a lot of us aren't."

"All I know is on Vron, our leaders have more respect for our people," Cranius said. "We just assume that everybody's capable of thinking and making up their own minds, and it's enough to provide all the pertinent information."

"Well, I'd be *very* interested in knowing how your species accomplishes that, because that's a wonderful philosophy, and I agree with it, but it never seems to work for our species."

———

Butch led Kaisman through the halls of the Civilian Hab. "Okay, let's go, Kaisman," he coaxed, his tone mocking.

Kaisman showed no concern about his sentence; in fact he seemed pleased. He walked silently beside Butch until they reached the brig.

"Harry, open the door please," Butch ordered.

Harry Marsh opened the brig door—then struck out and leveled Butch with a left hook. "All right, come on, Burt!"

"What is this?" the astounded Kaisman asked.

"I've got a fighter prepped and ready to go. Come on, hurry! Before security catches up!"

———

Tepper sat in an examining room in the Infirmary. He wasn't sick, but he had no desire to return to duty. "I don't know who I am anymore," he moaned.

Dr. Marfida Lazarev examined the results of Tepper's blood tests, tapped at her terminal. "Who you are is Elmer Tepper, Chief of the Dock Decks, Station Post One. The same person you've always been."

Tepper rubbed his forehead. "I've been duplicated so many times I can't even be sure if I'm the original anymore. I've been infested with the Darian nanites, I've been in contact with Fweery, I can't find *me* in all of that cloud of different identities."

"Well, I can tell you this much: biologically, you are Elmer Tepper. The nanites are gone, no trace of the Sev gene, so medically, you are the same person you were before you left for the Darian Central Space Station."

———

As they stepped onto Dock Deck One, Harry Marsh said, "Okay, just act natural."

Kaisman did his best, though he knew his was one of the most recognizeable faces on the Station. He hoped the fact that he was being escorted by a security guard would mitigate any suspicion.

Some people did look his way as he followed Marsh across the bay, but they were too intent on their jobs to pay him much mind.

They came to a fighter in launch position, its engine humming.

"All right, this is it," Marsh said. "Just climb in. Your course is preset to take you to a refugee ship that's on its way to Fantasia."

"What am I supposed to do when I reach Fantasia?"

"Keep sending your editorials to us, and you can report firsthand on the activities of the Sev Army. As soon as this thing blows over, we'll bring you back."

"I have no desire to leave my wife and daughter."

"We'll take good care of them here. The thing is, we've got to get *you* out and to safety so you can still play a part. It won't be long before this whole thing blows over. Now, quick, hurry, before somebody catches us! You want to spend the next two years in the brig?"

"All right." Kaisman climbed into the cockpit; he had to admit it was pretty cool to sit there behind these controls, and he wondered what it would be like to streak through the stars like the hero of a space opera.

The canopy whined down and clicked into position. Air began to blow from the vents, and he was aware of a change in pressure. He heard the whine of the engines rising, felt the pent-up forces preparing to unleash themselves. He looked out the front of the canopy, at the wide open launch tube beyond which was total, all-consuming blackness.

Then he was pushed backward into his seat as the engines fired, and the walls of the Station disappeared. As soon as the glare of the Dock Deck lights were gone, the heavens lit up with a dazzling myriad of stars, more than he had ever imagined.

As many years as he had spent in space, it had always been secure inside well-lit spacecraft; even in his brief jaunts in shuttlecraft, he had sat in the rear without a good view of the windows. Now he saw infinity spread before him.

He looked at the complex controls and hoped the computer knew what it was doing; he could make no sense of any of the touchpads, touchscreens, switches, buttons, knobs, and dials. The heads-up display was a confusing assortment of lines and numbers moving in meaningless directions. He felt a new respect for the pilots who had to learn all this stuff and work with it.

———

"What was that?" Kramer asked. "Did a fighter just launch?"

"One moment," Flynn said. "BHC, this is PHC."

"BHC here," the intercom answered.

"Did a fighter just launch?"

"Nothing was scheduled. Just a moment."

Kramer drummed his fingers on the command desk as he awaited the answer.

"Wait, confirmed, yes," the voice on the other end said. "A fighter did just launch from Dock Deck One."

"Well, who was it?" Flynn asked.

"There's no one on the schedule and they didn't have clearance. I don't know."

"Dock Deck One, this is PHC."

"Dock Deck One here."

"A fighter just launched. Who was that?"

"I don't know. We didn't grant any clearance. I assumed BHC did."

"No, nobody granted clearance. Who was it that left?"

"Well, I don't know. It was a D-4000. I heard the blast, I turned and looked and I didn't see who it was."

"This is some fucking martial law," Tobey said.

"Well, contact the fighter," Kramer ordered.

Clio Steele said, "Attention D-4000 that just left the Station. Who are you? What are you doing?" There was no response. Steele looked up at Kramer, then tried again. "Hello, attention, respond please."

The next voice, to Kramer's surprise, was that of Butch McCrae. "PHC, Civilian Hab, brig corridor."

Kramer hit the intercom tab. "Go ahead. PHC."

"This is Butch McCrae. I was just escorting Burt Kaisman to the brig and my assistant attacked me, knocked me out, and now he and Kaisman are gone."

Tobey rubbed the bridge of his nose. "God almighty, Kaisman got away."

"Kaisman can't fly a fighter," Kramer said.

"What's the explanation then?"

Flynn said, "That fighter's on course to rendezvous with the refugee ship *Pardo*."

"Refugee ship is on," Clio Steele said.

Kramer nodded, hit the communications icon. "Refugee ship *Pardo*, this is Station Post One."

"*Pardo*," came a voice that sounded almost human.

"There's a fighter on course to rendezvous with you. When it goes on board, take the pilot into custody please."

"Can you give us some more details please?"

"He's a fugitive from justice. Burt Kaisman. I don't think he's dangerous."

"Well, President Kramer, as soon as we departed the vicinity of your Station, we are no longer bound by your laws. We'll evaluate the situation ourselves and inform you of our decision. Thank you."

Kramer closed his eyes, acquienced to the alien's reasoning. "Understood. Station Post One out."

"That's appreciation," Tobey said, "considering all that we've done for them!"

"It's also understandable, considering that we just turned our Station into a police state."

The intercom blared, "Uh, PHC, this is Butch McCrae. I'd like to ask permission to check out a fighter and go after Kaisman."

"Butch, this is Kramer. You said your assistant knocked you out. Did you lose consciousness?"

Butch's sigh came over as a burst of static. "Briefly!"

"Then you get your ass to the Infirmary!"

———

Kaisman didn't know much about operating a fighter, but he was able to find the transmitter; communications, after all, was his career. "Refugee ship, this is Burt Kaisman from Station Post One. I wonder if you would be able to guide me in."

"Stand by," a voice replied, "we've locked on to your navigation system and we're bringing you in."

The voice sounded alien. *Almost* human, but definitely alien. "Thank you," Kaisman snapped in an unfriendly tone. He didn't like having to depend on aliens.

But whoever had taken control of his fighter knew was he was doing. Kaisman felt scarcely a bump as the craft set down in the refugee ship's landing bay. The pressure doors closed. He tried to open the canopy, but the heads-up display flashed a pressurization warning at him. Realizing the bay was not yet pressurized, he sat and waited.

Eventually a three-legged, three-armed thing entered the bay and cracked the canopy. Kaisman got up and hopped out of the fighter, hurting his ankles as he landed; the gravity was a little higher here than on Station Post One.

"Mr. Kaisman," the alien said, "welcome aboard. I am your evacuation director, Azman. We had a request from Station Post One to return you, but our captain decided it would be too big an inconvenience for our other passengers, so you'll be staying with us for the trip to Fantasia unless someone from Station Post One wishes to make a rendezvous."

Kaisman appraised his alien friend. It wore a loose brown tunic over its green, scaly skin. Its head was knobby, its eyes segmented, like a fly's eyes. It smelled like rotting steak. "Well, that's very much appreciated. May I be shown to my quarters?"

Azman led him from the bay, and he watched with fascination the movement of the three feet. "This is the passenger compartment."

The "passenger compartment" looked like a storage bay with bits of junk welded together into cubicles to give some measure of privacy. Creatures lay about on makeshift bunks; some were human, but most were an assortment of Kriddich, Zang, and whatever Azman was.

"I'm afraid we're pretty full," Azman said. "You'll have to find a space somewhere."

"Pardon me, but I am a rather important media personality," Kaisman said. "I'm used to traveling in more upscale conditions than this. Don't you have First Class accommodations? I can, of course, pay."

"This is a refugee ship," Azman said with a trace of irritation. "What you see here is all we have to offer. All refugees are the same status. You will excuse me while I attend to the other passengers."

The three-legged alien moved off down the row of jerry-rigged cubicles.

Kaisman tiptoed among the sprawled bodies, trying not to look at the alien faces. He was grateful when a human woman said, "Come, sit next to me."

"Thank you...excuse me...pardon me..." Stepping past several Vron, he eagerly entered her cubicle and sat in the offered plastic chair.

"Where did you come from?" the dark-haired woman asked.

"Station Post One. I stole a fighter."

"Aren't you that newsman?"

Kaisman smiled, pleased to be recognized. "Yes, Burt Kaisman."

She extended her hand. "Amelia Cortez."

He took her hand and kissed it. "A sincere pleasure, Madam."

She gave a vague smile. "So sorry they arrested you."

He shrugged. "Par for the course these days. The important thing is not to give up. What about you? You're human, right? How did you get on this ship?"

"I escaped. I couldn't feed my children, so I became a prostitute. When they declared martial law, I was arrested. A man broke me out and put me on this ship. He'll suffer for it."

Kaisman withdrew from her on the revelation that she was a prostitute, but he said nothing about it. "They'll *all* suffer for this outrage in time."

———

Butch cheerfully walked into Tepper's office on Dock Deck One. "Heya—"

"What the hell do *you* want?!" Tepper looked up at him, fire in his eyes.

Butch was startled. "Well, there's a fine hello—"

"I don't want any crap from you! I don't want to be—"

"Now, hold it, hold it!" Butch was bewildered. "Where's this all coming from?"

"If you're here to try to talk to me about how 'wonderful' it is to get rid of Fweery, I just don't want to hear it!"

"Whoa, whoa—"

"I've got my own problems and I'll deal with them in my own way!"

"That is not why I'm here! I'm here because I want to check out a fighter to go after Burt Kaisman! If you've got your own little identity crisis going on, that's your own business and I'm not going to get involved!"

"Well..." Tepper calmed himself. "All right, no—um, look, you can't just check out a fighter. You know perfectly well every fighter's allocated to a particular pilot. I've already got Corporal Peters barking at me because Kaisman stole his fighter."

"Well, we can't just let him get away."

"Well, why don't we let the commander decide what to do?"

Butch gritted his teeth. "Because we don't have time to go through any bureaucracy. We've got to go get him! Now, we need to take initiative."

Tepper glared at Butch, hit the intercom tab. "PHC, Dock Deck One."

"PHC, Dingell," the intercom answered.

"Tepper. Requesting permission to take the *Frontier* to go in pursuit of refugee ship *Pardo*."

"Yeah, I was just about to notify you, they have elected not to return to Station Post One. They're on their way to Fantasia. You're authorized to follow them there and pick up Kaisman there."

"Thank you." Tepper stood, still staring at Butch. "Well, you got your way."

Butch nodded. "Okay, then. You're okay with me coming with you, then?"

"Well, what the hell difference does it make what I want?"

Tepper brushed past him into the Dock Deck. Butch turned and bellowed after him, "Hold it there! I've heard just about enough out of you!" He set off after Tepper. "Now, hold it! Tepper! Hold it!"

Tepper did not slacken his pace.

"Tepper! Listen to me!" He reached Tepper and grabbed his arm.

Tepper yanked his arm away and whirled on Butch, his eyes wet with tears, and shrieked, "I don't want to listen to you or anybody else!"

Heedless of all the flight crews staring at them, Butch shouted, "Fuck you! You and I have been through a lot together not to be able to talk straight with one another!"

Tepper was once again storming across the bay toward the pressure snake. "You don't know the half of it!" He reached the pressure snake and gripped the rim as though afraid he would blow into space if he didn't let go. "I don't know who I am, so *you* sure as hell don't know who I am!"

"I'll tell you who you are!" Butch shouted. "You are a *pilot*. That's who you are, that's what you are. That defines everything about who you are. Rail all you want at the God above and all that other bullshit, but you're a guy who climbs into a cockpit, takes a set of controls, and flies his machine through space. That's always been enough for you before. And if you let go of all the goddamn baggage, that's enough for you right now."

Tepper appeared to mull over what Butch had said, but then he shoved him and set off down the pressure snake. "Get away from me! You don't know a damn thing!"

Butch started through the pressure snake after him. "Tepper—hold it. Tepper! I want to go with you. I want to go with you! I've got a personal score to settle with Burt Kaisman."

Tepper raised both hands and said, without turning around, "Fine, come on."

They entered the *Frontier*, passed through the lounge and sat at their old familiar stations in the cockpit. To Butch it felt good, and he hoped the long journey to Fantasia would loosen Tepper up.

"*Frontier*, PHC," Flynn's voice said over the speaker, "you are cleared for departure."

"Marked," Tepper replied, "clear for departure."

There was a series of clanks as the power ubilicals, mooring lines, and pressure snake disconnected, then Tepper pushed gently on the sensitive yoke. "Now departing."

Butch watched as Station Post One drifted out of view, and he looked across at Tepper and smiled.

Tepper did not return the smile.

———

Kramer and Tobey entered the Wheel, found DuBois in his cubible. "Ebor," Kramer said, "we'd like to talk to you."

DuBois sat back and rubbed his eyes. "And I could use a break. What's on your mind?"

"You really think the Darians are our allies now?" Kramer asked.

"They said they are. If they are infected with the Sev gene, I don't think it's likely they'd lie about that."

"According to Tepper," Tobey said, "even when the Darians were set on their extermination of all organic life, they were not programmed to lie. Deception was just not part of their makeup."

"Well, they obviously came to understand deception," DuBois said. "They were exposed to it enough times through contact with humans and other organics."

Kramer said, "So what can we look for from them? Are they going to actually aid us in battles against our enemies? Or are they simply going to sit by passively and not bother anyone?"

DuBois shrugged. "Frankly I just don't know enough about the Sev to say. I would suggest that if we had left Tepper contaminated with the Sev gene—"

Tobey objected vociferously. "We've crossed enough moral lines."

"Dr. DuBois makes a valid point," Kramer said. "We could use a contact with the Darians."

"Contaminating one of our own people with those goddamn, icky, freaky nanites is not an option."

"Well, we certainly have Sev allies on Fantasia."

"*Allies?!*" Tobey asked.

"If I understand how it works right, they are now in contact with the Darian Empire."

"Yes, they should be," DuBois agreed.

Tobey was appalled. "You're calling them allies?"

Kramer nodded. "The ones who were infected with the Sev gene, yes, I think wanted to be our allies. And that's where Butch and Tepper are headed right now."

"Are you suggesting that Tepper's going to want to go and have sex with one of them and become reinfected?"

"I'm suggesting that a little bit of open-minded-ness might help. Ebor, you know that I dropped all charges. You are now in no danger of prosecution for anything that went on in relation to Zach Mortimer's case. Can you tell me—is Zach Mortimer dead or alive?"

DuBois thought for a full thirty seconds, then said, "I can honestly tell you I don't know."

Kramer was about to press the point, then changed his mind. "All right. We'll leave it at that." He turned to leave.

Tobey started after him. "Damon, hold it, are you actually going to suggest—"

"I going to do everything I can to get this state of martial law lifted as quickly as I can. If making contact with the Sev and allying ourselves with them will do that, I'll do it."

———

Cranius had worked with the Civilian Hab's victualling department to prepare the distribution center in the converted Rec Pod. It had been challenging to increase the pod's volume to accommodate a large crowd. All the tables and chairs had been moved out, and the walls stripped to make more floor space. That left an entire half of the chamber exposed to the ugly innards of the Station—pipes and semiconductors and a silver oxygen tank.

"We are honoring our word to you," Cranius said to the milling crowd. "We have food and water and extra canisters of oxygen!"

Flynn tried to organize the crowd. "Let's form four separate lines! We have salads here, carrots, green beans, apples, oranges, steak-flavored protein, chicken-flavored protein, fish, we have water, and fourteen different flavor combinations."

Cranius sat while Flynn opened the gate at the end of the aisle. A man stepped up to the counter.

"You want steak?" Cranius asked.

"Yeah," the man said. "How much this gonna cost?"

"Your taxes already paid for this."

———

In the Prime Hab Center, Tobey approached Kramer's desk and handed him a digifile. "Repair status report on the *Phoenix*."

Kramer slipped the digifile into a slot and read the report that appeared on his realscreen. "Well. She won't be fighting any battles any time soon."

"Nope. This is going to have her laid up for at least two more weeks."

Kramer sighed. "Well…we functioned for a long time before we built the *Phoenix*. The Darians are under control."

"Yeah…no telling when the Hyrons are going to act up next."

"Nothing we can do about it but repair it as fast as we can."

"And get on building more Space Stars." Tobey was not joking. Two more Space Stars, larger than the *Phoenix*, were in the planning.

"We need to move on to the next phase of expanding Station Post One," Kramer said, "*then* we can focus on building the new Space Stars."

———

Cranius, who had been beaten up several times by Human Power, was growing nervous as the food lines grew and his supply of food grew smaller. "This is getting out of hand," he said to Flynn. "We're going to run out of food before the crowd disperses."

Flynn agreed. "People are taking too much."

To the next woman in line, Cranius said, "I'm sorry, I'm going to have to limit you to just one chicken."

"I've got a family of four!" the woman protested.

"Sprog. I'm sorry, we're running low. We have to conserve for everybody else."

Flynn stood up and waved his arms. "No more steak, everyone! No more steak!"

The crowd grew rowdy, many shouting their protests, some making threatening gestures, and in general they began to surge forward toward the counter.

"Apples are all gone," Cranius said to the next person.

"You've got plenty back there!" the young man shouted.

"What you see is all there is."

The old man three places back shouted, "You promised us enough for everybody!"

"I'm sorry," Cranius said helplessly, "this is all we have left!"

"We don't have to take this!"

Flynn got up, saying, "I'll alert security."

"Come on," a young man in the next line said, "let's get 'em!"

Cranius stood, grabbed a steak knife and stood his ground. "Sprog it, get back! Get the sprog back!"

Fortunately security arrived before things could get completely out of control. "All right, come on, people," Lieutenant Balderson shouted, "let's get back to your privacy pods!"

Ten security guards tried to usher the crowd out of the pod, but one especially temperamental man lashed out, *"Get out of my way! I want food!"*

Balderson had planted himself next to Cranius and drew his sidearm. "Stay back or I shoot!"

The man was not deterred, and was promptly cut down by the flash of Balderson's sidearm.

Caught in the mob mentality, many of the others surged toward the counter—some driven by anger, others just caught in the movement of the crowd. The other security guards opened fire.

In the ensuing mayhem, Balderson shouted fruitlessly, "Keep order! Keep order! Get back to your privacy pods!" But the louder he shouted, the more he was drowned out by the angry screams of the increasingly violent mob.

Balderson and the others continued to fire. Cranius's eyes flicked with sudden panic to the exposed oxygen canister.

And then there was a low *boom*, and a fragment of the wall blew out. A moment later the Red Pod was a hurricane, the atmosphere rushing out into the cold blackness of space, carrying with it bits of food, eating utensils, plates, and any other loose object caught in the windstorm.

———

"What the hell's going on?" Kramer demanded as alarms sounded.

"Civilian Hab," DuBois said, "there's been an explosion.

Tobey pounded the intercom tab. "Civilian Hab, PHC. What's going on?" There was no reply. "Civilian Hab, PHC. Report."

"This is Cranius!" The voice was barely audible over roaring wind. "Security opened fire and hit one of the oxygen canisters! We've got an air leak down here! We're working right now to seal the bulkhead!"

"Those bulkheads should seal automatically." DuBois' comment was exceedingly mild, though the import behind it was not.

"If an oxygen canister blew up at one of the juncture nodes," Kramer said, "it would have blown out the bulkheads."

"The other bulkheads could have sealed," Tobey said. "The Manway could have sealed off and the bulkheads to the other sections could have sealed off. All those people could be stuck in a decompressing section with no way out."

Kramer tried to put out of his mind the fact that Cranius needed more oxygen than humans. He directed his attention to solving the problem.

DuBois remained calm. "Cranius, this is DuBois. Try to move to an inboard section, and if there's no open passageway, there are life support closets every three meters down the hall."

"I just found one!" Cranius was almost impossible to hear. "But it's not large enough for everybody!"

"No time to lose," Kramer said. "Nautabots out there, seal the hole."

DuBois was on his feet before Kramer finished speaking. "On my way."

Kramer looked up from the command desk, glanced to his left, where Tobey sat stunned.

"Well, Tobey, you see? The 'calm' resulting from martial law was temporary and forced."

———

Cranius whipped an oxygen mask away from a frightened woman. "No, no! Don't suck on that oxygen! If you fill your lungs with oxygen in this depressurization you could rupture your lungs!"

Flynn ran up to Balderson. "Inboard bulkhead sealed. Here, give me that sidearm."

Balderson handed him the sidearm. Flynn set it to narrow beam and used it to cut open the bulkhead. "Cranius, help me with this!"

Cranius ran to his side. Together, huffing and puffing in the thinning air, they lifted the heavy bulkhead, silently cursing the downside of artificial gravity.

"All right—everyone, go on through!" Flynn shouted.

Balderson stood at the now-open door and directed the masses as they fled. The wind had died down as the air thinned, but with the opening of the bulkhead it was back to hurricane strength. People fought to stay on their feet as they clamored into the hall, pummeled by loose items that whipped unpredictably through the door.

"Can't hold on much longer!" Cranius cried through gritted teeth.

"All right, they're through!" Balderson shouted, ducking through the door. "Come on."

Flynn looked at Cranius. "Ready? One, two, three!"

Together they ducked under the bulkhead into the cooridor, then let go. The bulkhead fell with a loud *slam!*, and all at once the wind was cut off.

Cranius knelt down and felt the base of the bulkhead. Air was seeping underneath. "That's not airtight, you know."

"It's the best we can do for now," Flynn said. "I'll check and make sure everyone got out safely."

Cranius looked around, located an intercom. He signaled the Prime Hab Center. "We cracked one of the bulkheads open. Flynn got it open, we got everybody through, got it shut again. Of course we have a minor leak here, but we're safe for the time being."

Kramer replied, "Any losses?"

"Flynn is taking a census right now. I'm guessing that the three civilians who were stunned were lost, and of course we lost all the food."

"Thank you, Cranius. Dr. DuBois is going to seal up the hole and we'll have the Civilian Hab repressurized soon. Hang in there, try to keep everyone calm."

———

The *Frontier* was not a very big ship for two men to hide from each other, and things remained tense between Butch and Tepper. Fortunately there were enough housekeeping chores to keep them busy during the trip to Fantasia, but Butch hoped to break through Tepper's anger and make him see that he and DuBois had given him back his freedom, not taken it away.

It was a relief when they dropped out of light speed.

"There's Fantasia, right on the nose," Tepper said.

Butch watched his instruments. "Yeah, our current trajectory is going to take us into a forty-five-degree orbit, one hundred nine kilometers perigee, three thousand one hundred seventy-three point six apogee."

"All right, let's just trim that a bit…and we've got a perigee of ninety-three. That should allow us to brake, then we'll circularize at one hundred, trim her again and get atmosphere entry on the far side. Then we'll have discretionary maneuver after ionization and we can just, uh, locate the encampment and land."

"Any sign of that refugee ship?"

"I didn't see anything of it when we came out of light speed, but…there. I got its fuel trails. Yeah, looks like it already made atmosphere entry. Probably on the ground by now."

"And we're supposed to make contact with the Sev," Butch said cautiously, "and find out if they can help us with the Darians. I don't get that."

"They're really very peaceful and wise people," Tepper said in a flat tone.

"Don't give me that! Don't get sucked into that whole thing like Zach Mortimer did."

"Well, I *can't* now, can I?" Tepper grew thoughtful. "It's a tempting thought, though, go down there, join their community, have sex with one of them…"

"I hate that! I hate that, Tepper!" Butch sighed. "My job is to get Burt Kaisman, that's what I'm fixed on doing. I guess you can go and talk to the Sev if you want to, but you've got an obligation to Station Post One. I want you to come back."

In a small voice, Tepper said, "I will."

———

Burt Kaisman wished he had his linkpad with him. The Fantasia colony, home of the Sev Army, would be red meat to his viewers—and to SSBC management. But then again, it was a calm and peaceful place; no military training camp, no charismatic leader urging the masses to violence, altogether nothing *exciting* to drive ratings.

After landing, Azman had handed the refugees over to one of the Sev, a young man named Beerman, who had been taking refugees' names ever since. But one of the Sev recognized Kaisman and invited him to meet their leader.

He followed the young Sev into the heart of the settlement, a conglomeration of wooden huts, many of them built in the trees. He was escorted onto a wooden platform where a ghastly pale man said.

"This is one of the refugees. He's Burt Kaisman."

Kaisman looked at the a pale face, the almost yellow eyes, and recognized him: Arnold Livingston.

"Burt Kaisman," Livingston said. "You spoke against us a great deal."

"Yes, I did," Kaisman said unapologetically, "but I have been forced to flee Station Post One because your ally, 'President' Kramer, declared martial law and placed me under arrest for voicing dissenting views."

"Now you wish to take sanctuary with *us?*"

"No, I desire no such thing. I still consider you a great threat to the human race. But this is where the refugee ship brought me. If you could permit my staying until I could find passage to another world, I would be grateful."

"Well, you're welcome to stay with us." There was no irony or anger in Livingston's voice. "As you do so, I hope you'll take time to learn more about us and come to understand how seriously you've misjudged us."

Kaisman had no interest in learning anything; his mind was made up. "I would appreciate just a private tent or room or whatever you have available, so I can work on my writing."

"As you wish."

———

Tepper set the *Frontier* down at the landing field, which after months of inactivity had come to life again. The refugee ship sat nearby, its engines still steaming and various aliens working on prepping it for takeoff.

Tepper disembarked first, followed by Butch.

"Okay, Tepper, now matter how peaceful you think the Sev are, just remember what happened earlier this year when the *Saviour* came here."

"I haven't forgotten, Butch," Tepper said in a weary tone.

Butch pointed into the woods. "Settlement's that way."

———

DuBois's message was not what Tobey wanted to hear: "This is a pretty big hole."

Tobey had been consoling himself with the probability that the hole was small, otherwise the Rec Pod would have depressurized before anyone could have gotten out. But the strain of the escaping air and the jetsam pummeling out into the void must have widened it. "Can you fix it?"

"I'm applying the plasteel now."

DuBois extended the nautabot's arms, placing the plasteel patch against the jagged crater, and then sprayed it with sealant.

"Okay, we had some bubbles," DuBois said, "but it's sealed and it's holding. I'll put on another treatment just to be sure."

Kramer signaled the Civilian Hab. "Cranius, outer hull is sealed. The leak should be stopped."

Cranius's voice replied, "Right, Flynn confirms the leak is stopped."

The next voice was Flynn's. "Yes, and the scrubbers are functioning."

The sound of applause carried over the intercom; Kramer could imagine the relief. It was no wonder the people on the Station were going insane; they had been through so much.

———

Butch was angry. Tepper had gone off to "mingle" with the Sev, and would no doubt soon be in bed with one of them.

Some questioning led Butch to a hut on the edge of the settlement. There was a young Sev standing guard. In his typical belligerent manner, Butch strode up to the Sev and demanded, "I'm looking for Burt Kaisman!"

"What are you going to do with him if you get him?" the young man asked.

"I'm taking him back to Station Post One. He's supposed to be serving a two-year sentence."

A young woman leaning against a tree chimed in, "About time if you ask me! Why don't you turn him over, Brad?"

"Burt Kaisman's a guest," Brad said. "I don't understand the reasons, but I trust Fweery."

Butch clenched his fists at the mention of Fweery. "Well, I don't! I'm taking Burt Kaisman out of here and I'm taking him now, or you people are going to be facing a heap of trouble!"

A woman came out of the hut. "Mr. McCrae?"

Butch glared at her, but held off saying anything until he knew whether she was Sev or refugee.

"Please. I am Amelia Cortez. I escaped from the brig."

"What do you want?" Butch asked crisply.

"I would like to make a deal."

"I don't make deals."

"Please. My crime is prostitution. I needed to feed my family. Please. Take me instead of Burt Kaisman and see that my family is fed."

Butch's expression softened; he sympathized with this woman, but he had a job to do. "I'm not letting Kaisman go."

"Please. My children did no wrong. Please."

"I'll do what I can for your children, but I'm not letting Kaisman go."

———

Tepper had mingled with the Sev for an hour, but found none who actually held the Sev gene. Finally someone offered to take him to Arnold Livingston, their leader, who did indeed carry the gene.

"I'm sorry, Mr. Tepper," Livingston said after listening to his story, "I'm afraid you've been misinformed. I know nothing about the Darians."

"But that's impossible—I was infected by Darian nanites when I was on the Darian Central Space Station, and Brandi Taylor had sex with a Darian and infected him. I felt Fweery. She became part of me."

Livingston smiled. "Oh, I see. Yes, of course she did. You became infected with Darian nanites, you said; the Darians became infected with Fweery. They have no communication with us."

"Oh, I see." Tepper felt stupid for not having thought of that himself. "Dr. DuBois should have known better! He's the one who's always saying there's no such thing as telepathy."

"Perhaps the Darians transmit some sort of frequency that their nanites respond to, but we can't receive it."

———

Butch took Amelia Cortez to the *Frontier*. He could have charged the hut and extracted Kaisman, but only at the risk of raising the ire of the whole colony. He didn't want a replay of the *Saviour* incident. So he needed time to think.

He wished Tepper would come back, but he wasn't counting on that. No, soon Tepper would be gathered with the others at sunset, singing the songs of the Sev.

He sat in the pilot's seat, Amelia next to him. But he frowned as he heard footsteps in the lounge. He clutched his sidearm as he heard footsteps behind him.

"Put down your weapon please," said the voice of Burt Kaisman. Butch saw the glint of a weapon out the corner of his eye, a metal gun that fired lead projectiles. A revolver, if he wasn't mistaken.

"I know that ugly voice."

"Are you all right, Amelia?" Kaisman asked.

"Yes," she said.

"Then go on. Get out of here."

"Please, Burt, you cannot give in."

"I won't. Now, go on, get out. I will handle this thug."

Amelia left.

Butch sat with his hands on the armrests, staring forward, feeling stupider than he had in his entire career. To have allowed an intruder into the ship, and to be caught unawares by, of all people, Burt Kaisman, was an all-new low point in his life.

And Kaisman was determined to rub it in. "Well, there's our chief of Civilian Security, not only leaving the door unlocked, but open."

"Yeah. Well, I'd like to say that it was a trap to lure you in."

Kaisman laughed. "Ah-ha, yes. So, what have we here? The great and powerful Butch McCrae taking innocent hostages."

"Ah, well, she wasn't exactly 'innocent,' was she? She was a refugee from justice. But that's okay; I've got you."

Kaisman laughed again. "Oh, on the contrary! It appears *I've* got *you!*"

"Yeah, what are you going to do? Shoot me?"

"That's not my style. That's more your 'president's' style."

Butch turned and stared down the pistol. "Right, no, no, no, no, your style is to go on SSBC and tell all sorts of lies. Let me just speculate a minute about how you're going to interpret my actions here…um…you escaped from our brutal regime, uh, our torture chamber on Station Post One, you fled here and hid out among the Sev, who welcomed you with open arms—and then in rushed the *Frontier*, strafing the city! Boom! Boom! Everything blew up around you! Then I marched in, took over the town, threatened to level everything and kill everybody unless they turned Burt Kaisman over. And to prove my point, I took Amelia hostage. Ah, but you came to the rescue, didn't you? Have I got that about right?"

"Well, you've got an interesting idea there," Kaisman chuckled. "But no, I simply report the facts as I see them. At the moment, my only desire is to go back to Station Post One, where I can do the most good."

Butch raised an eyebrow. "*You* do *good?*"

"Your assistant broke me out of the brig. He wanted me to come here and report on the doings of the Sev Army. It was never my idea. I had reservations about it from the start. I'd rather go back to Station Post One, be reunited with my wife and daughter, and report firsthand about the Station Post One Imperial Regime."

Suddenly a sidearm stabbed into Kaisman's back. "Weapon down, Kaisman," Tepper said.

Kaisman raised his hands, dropping the pistol. "Ah. Reinforcements arrive. So be it; I'm yours."

———

DuBois reported to the Prime Hab Center, linkpad in hand. He interrupted an intense conversation between Kramer and Cranius.

"Got your report?" Kramer asked.

DuBois handed him the linkpad. "Stress tests are complete. The sealed portion is airtight, but that's always going to be a weak spot. A number of the pods were damaged. We can erect new bulkheads and walls. It won't be reinforced quite as strongly as before, but we can work that out with sealants and insulation and so on. The expansion and contraction of the Civilian Hab won't really be as efficient as before."

"Well, that's not really a big deal," Kramer said.

"Mr. President, *everything* is a big deal in the construction of a space station. The Civilian Hab was designed to be a hive of pods which inflated when deployed in space. Now the configuration has been disrupted. Now, that's no problem in the short term, but over the long term—"

Cranius interrupted, "Over the long term, we can replace the entire Civilian Hab. Over the short term, the important thing is we have to end martial law!"

Tobey looked up from his console. "Cranius, I admire your ethics, but we were forced into—"

"Tobey, let's not play the victim," Kramer said. "Yes, the situation got ugly. Yes, Burt Kaisman is insufferable. Human Power's ideas are despicable. But we need to face the hard fact that we are in power. We can't pretend that we're the victims here. We are in power and we chose the course that we're on!"

The Aftermath of Revolution

Butch and Tepper had been back on the Station for a week, Burt Kaisman sat placidly in the brig, and Civilian Security patrolled the halls and kept the peace at the price of every human freedom that the Republic charter honored.

But then it finally happened. Open fighting broke out between Human Power and Civilian Security.

"Where the hell did they get sidearms?" Kramer demanded into the intercom.

Butch's voice was muffled by the crackle of static caused by sidearm fire. "I don't know! You know some of my security guys are Human Power sympathizers. Maybe they distributed them!"

"We need to get the situation under control. We don't need another hull breach."

"Yeah, I'm working on it! If you'd quit bugging me, I could get on with it."

Kramer decided to forgive, and not mention, the moment of insubordination. During a crisis, Butch was just a little more Butch than usual.

"It's all confined to the Civilian Hab," Flynn said, "outer ring, security corridor one, habitation corridor two, rec corridors three and four, and security is holding them off at the top of the grapple shaft."

"So far damage is superficial," DuBois said, "but I remind you, outer structure is still weakened from the last hull breach."

"Ready to deploy anesthetic gas," Kramer ordered.

"Anesthetic gas is ready to deploy," Tobey said.

"Butch, this is Kramer. We're going to deploy anesthetic gas."

"Right," Butch replied. "About time, too. Okay, boys, gas masks on!"

The sounds of clicking and hissing carried over the transmitter as Butch applied the facemask. Then his heavily muffled voice said, "Okay, gas masks are on."

Kramer nodded at Tobey, who hit the "discharge" icon.

In the next three minutes, the Human Power activists inhaled the gaseous fentanyl-benzodiazepine combination and lapsed into unconsciousness.

Dr. Lazarev was alerted, and she and her medics quickly arrived on the scene to keep the terrorists' airways and hearts stable until they woke up.

————

Burt Kaisman watched with a bemused expression as the Human Power activists—drowsy, sore, and itchy from the anesthetic gas—were herded into the brig by Butch McCrae.

Tobey Dingell arrived shortly after to call him out on instigating the violence.

Kaisman only chuckled at the accusation. "This bold revolutionary activity can certainly not be attributed to me. I have been locked here in the brig."

"I know perfectly well you've been getting articles out."

"Ah, and I've noticed that Derek Winchester's not been around here lately. You must have figured out that's how I was getting my articles out."

" 'Free Speech Galaxy' is shut down."

Kaisman laughed. "Oh, I'll say it is!"

Tobey pointed a finger at him. "You're cut off, Kaisman! You can't influence events anymore!"

"Oh, yes I can! I can influence events more loudly than I ever have before—through my silence!"

————

DuBois, Lazarev, Tobey, Flynn, and Cranius sat around the conference pod table, each in turn reporting on the aftermath of the violence. Butch and Tepper sat at the far end of the table, too tired to inject sarcastic comments.

"Three are dead due to complications from the gas," Lazarev said in an accusing tone.

Kramer rubbed his temples. "Oh, God."

"Heart failure was one problem, people vomiting into their throats and suffocating was another. You cannot simply deploy anesthetic gas willy-nilly, Mr. President. There is a reason we who have *medical degrees* only anesthetize people under controlled conditions!"

"This situation was anything but controlled," Kramer said, keeping a rein on his temper. "What happened to those people was a tragedy, but I judged that the risk from the gas was less than the risk of ongoing armed conflict aboard our Station, and I would do it again. Dr. DuBois, what did it do to the Station?"

DuBois said, "Structural strain on joints four, seven, and eight, on the outer rim, and joint two and four on the upper section of the grapple shaft, and of course the scrubbers will need to be replaced."

Kramer turned to Flynn. "You get on that."

Flynn was on his feet as Kramer spoke. "Yes, sir."

DuBois continued, "Semiconductor rupture in corridor two, so there are no lights in pod eight—that's Jeremy and Felicia Halpern."

"Are they among the rioters?"

"I don't know."

"All right, one thing at a time. Flynn?"

"The new scrubbers are in place now. Give it about an hour before we can open up the hatches."

"How many of your own people are you going to confine to the brig?" Cranius asked.

"As many as I have to," Kramer said.

"You have more of your civilians in the brig than out! It's time to reexamine your system of government."

"I've *been* reexamining it, Cranius."

"Lift martial law, no questions asked. If you do it now, the people will be grateful for their newfound freedom."

"No, the anger is still too great. It needs to be propitiously timed. If I do it now, it will send a signal that violent revolution is legitimate political discourse."

DuBois said, "While all this was going on, Republic intelligence had the Hlthlishtl on the newsfeed. It says that the Skobee have scored a major victory and the Braydon have agreed to establish two separate countries."

"Right, I was looking at that," Tobey said. "Several of the planets of the Hlthlishtl Confederation brokered a peace between the Skobee and the Braydon and both sides agreed to a cessation of hostilities whereby both would occupy the planet but different regions."

Tepper said, "It seems so simple."

"Amazing what you can do when you stop bombing civilians," DuBois said.

"You know, Fish-Head never wanted to bomb civilians. It was the more extreme elements."

DuBois disliked referring to the Skobee leader as "Fish-Head," but as he had never mastered the pronunciation of D'quan'k-modk-vu d'sa, he said distastefully, "Well, Fish-Head's no longer in power there."

"No kidding! What happened?"

"If I understand the information correctly, he was just old and he decided to step down and become a shopkeeper. That was another facet of the message. We got word that Fish-Head died and you and Butch were invited to the funeral."

"Aw, man," Butch said. "I really liked him."

Tepper cast him a sidelong glance. "I guess he was the nicest and smartest terrorist leader I ever met."

"Was he a terrorist or was he a freedom fighter?"

"Well, the families of the civilians who were killed would certainly say he was a terrorist."

"Yeah, but Fish-Head didn't do that stuff."

"Well, do you want to come with me to the funeral?"

"Yeah, of course I'll come with you, yeah. Any chance to get away from all the damn civilians."

Tepper turned to Kramer. "Yeah, who's going to keep an eye on them while we're gone?"

"I think all the real troublemakers are in the brig right now," Kramer said.

———

Fabian Marshall, the Human Power leader in the next cell, approached the plasma-charged bars and reached through to shake Kaisman's hand. "It's an honor to meet you, Mr. Kaisman. We did our best."

Kaisman tentatively grasped Marshall's hand, but didn't shake, fearing to singe Marshall's skin on the bars. "You certainly did. I would never condone armed rebellion, but this government has given us no choice."

There were murmurs of assent from the other Human Power prisoners.

"Yet you did make one miscalculation," Kaisman said. "Such an open and violent and widespread revolt has resulted in all of you being placed here in the brig. Who is going to continue on our work now?"

Marshall grew defensive. "What else could we have done?"

"When we're subjects of an overreaching government, we must act with cunning. We must infiltrate their system. We need spies, double agents, sabateurs. We can't let them know who our leaders are. So long as they are better armed than we are, any open combat will result in defeat for us."

"How long do you figure we'll get in here?" asked a young man—probably no older than eighteen— behind Marshall.

"I got two years merely for speaking out," Kaisman said. "You people may get life—or death."

The prisoners fell into a hushed murmer.

Kaisman gave them a reassuring smile. "But don't fret. I don't think they'll actually do that. They know resentment runs deep. They can't be executing a full quarter of their civilian population, nor can they afford the resources to keep us fed and sheltered in the brig for an indefinite period of time. The most helpful thing would be if one of you could pose as someone who was dragged into this against your will. Contrive a convincing enough story to be released. Then you can spread a more equitable plan for the rest of the civilian population."

———

The *Frontier* detached from Station Post One and, under Tepper's skillful hand, steered in the direction of the Hlthlishtl Confederation.

"We're clear," Tepper said. "We have discretionary maneuver."

Flynn's voice replied, "We show your optimum light speed point at fourteen point seven."

"Marked. Confirmed on this end."

Butch gestured out the window at the huge, triangular hulk bathed in spotlights from Dock Deck Three. "And there's the *Phoenix*, still under repair."

"Yeah, give it another week, it'll be ready," Tepper said.

"Sure quite a blow, though."

"Well, let's just hope Zoran has other things on his mind."

"What mind?"

"All right, ready for light speed."

"Okay."

Tepper pushed the slide lever forward. "Accelerating to light speed factor nine."

———

Kramer scrolled through the summary of the day's Council Session as he listened to Cranius's objections.

"I can't understand your attitude, Cranius," Kramer said. "It was you that these people were targeting. You should be delighted at this turn of events."

"Well, sprog, I don't want to be targeted anymore. I just see a system that isn't working. It seems like both sides are just on this determined sprogging spiral to make this thing accelerate beyond all control. I don't understand why. You're both reacting to each other in the most unproductive way possible."

"What would you do in my place?"

"Now that the actual revolutionaries are in the brig, lift martial law. The security threat is over. That will allow the civilians to see that this isn't a power grab; it was an attempt to save their melchers."

Kramer smiled. "The Gandhi approach. Fight violence with peace."

"Well, I don't know what a gondy is, but sprog, yeah, I'd put it that way."

"You may be onto something, Cranius. I'll give it a little thought."

———

The alert sounded in the *Frontier*'s cockpit. Butch set down his paper copy of Paul Theroux's *The Mosquito Coast* while Tepper shut off the alert and said, "All right, there it is. We've crossed the boundary. We're in Hlthlishtl space."

Butch activated the scanner. "All right, I don't see any signs of their patrol ships—I take it back. I've got one rushing in on us right now."

The disconcerting mechanical voice of a Hlthlishtl announced, "Attention *Frontier*, state your intentions and destination."

"This is Elmer Tepper and Butch McCrae out of Station Post One," Tepper replied. "We're on course for the planet Skobee. We've been invited to the funeral of Fi—the Skobee leader."

"Information confirmed. We will escort you to Skobee."

"Much obliged." As he took manual control and prepared to follow the patrol ship, Tepper asked, "Got a Shakespeare quote for this, Butch? Wasn't there a situation similar to this in *Hamlet* when, uh, King

Claudius sent those two idiots to reach some sort of a deal with King Fortenbras?"

Butch grinned. "Well! I didn't know you actually knew the story of *Hamlet*."

Tepper shrugged. "Well…I've started to get into Shakespeare lately, believe it or not."

"You have?!" Butch was astonished.

"Yeah, I've found a lot of his stuff kind of has parallels to our situations."

Butch smacked his forehead. "God. That is the weirdest damn thing, because—for the first time in my life, I've found I don't have much of a stomach for Shakespeare anymore."

"*Really?!*"

"Yeah. Just, after all we've been through, all the things we've seen, he just seems to have such a limited perspective on the universe. I read his plays now and… just a little bit of communication and understanding could have tidied up the situations. I just lose patience with it nowadays."

Tepper shook his head. "God. We just can't seem to get ourselves aligned."

———

Kramer stood at the podium in the press pod, his fingers shifting nervously along his linkpad and leaving sweat stains.

"People of Station Post One. As you're no doubt aware, violence broke out in the halls of the Civilian Hab. Protesters fighting against the imposition of martial law and affiliated with Human Power openly fought our security people. Despite some small damage to the Station, hull integrity was not compromised. All damage has been repaired and the civilians are in no danger.

"Those who perpeatrated this uprising are now in the brig, pending trial. After an investigation, it has been determined that the danger of further uprising and violence has been diminished. Therefore, as promised, I am hereby lifting the state of martial law and returning this Station to Congressional control. I will no longer be in operational control of this Station. Commander Tobey Dingell is once again the operational commander.

"Now, since such a large portion of the civilian population was involved in the revolt, I believe that we are best advised to forego the usual methods of reaching the truth in such matters. Instead of a hearing before a formal court, I should like the Human Power activists who participated in this revolt to be tried by their own peers. This will be the first jury trial since the destruction of the Earth."

———

When the Human Power prisoners began verbally, and then physically, assaulting a young woman in the cell with them, security officers Schell and Perkins made the decision to pull her out.

A short time later, DuBois escorted her into Tobey's privacy pod.

"This is Arlyn Fisher. She claims that she was just kind of caught in the middle of things when the fighting broke out, and she wasn't with the revolutionaries."

"Ms. Fisher," Tobey said with a nod. "What's your story?"

"I'm a botanist," the woman said in a German accent. "I was on my way to the outer ring to check on my hydroponic gardens when all of a sudden all these people started shooting sidearms, then security came from the other direction and they started shooting sidearms. I ducked for cover, and next thing I knew, the gas came down and I woke up in the brig. I don't belong there with those people. I don't share their politics and I have my gardens to attend to. Is there any way that we can work something out?"

"Well, if it was up to me the answer would be no. You all stand accused of fomenting insurrection, and I would want to see some solid proof that you were not involved, but it is the President's decision that you are all innocent until proven guilty, and that anyone who comes forward with a story like yours is to be released. So, against my better judgment, go back to your gardens."

The woman smiled brightly—too brightly for the lecture Tobey had just given her—and said, "Thank you, Commander! Thank you, I'm truly grateful."

"Get out of here."

DuBois escorted her out.

———

Skobee was a cold, dark planet whose heat emanated mostly from volcanoes rather than the pittance of sunlight that managed to penetrate its thick clouds.

A squid-like being was waiting for Butch and Tepper as they climbed out of the *Frontier*. It spoke in its wet, gulpy language. Their translation fibers provided a human-sounding voice.

"Welcome back to Skobee, Captain Tepper, Mr. McCrae."

"Thank you," Tepper said. "I wish it could have been under happier circumstances. I'm sorry about the death of Fish-Head."

"It was its time. It lived a good life." The Skobee were asexual and content to be referred to as "it." "I am Nu'naka'a'ga'aga'am. Please come with me."

"How 'bout if I call you Frog-Face?" Butch asked. "I can't pronounce your name—or even remember it."

"So be it."

Nu'naka'a'ga'aga'am—or "Frog-Face"—led them to a car of Braydon design and held the door open for them. Once they had climed in, Frog-Face got into the front seat, placing four tentacles on the floor and four on the steering wheel. It drove effortlessly with its tentacles, taking them deeper into the city.

Noting the bright lights, the traffic, the shops and markets, Butch tried to equate this place with the swamps and forest he remembered from their previous visit.

"This place has changed," Butch remarked.

"Sure has," Tepper said. "They didn't have this kind of development before."

"Uh, Frog-Face, all this development, the high-rises and stuff, that doesn't quite fit with what Fish-Head told us about how you people like to just live in harmony with nature."

"Things have changed since your last visit," Frog-Face said. "We can explain after the funeral."

———

Tobey was livid. It took all his self control not to scream at Kramer. "So we're just going to let her go! We don't have anything but her word that she wasn't involved in the mutiny!"

"That's all we have," Kramer replied calmly. "The security cameras were shot out in the battle. Now, we could go through all the security officers' personal helmet cams and see if we can get a shot of her, but what good would that do? She's one woman. From what the guards were saying, the others were beating up on her."

Tobey was not convinced. "Those people seem willing to beat up on anybody and anything."

"Tobey, they're not a force of nature. They're our people. Our job is to serve them. We're not their overlords."

"Somebody's going to have to be."

"Our job is to represent them—even if they're wrong."

Tobey's face reddened. "*Why?!*" he demanded.

"Because what they are is what we are. We're trying to preserve our species. They are our species."

"This continual fighting can only result in the end of our species! What's the point in preserving the worst of us if the worst is going to destroy us?"

"What's the alternative? Confine sixty percent of the civilian population to the brig?"

"The alternative is a firm hand of justice, not just taking the word of some chick who says 'I didn't do it!'"

"So we'll watch her, all right? What's she going to do? Blow up the Station that she lives on?"

"I wouldn't put much past these people."

"All right, maybe you wouldn't, but I would. These are human beings with their own concerns. They may be misguided, they may have been misled, but they have their own concerns, and we have to treat them fairly, treat them with respect, treat them as human beings."

"They don't treat you that way," Tobey pointed out.

"That's the job," Kramer said firmly.

————

The funeral was held at the same riverbank where Butch and Tepper had met Fish-Head on their last visit. The trees had been cleared out and some buildings erected, with electrical and phone wires and a small parking lot, but the area was still lovely, open, and natural despite the dark clouds.

A Skobee played a strange musical instrument composed of long bells hanging from a rack and shelf arrangement. Butch actually liked the haunting melody the creature was playing, but Tepper's mouth wrinkled in disgust.

Seeing no sign of a coffin or a body, Butch gripped one of Frog-Face's tentacles and asked, "Isn't there any kind of a viewing or anything?"

"What do you mean?"

"Well, I mean to pay our last respects to Fish-Head?"

"That is what we are doing."

"So we're not going to see the body?" Tepper asked.

"Certainly not! Why would you wish to do that?"

Butch was embarrassed. "Uh, customary in our culture, I guess...." The bells continued to ring out their simple, sweet melody. "There's no speech or eulogy or anything?"

"No. A funeral is a solemn affair. The body has been enclosed in a firebox."

As Frog-Face quietly explained, four Skobee carried the coffin—or firebox—toward the river, along the row of attendees while each silently paid its respects. Upon reaching the river, an eight-meter wooden paddleboat received the firebox. The Skobee on board placed it in the stern.

As the Skobee gathered at the riverbank, the boat set off, the paddlewheel rotating faster, propelling the boat downstream toward the sea.

As the boat dwindled into a speck on the horizon, it suddenly lit up with a bright flame, brilliant in the darkness of this cold and forlorn planet.

At that moment all the Skobee bellowed a musical tone into the air.

Frog-Face explained, "We announce to the gods below that a fine Skobee is on its way."

When the ceremony had concluded, Frog-Face escorted Butch and Tepper to the sleeping quarters next to the river, explaining, "After we reached the agreement with the Braydon, all Skobee were relocated to our side of the planet. This included all Skobee who were workers, secretaries, and so on, in the Braydon cities. Those of us who had been trained to work hard, to aspire to be something, to build things, were naturally the dominant Skobee. Once we arrived here, we constructed an infrastructure rivaling that of the Braydon."

The sleeping quarters contained six beds—the mattresses secreted water when compressed—and a kitchen. There was a television set and a computer with a large keyboard fit for the Skobee tentacles.

"We were a group of do-nothings," Frog-Face said, "content to sit by the river and waste our lives away, but now we're hard workers aspiring to be something. Those who don't merit success don't succeed."

"Don't you see what you're doing?" Butch asked. "You've become your own enemy!"

"Butch, let's not press it," Tepper warned.

Frog-Face said, "We have already succeeded in taking over our side of the planet. The fact that we succeeded indicates that we merit that success. Wouldn't you agree?"

"No, I would not agree," Butch said. "By that reasoning, the Braydon merited their success when they took over your planet."

"The Braydon taught us the value and the dignity of hard work."

"That's natural for the Braydon! That's what you were fighting against! That's not natural for the Skobee!"

"Yet we *are* Skobee, and that is the way *we* have chosen to live."

"Not all of you have. You just mentioned the ones who haven't embraced this way of life. What happens to them?"

"Those who are too lazy to work hard do not merit success."

Butch sighed. "Do you think this system is something that Fish-Head would have condoned?"

"Fish-Head is dead."

———

President Kramer walked up to the brig. "Burt Kaisman?"

Kaisman walked toward him, grinning. "Well! Mr. President!"

On Kramer's signal the guard unlocked, decharged, and opened the door.

"Please step out here," Kramer said.

Kaisman obeyed. He stood face-to-face with Kramer and said, "Well, if it had been Commander Dingell, I would have assumed I was being spaced. What could you possibly want with me?"

"You're free."

Kaisman raised an eyebrow. "I beg your pardon?"

"Martial law is lifted. You're free."

"Under what conditions?"

"None. Go back to your show. Do whatever you want. You're free."

Kaisman studied him, then slowly walked away. At the door to the cell block, he turned, gave Kramer another puzzled glance, then left.

———

Arlyn Fisher entered the Rec Pod, looked around, and chose someone at random. She walked up to the young man's table, gave him her most charming smile, and said, "Good afternoon."

The startled man smiled back. "Hey! What's going on?"

"Nothing. I don't think I've seen you around before. I'm Arlyn Fisher."

The man extended his hand. "Bartolo Rasoulis. Good to meet you."

Arlyn sat, folded her hands on the table, and continued to smile. "Things are crowded in here today."

"Yeah, I guess so. I'm surprised. With so many civilians in the brig, you wouldn't think there'd be so many people running loose….On the other hand, with martial law lifted, everyone feels like celebrating."

"What do you make of all that?"

"Me?" Rasoulis shrugged. "Well, I guess all those dissidents are taken care of, so the President sees no more need to impose martial law."

Arlyn leaned forward and whispered conspiratorially, "You don't suppose that this is all some sort of grand plan, do you?"

Rasoulis casually reached across the table and placed his hands over hers. "What do you mean?"

"Well, supposing he was lifting martial law just to get everybody's support, and then he plans on cracking down in a more subtle and insidious way?"

Rasoulis drew his hands back. "No, I don't buy all that stuff that Burt Kaisman has been saying."

Arlyn continued cautiously. "No? Well, what if it's true? I run the hydroponics section. Do you know how much trouble I've had getting ahold of seed?"

"Well, yeah, this is a space station."

"Exactly my point." Arlyn tried not to lay it on too thick; she kept her tone soft, her smile warm. "We're all being forced to live in a space station because it's no longer safe to live on planets. And why is it no longer safe to live on planets? Because it's now Republic policy to stand by and do nothing about the Thermians."

"No, that's not true." Rasoulis was clearly losing interest—in the conversation and in her. "We still fight the Thermians with P-SARs."

"Yes, swat them out of the way, sure, but they always come back."

"Yeah, well, that's true." Rasoulis was looking down at his meal now; Arlyn realized he was agreeing with her merely to avoid an argument.

"I'm not saying anyone should go out in the halls and shoot anyone like those wackos who are in the brig now," she said with what she hoped was an adorable little giggle, "but we've got to stay vigilant, keep an eye on what our government is doing."

"Well, I'd much sooner get my information through legitimate sources than through Burt Kaisman."

"What do you consider legitimate sources? The President?"

"I have friends on the command staff. News trickles down to me."

She shrugged. "Perhaps the news they want you to hear."

"Well, yeah." Rasoulis rose, tossed his half-eaten lunch into the recycler slot. "Well, I'm running late for a meeting, so…it was good to meet you."

"Good to meet you, Mr. Rasoulis." Arlyn watched him go, discouraged. Evidently Bartolo Rasoulis was so brainwashed that even her feminine wiles failed to break through his defenses.

She tried three more people—two men and one woman—and met with similar results.

That afternoon, she was surprised to receive a visit in her privacy pod by Burt Kaisman.

"Mr. Kaisman!" she said, awed. "How did you get out of the brig?"

"Damon Kramer came by personally and let me go."

"*What?*"

Kaisman laughed at her reaction. "Yes, he just set me free. He told me martial law is lifted and I was free to go. I've already been to the SSBC Studios, and I'm delighted to say that *Kaisman and Friends* will be back on the air tomorrow."

"Oh, that's wonderful! Will Derek Winchester and Shellie Hurlburt be with you?"

"I don't know. I haven't gotten a confirmation on that yet. So tell me, how have you been doing with your…" Kaisman grinned. "…top-secret assignment?"

She told him about her encounters with Bartolo Rasoulis and the others.

"It's hardly surprising the people you've spoken to have not been very receptive," Kaisman said. "Remember, all those who agree with us participated in the…demonstation. They're all in the brig."

"Then what more can I do?"

"Exactly the opposite of what you've been doing. The idea of getting you out of the brig was to get you trusted by the command staff. Go back to your hydroponics. Play the system. Become one of them. And then you, on the inside, can feed me reports to expose what's going on in the upper echelons."

Arlyn felt foolish. "I understand."

"Good luck, and well done."

"Thank you."

Kaisman turned and left. Arlyn sat down at her desk to think. She had a difficult task ahead; to suck up to people she despised would be a challenge.

Butch McCrae stood before a crowd of Skobee on the riverbank. He had persuaded a few to listen to him, and as he spoke, others grew interested and joined the crowd.

"It's called collective bargaining," he explained. "All you've got to do is refuse to work until your employer gives you certain concessions. A living wage, better working conditions, whatever."

A Skobee in the front row protested, "That hardly helps those of us who don't wish to work in their industries."

"Okay, no, no, it doesn't. But there are certainly other alternatives to going out and killing people. That's why you all need to organize and try to effect change through legal means—"

"Butch!" Tepper stomped through the reeds. "Could I talk to you please?" There was no missing the anger in his voice.

"Uh…sure." To his audience, he said, "I'll be back."

He followed Tepper through the reeds and behind a tree in view of the parking lot.

"What is it, Tepper? I was just getting them motivated—"

"What the hell do you think you're doing?"

"Look, you see what's going on around here—"

"It's none of our business!"

Butch ground his teeth. "It's certainly our business! We got involved when we struck up the treaty with Fish-Head."

"And now our treaty is with Frog-Face!"

Butch turned to leave. "Mine sure ain't." Then he paused, his anger enflamed, and said, "What they've formed here is an oligarchy! They've consolidated their power and they're going to oppress the other Skobee!"

Tepper held a hand up. "Not our business, not our business."

"Look, this is the whole reason they broke away. The Braydon were oppressive. And now—now they're just as oppressive!"

"Well, that's the way it usually works. Revolution sounds like a wonderful thing, but generally after the revolution, whatever steps in to replace it turns out to be just as bad—or worse."

"Right. So maybe we can set them on the right path, prevent another bloody conflict, transition them into a new and more equitable—"

"Butch, you're not listening to me! It's not our business!"

"They're supposedly our allies."

"They're also a sovereign civilization."

"Sure, they're kind of a new and unstable civilization. They just reached—"

"*We're* a new and unstable civilization," Tepper shouted. "The Unified Republic is less than a year old. We still have not recovered from *the destruction of our planet*, Butch! We can't go around policing the galaxy."

Butch turned and walked off. "I can do whatever I want."

Tepper ran after him and grabbed him round the torso. Butch shook him off, prepared to fight. Tepper stepped back, raised his hands in surrender.

"This is *their* civilization," Tepper said. "They'll do what *they* want, not what *you* want."

Butch calmed himself. "I'm helping people who need my help."

"We came here to attend a funeral. We've done that. It's time to go back to Station Post One."

"Why don't you go on ahead, leave me, I'll take care of this myself—"

Tepper laughed. "No, no, Butch, Butch, that's not the way it works. Look, I hate to pull rank on you, but I am in command of this mission. I call the shots. We're leaving and I'm ordering you to come with me."

Butch was taken aback. "*You* are pulling rank on *me!*"

"That's right. What are you going to do? Quit again?"

"That was a low blow!"

"Come on, Butch, let's go."

Butch gestured at the squid-like beings who were still gathered at the riverbank. "And we're just leaving them in the lurch?"

Tepper nodded. "It's the way it's got to be."

Butch looked at the Skobee, at their imploring eyes—or what he saw as imploring—and their miserable conditions at the hands of a greedy few.

"Well?" Tepper pressed. "What's it going to be? Are you going to come along or are you going to quit? Those are your only two options."

Butch thought about pointing out that he had already quit, that he was a civilian now, that he didn't have to obey Tepper's orders, but he wasn't angry enough to leave Station Post One again—or perhaps he didn't truly care enough. "Right. I'm coming."

———

As promised, Burt Kaisman returned to his show at noon, greeting his viewers with a proud smile.

"Good afternoon, everyone!" he began with more than the usual enthusiasm. "Welcome to *Kaisman and Friends*. I'm Burt Kaisman, here once again with Derek Winchester and Shellie Hurlburt. We…are…*back!* Thanks to all of *you*…" and with that he pointed at the camera. "Thanks to *your* protests, thanks to your participation in the democratic process, the state of illegal martial law has been lifted! And we are back on the air, here to report to you the objective truth, the *facts*, which 'President' Kramer and Commander Dingell don't want you to know.

"But today we can bask in a number of victories. Not only has martial law been lifted, but there will be no more aliens on Station Post One. Oh, we still have a few. We still have Cranius from Vron, we still have Ophelia from the Etuknip Hegemony, but the invasion of our Station seems to be over. How about that, Derek?"

Derek Winchester said, "That's true, Burt, but we must be vigilant. We can't let down our guard. Damon

Kramer's allegiance is still with aliens, and as long as he remains in power, there's still danger."

"Very good point, Derek. And what do you have to say, Shellie?"

"Well, I say Derek is absolutely right!" Shellie Hurlburt shrieked. "As long as Cranius is here to whisper in Damon Kramer's ear, there will always be danger! I mean, even now the Vron are massing for a major strike on Klym Valdor!"

"That's right, Burt," Winchester chimed in. "The Valdor have been preparing their own pre-emptive strike which could rid this galaxy of Thermians, but the Vron won't have that."

"Right! Right!" Shellie shrieked. "And I remind you that Damon Kramer talked the Centralized Committee into endorsing the Vron's actions! I mean, the Centralized Committee used to be the central government of the Valdor! I mean, what is going on here?! They've betrayed the very civilization that was responsible for its existence!"

"You are absolutely correct," Kaisman said. "So though we may be winning the fight against 'President' Kramer, we are losing the fight against the Thermians. And that is why we all must urge a strong response to the Vron! And I don't mean a slap on the wrist; I mean a full military response! And it must begin by either removing Cranius from the Station or placing him in the brig. For so long as he is present to influence our 'president,' this galaxy shall fall to the Thermians!"

———

Tobey visited the Presidential Pod after Council Session adjourned for the day, as had become his habit lately. He was in a rare good mood.

"Did you see SSBC's ratings for Burt Kaisman's show? They are piss poor."

Kramer did not follow SSBC's ratings. He cared about Burt Kaisman's blathering a lot less than Tobey did. "Well, there's no surprise there. All his viewers are in the brig!"

"Well, I guess that's true."

"What I'd like to know is how he found out about the Vron's plans for an assault on Klym Valdor. That's top secret."

Tobey sighed. "He's a journalist. They've got their ways."

"Yeah, he's still a force to be reckoned with, that's for sure. But whatever's going on with the Vron and the Valdor, we can't take our eyes off the ball."

"What are you talking about? That *is* the ball!"

Kramer shrugged. "Well, you're right. But I'm still thinking about Zoran and the Hyrons."

"Well, intelligence shows that it's true that they've backed off of Drayonne. And with President Frodax removed, Keilah and Eilonwy are running things. The Hyron Empire is back on our side."

"Well, but Zoran is not, and no one is ever able to control him."

Tobey had no answer to that.

———

The *Frontier* sped away from Skobee. Butch and Tepper sat in the cockpit, silent, morose. Neither liked to leave the Skobee civilization in the situation it was in, and neither liked to be on opposite sides of what to do about it.

"We're going to outphase transition at seventeen thirty," Tepper said, "aq beac at seventeen thirty-one. Right now field tension is thirteen point eight two six. And we've got a positive field flow of point one eight two. Gravimeter shows a one eight six point four two seven contraction forward and we're on trajectory one. Our ETA is seventeen hours. All right, she's on autopilot. I for one am ready to get some sleep. How 'bout you?"

Butch just grunted in reply.

"Come on, Butch, it's over."

Butch was so outraged by Tepper's remark that he fumbled for ten seconds on how to reply. After an endless series of incoherent sounds, he said, "The fact that we turned our back on them and ran out does not mean it's over. It is in full swing. It's going to be in full swing for, God, who knows how long? Generations maybe."

"Well, there's nothing we can do about it."

Butch let out a deep breath, then said with exasperation, "A little assistance!"

"There's no such thing as 'a little assistance' in something like this. Try and we'll end up in a deep quagmire that we won't be able to extract ourselves from. It's happened before. History is full of examples."

Butch knew full well how true that was. "Mr. Wise, aren't you? Since when did you read history?"

"You saying I'm wrong?"

"I'm saying…" Butch fell silent a moment, then voiced what he had been thinking of ever since leaving Skobee. "…that throughout its travels, the *Silver Streak* came across a lot of planets that were in trouble, and Captain Cameron never shrank back from stepping in and lending a hand."

"The fact that Captain Cameron did it doesn't mean it was a good idea."

"What's that supposed to mean?"

Tepper licked his lips and said, "What that's supposed to mean is, we never revisited any of those planets. How do we know? He could have made the situation worse. See, that's what I'm talking about. Captain Cameron stepped in, took a unilateral action, and then they left, and we have no idea what happened to the planet next. But I can guarantee one thing: probably who's ever in charge of those planets didn't think too fondly of Captain Cameron and his interference."

Butch was suddenly intensely curious to visit Omicron Andromedae-4 or the Flat Planet or Cincinnatti-10 or Trillion or Planet Mexico and find out what had happened there after the *Silver Streak*'s influence. "You're awfully sure of that. You can't just take a guess and say that's how it is."

"Well, that's what you wanted to do back on the planet."

Butch exploded, "Where are you getting all this stuff, Tepper?! When did you start thinking and reading?"

Tepper grinned. "I told you. I've been reading Shakespeare." The grin vanished. "Apparently you haven't been."

Trial by Fire

Dr. Ebor DuBois sweated in the overheated Nautabot as he hovered over a portion of the Space Star *Phoenix*'s thermoplast hull. He extended the Nautabot's arms as he examined the target area. The arms gripped a black box about the size and shape of a fisherman's tackle box.

"Mark twenty-four, system P, Z-47. Inserting unit CRS-16 into unit ALG-14."

The box slipped into the slot, and the LEDs along its side illuminated, showing that it was active.

"We have a baby," he said with a smile.

"Marked," said the cheerful voice of Reve Ruchinsky, who was at the helm of the *Phoenix*.

"And some serious goddamn congrats," came another voice, a delightfully familiar, booming, gruff voice.

DuBois looked up through the transparent bubble of his Nautabot at the other ship that drifted near the *Phoenix*, a Space Star of identical design that had been Station Post One's unexpected companion for the past two days. "Thanks, Mr. Hasta, and thanks for the parts!"

"Goddamn!"

Repairs on the Space Star *Phoenix* were nearly complete, thanks largely to the timely arrival from deep space of the Space Star *Exodus*, laying over for maintenance, upgrades, and extended shore leave. Captain Philippe Stargazer and his first officer, Jack Hasta, had proven invaluable in both repairing and upgrading the *Phoenix*.

———

Philippe Stargazer had many outstanding qualities. His singing voice was not one of them. As he looked over some of the equipment in Station Post One's storage bay, he idly sang,

"*Auprès de ma blonde*
"*Qu'il fair bon, fait bon, fait bon,*
"*Auprès de ma blonde*
"*Qu'il fait bon dormir—*"

until Jack Hasta begged him to stop. "And don't ever goddamn sing ever again!"

"You know, Servanne told me that my singing voice was like nothing she had ever heard before."

"Yeah, I can believe it! Goddamn! You sound like a dolphin being run over by a steamroller! Goddamn!"

"Well, the point is we have finishèd the repairs!"

"Well, goddamn, we did, didn't we? Not a bad pair of mechanics, are we?"

"Well, we have been known to slap a few ships into shape now and again, haven't we?"

"You goddamn better believe it! Aw, goddamn." Jack looked around at the cramped and dark environment of this ramshackle space station parked here in the center of the Unified Republic. Most of the damage they had helped to fix had been caused by angry mobs of civilians shooting things and breaking things and otherwise causing trouble. He shook his head as he pondered life on Station Post One. "The goddamn stuff that's been going on on this Station."

Stargazer agreed. "Things never got to that point aboard the *Silver Streak.*"

"Figure it the hell out. Maybe a bunch of goddamn civilians feel better when they're on board a goddamn spaceship *going* somewhere as opposed to sitting on a goddamn space station that just goddamn sits there."

"Well, we do not know how Kramer and Dingell handle things around here. Maybe they really are a little overbearing."

"Shit. More overbearing than Dick?"

Stargazer laughed at that.

———

After completing the repairs, Stargazer went to meet with President Kramer while Jack Hasta headed to the Intercore offices to deliver the repair report. Cranius was working in the Intercore reception pod when Jack arrived.

In their brief encounters in the past two days, Jack had decided that he liked Cranius. As they reviewed the report, his thoughts wandered to the multiple times Cranius had been assaulted, and it made him angry.

"The *Exodus* is now alongside Dock Deck One," Cranius said. "Pressure snakes are attached to the Hangar Deck. All your equipment is prepared, so if there's anything more you need, just let me know."

"I'm doing just goddamn fine, Cranius," Jack Hasta replied. "Listen, a lot of the goddamn trouble that's happened on this goddamn Station is because a bunch of funky civilians have a problem with you."

"I'm very well aware of that," Cranius said in a tired voice. "I was physically assaulted a few times."

"Well, goddamn, I trust you know that kind of goddamn crap would never happen aboard the *Exodus*. Philippe wouldn't allow it, our security chief wouldn't allow it, and *I* wouldn't allow it! So listen, as long as the civilians are all in a goddamn uproar around here, acting like a bunch of Nazis, why don't you leave this place behind, all the ugliness around here, and come on board the *Exodus*? We've got a nice, happy environment. We're very open and welcoming of everybody, even goddamn aliens."

Cranius turned away and walked across the room, pondering. "That's a very interesting proposition. You know, I have noticed this place isn't really very friendly."

"Goddamn, I don't know what the hell's goddamn happened around here! Let me ask you this: what kind of a commander is Tobey Dingell?"

"I actually don't have much contact with him. Most of my contact is with President Kramer, who—I really like him. He's been a very good friend, very supportive, and he's wise and he's a good leader—"

"Ultimately, though, it's Dingell goddamn calling the shots. Now, I don't mean anything against Dingell; he was a good, capable officer on the goddamn *Silver Streak*. But from all I've goddamn heard, I don't know if he is goddamn up to commanding this Station. And keep that between you and me; it's not my goddamn call to make."

"Well, as long as we're being honest with each other, if you want to know the sprogging truth, I'm not sure he is up to command. I've noticed any time he's *not* in command, he's gentle, humorous, laid-back—but when he *is* in command, he's tense and irritable and temperamental and dogmatic."

"Well, goddamn, Philippe's a real laid-back captain. He runs things real smooth—probably because I'm always telling him what to do!"

Cranius laughed obligingly, though he didn't really understand. "Well, Mr. Hasta, I'll consider your offer. I have to think about it because—"

"Sure!"

"—I already lost my life on Vron and I've worked hard to—"

"I gotcha."

"—make a new life for myself here."

"I hear ya, Cranius, take your goddamn time. No goddamn pressure."

"What kind of position do you have in mind for me on the *Exodus*?"

Jack shrugged. "I dunno. Whatever you've been goddamn doing here, I guess."

"Well, I can't be the President's chief of staff from the *Exodus!* But aside from being a part-time software engineer for Intercore, primarily I've been an intermediary with the Vron."

"Well...maybe we need a goddamn intermediary with the goddamn Vron, or, hell, you could be our intermediary with goddamn Kramer. I don't know. I'm making bullshit up. I'll talk to Philippe about it—if you want me to."

"If you raise it as no more than an inquiry."

"Sure, sure!"

———

"I want to thank you for all the help you've given us in upgrading and repairing the *Phoenix*," Kramer said.

Standing before the President's desk, and bouncing up and down on his heels, Philippe Stargazer said, "Oh, it has been our *plaisir*."

"I'm sorry I haven't had a chance to work with you more closely, but we've had some internal problems."

"*Oui*, the Human Power. I remember we had similar anti-alien sentiment aboard the *Silver Streak*. I remember that from my days in Domestic Relations."

Kramer was surprised. "I don't remember anything like that!"

"It happened after Dr. Geeson and the Bolyrians came aboard."

"That was a pretty low-profile event in the Civilian Section as I recall."

"For the most part," Stargazer agreed, "and it did not get much news coverage in *StarQuest* or SSBC. But there definitely was an element that was looking to get the Bolyrians off the *Silver Streak*, felt they were taking up rooms and food and water."

"Well." Kramer raised his eyebrows, digesting this. "Henry Walden would have been President at that time. How did he handle it?"

Stargazer laughed. "Well, he buried it by proposing anti-alien bills that were so deep in bureaucracy that they never saw the light of day. That way he could honestly say to his constituents that he was representing their interests, but at the same time making sure that they did not surface."

Kramer had never imagined the legendarily stupid Henry Walden capable of such duplicity. "Pretty slimy."

"He was a slimy man."

Kramer's smile disappeared and he looked into the distance. "Politics is a slimy business." The desk intercom chirped. "Excuse me." He reached over and tapped the intercom tab. "Kramer here."

"This is Petrov aboard the *Phoenix*. We have completed our systems checkout and trial run. I believe we are ready for business."

"Well, excellent. I'll be sending you to Klym Valdor to mediate the disagreement between the Vron and the Valdor. As soon as you finish your checklists I want you back on Station Post One for final briefing."

"Yes, sir."

Once Kramer had cut the transmission, Stargazer leaned against the desk and said, "I'd heard about this. The Vron are actually planning on attacking Klym Valdor?"

"Yes," Kramer said. "It's not entirely pre-emptive. The Valdor are planning on a major strike using the Thermian Destroyer against Thermians throughout the galaxy. The Vron want to step in to prevent this. The Triumvirate Council supports that action."

"*Oui, oui*, I suppose I do too. I would be interested in testing the *Exodus*'s new systems by participating in that mission."

Kramer was initially uneasy about sending two Space Stars into a potentially explosive situation, but finally decided, "Well...we welcome the help."

The *Exodus* was identical to the *Phoenix* in design and specifications, but Jack Hasta and Philippe Stargazer had made many changes to customize it to their particular purposes—and taste. For instance, the bridge was painted beige instead of the stark grays and whites of the *Phoenix*, and a ficus plant grew in the center of the central control console.

Fred Dexter, the ship's helmsman and bartender, said, "Course is programmed in. We're at one-quarter fusion power. Light speed entry in five minutes, twenty-six seconds."

"*Merci.*" Stargazer sat not in the command chair, but at the science station. Although the ship had a chief science officer, Dr. Scarlett Bremmel, Stargazer himself insisted on taking on the bridge science duties.

At the command intelligence station, Jack Hasta monitored communications. "*Phoenix* signals they're ready to get under way too."

"*Merci.*" Stargazer turned and looked at President Kramer, who stood with Cranius at the rear of the bridge. "All set, *monsieur* President?"

"I'm all set," the President said with a nod.

Cranius fidgeted nervously. "I hope you don't mind my observing."

"No, of course not, *monsieur* Cranius," Stargazer said. "Jack, what is our EGI rate?"

"Four-two-one. Goddamn G-32 monitors twenty-seven."

Dexter said, "We've got full operational status on engines. Singularity's looking good. Drive field seven-one-two-zero-six. Reactors eight-three-zero-one. Coolant systems full power. MGS active, deviation forty-six."

"*Merci,*" Stargazer said. "Jack, what does the *Phoenix* say about their own light speed entry?"

"Just a sec." Jack inserted an earpiece into his ear. "*Phoenix*, this is *Exodus*. When are you going to enter light speed?"

Strom Gielgud replied, "We are calculating light speed factor six in two minutes, fourteen seconds."

"Markeroonied. Make that two minutes and ten seconds."

"*Merci,*" Stargazer said. "*Monsieur* Dextay, we will follow them into light speed."

"Righto," Dexter said.

"Move us into acute eighty-seven."

"Acute eighty-seven."

"Radiation shield's up full," Jack said.

Two minutes later, there was a flash of light on the main screen. At the same time, Stargazer monitored a burst of spacetime turbulence.

"*Phoenix* just went to light speed," Dexter said.

"*Merci*. Now eighty-two degrees port."

"Eighty-two degrees port."

"Again, we just absorbed their light boom," Jack said.

"*Merci*."

"Quantum radar shows them on course and we've still got their TM."

"All right, and we are in position," Dexter said.

"Engineering, stand by for light speed."

"Engineering," the voice in Jack's earpiece said, "all systems go. We're ready for light speed."

Kramer leaned over and whispered, "Like it, Cranius?"

Cranius was absorbed in watching the *Phoenix* bridge crew and was startled by Kramer's question. "Hmm? Oh, yeah, yeah."

"Let's put the Z-27 on priority," Stargazer said.

Jack nodded. "Yeah, I was going to suggest that, yeah. Fred, toss me some pre-advisory data, would you?"

Dexter fingered his controls. "On its way to you."

"And I got it! Nice-looking pre-advisory data!"

"I aim to please!"

"Philippe, angle of light speed entry is going to be fourteen point two mark three. Field tension's going to reach max-asym fourteen point three subjective seconds after light boom. Two mid-course corrections, one at twelve hundred hours, the next at twelve-twenty-seven to avoid a neutron star. Other than that, smooth goddamn sailing."

"Okay, she's a go," Dexter said.

Stargazer got up and went to the command chair. "Very well. Ahead light speed factor six."

"Factor six!" Dexter moved his finger along his touchscreen, and the ship vanished from normal space into the blur of hyperspace.

"And we have light speed factor six!"

"Light speed factor six, everyone!" Stargazer announced.

Kramer and Cranius were most surprised when Stargazer, Jack, and Dexter simultaneously burst out singing, *"Light speed! Light speed! Light speed! Light speed! Light speed! Light speed!"*

Red-faced, Stargazer said, "Your pardon, *monsieur* President. We, eh, we always...do that."

Over Jack's and Dexter's sniggering, Kramer said, straight-faced, "Uh-huh."

————

Once the ship was on course and the post-light speed checklists were done, Kramer and Cranius had lunch together in the rec room.

"Why don't we ever have fun like that on Station Post One?" Cranius asked.

Kramer took a bite of his sandwich and said, "Because we all take life so damned seriously."

Cranius hesitated, then said, "I didn't want to tell you this just yet, but sooner or later I was going to have to. Jack Hasta asked me to transfer to the *Exodus*."

Kramer's expression fell. "Oh. You going to do it?"

"I haven't decided yet. I think this would be a good opportunity to get the feel for what life is like here."

"Do you like the looks of things here?"

Cranius answered with the Vron snarl that passed for a smile. "Yes, I do. On the other hand I—I've sort of connected to Station Post One. Despite all that's gone wrong, I do kind of feel like I do have a stake in things there."

"Well, I won't attempt to influence your decision one way or the other, Cranius." But Kramer's tone betrayed his intense disappointment.

————

At the apex of the great hollow sphere that was Klym Valdor, Capitol Control monitored all the goings-on both inside and outside the vast artificial world. Dugrow, high commissioner of the Valdor, stood on his eight legs at the center of the circular command chamber, assimilating the reports, some of them verbal, some transmitted directly into his receiver nanites.

"Vron ships are standing off every quarter," said Deputy Commissioner Sudred. "It is not physically possible to launch any craft without being intercepted by Vron ships."

"How can the Vron have cut off an entire artificial world?" Dugrow demanded. "How long before our reserve force gets here?"

"Eighteen *kofacch*, but it won't be enough, not unless we recall the Thermian offensives."

"That would be as much as admitting defeat!"

A signal beckoned their attention. It manifested as a tingling behind the eyes. Sudred clattered over to the external sensor station, though the data was already implanting itself in his brain.

"Two large ships just emerged from light speed."

"Who are they?" Dugrow asked.

"Human Space Stars *Phoenix* and *Exodus*."

———

The giant form of Klym Valdor took shape on the center screen as the *Exodus* dropped out of light speed. Kramer and Cranius stood behind the command chair, taking in the sight of the world-sized structure and the myriad tiny dots of Vron vessels surrounding it.

"Klym Valdor dead ahead," Fred Dexter said. "*Phoenix* is just ahead of us."

"Goddamn," Jack Hasta said, monitoring the activity ahead, "Klym Valdor is completely surrounded by Vron ships. Ghost fighters, frigates, heavy cruisers, planetary patrol ships, and a few that the computer doesn't identify."

Stargazer got up from the science station and assumed the command chair. "Well, if they want to take on an artificial world, you had better have a lot of firepower. Hail Klym Valdor."

Jack turned toward the screen, extended his hands, and bowed. "Hail Klym Valdor!"

"Jack!"

"Goddamn, Goddamn. ...Klym Valdor, this is Space Star *Exodus*. Come in please."

Dugrow's guttural voice answered, "This is Dugrow. What to you want?"

Kramer approached the command intelligence station and put a hand on Jack's shoulder. "Let me talk to him. I'm used to dealing with Dugrow."

Jack got up and gestured at his chair. "All yours."

Kramer sat, grabbed a fresh earpiece from the cabinet, and inserted it in his ear. "Dugrow, this is President Kramer."

"Well?" Dugrow demanded. "What do you want?!"

"No one wants this situation to escalate into a situation of war. I'd like to ask permission to come aboard Klym Valdor to discuss the situation with you and the Vron."

"No! No Republic member is going to set foot inside Klym Valdor! The Valdor are autonomous, and our policy regarding the Thermians stands!"

Jack Hasta muttered, "Can you believe these guys recruited us into the Community?"

Seeing that the transmission was terminated, Kramer removed the earpiece, tossed it into the recycler, and got up.

Jack sat, frowned, and looked at a suddenly very active readout. "Hold on a second. Just got a whole bunch of quantum pings. Valdor TSRs, a bunch of them approaching from deep space."

Dexter said, "Looks like the Valdor called for reinforcements."

Kramer's pulse thundered. "We've got to defuse the situation before it explodes into all-out war." An idea occurred to him. "Cranius, could you talk to the Vron commander? Get a few concessions, get him to at least allow Valdor trade?"

Cranius stared wide-eyed at him, groaned and said, "I'll...try." He stepped up to Jack's station and asked, "Can you connect me to the Vron commander?"

"I'm trying," Jack said.

As they waited for Jack to make contact, Kramer watched the distant spots of the approaching ships. How odd, he thought, to come under attack by vessels of the same design as his own *Saviour* and *Frontier*. Things had certainly changed since the Valdor had given those ships to Station Post One for free.

"Okay, I got it," Jack said. "You'll be speaking to Lizette, Supreme Commander of the Vron Space Enforcer Fleet."

Cranius leaned over the console. "Commander Lizette, this is Cranius, former secretary to the Minister of Offworld Affairs and currently chief of staff to the President of the Unified Republic. In the name of interstellar diplomacy, I would like to ask that you cease your activities here at Klym Valdor and at least allow the Valdor through for trade with other sovereign worlds."

"No!" Lizette's sharp voice answered. "I refuse!"

"Commander Lizette, I'm speaking with the authority of the President of the Unified Republic. Now, what you're doing here is risking interstellar war."

"Sprog that! I refuse to let any Valdor leave!"

Cranius turned to Kramer and gave his best impersonation of a human shrug. "Sorry."

Kramer looked at the main screen and sighed. "Well, the Valdor won't let us in, the Vron won't talk. There's really nothing we can do.

———

DuBois leaned over toward Tobey's command desk and whispered, "I've got a message for you from Senator Kaminsky."

Tobey saw the message icon appear on his screen. He expanded it and read the brief message. "Jury selection's complete."

A familiar tune sounded. It was the theme to *Kaisman and Friends*. Jay Touffet, the external systems officer, was watching it at his station. "Sorry," he called, "forgot to switch on my headset."

"Leave it up for a minute," Tobey said. "I'm curious what that blowhard has to say."

Burt Kaisman appeared on the screen. Touffet's station was down in the Trench and two rows ahead of Tobey, but his better than 20/20 eyes saw Kaisman's face clearly.

"Good afternoon, everyone," Kaisman said to his adoring audience, "and welcome to *Kaisman and Friends*. Hello, I am Burt Kaisman here with Derek Winchester and Shellie Hurlburt. And jury selection is complete for the trial of the Human Power patriots who had the courage to stand up to 'President' Kramer's tyrannical regime. And SSBC has managed to obtain secretly a list of the jurors selected. Now, we will not reveal those names on the air, but I will say this: none of the jurors selected are members of the Human Power movement. What do you say to that, Derek?"

Derek Winchester laughed and said, "Well, Burt, I find that significant and disturbing and very telling about our judicial process. Without representation on the jury by Human Power, what guarantee is there that this will be a fair trial?"

"Excellent point, Derek. Has Senator Kaminsky stacked the jury against Human Power? What do you say, Shellie?"

Shellie Hurlburt shrieked, "Yes! Yes! We're going in with a jury already prejudiced against the defendants! This is a show trial! Damon Kramer chose a jury trial for show! He did it so that the people would believe that he's some sort of magnanimous leader treating us all fairly when he is nothing of the kind!"

"You are fired up today," Kaisman said. "I love it. You are absolutely right, Shellie, and this rigged trial will prove it."

"That's enough," Tobey said. "Turn that bullshit off."

Touffet did so. "I only tuned in out of curiosity, sir. I don't believe a thing that bastard says."

"Good to know." Tobey slammed his palm onto his console, got up and paced the command tier. "Goddamn bastard. *Of course* there are no Human Power members on the jury. All the Human Power members on the Station are on trial!"

DuBois made shushing noises. "Tobey, you've got to stop letting Kaisman get to you."

"I'm not *letting* him get to me—he just gets to me! He's very good at that."

"And the more you act like that, the more ammunition you give him."

"Well, who gives a fuck? He's going to say what he wants. He's going to interpret everything—"

"He's getting desperate now because all of his viewers are on trial. Just let it go. You're doing the best you can to command this Station, right?"

Tobey sat down, his energy briefly dispelled by his outburst. "See, that's the thing. The one thing that Burt Kaisman is right about is I'm not qualified to command this Station. It should be Damon in charge. He never should have run for President."

"This will blow over, Tobey," DuBois said. "Nothing lasts forever."

Tobey ran a hand over his bare scalp, hoping DuBois was right; the endless series of crises certainly seemed to be lasting forever.

———

"No change," Jack Hasta said.

The Vron and Valdor ships still encircled Klym Valdor, and the *Exodus* and *Phoenix* were hemmed in by more Valdor ships.

"The Valdor TSRs can't get in," Kramer said, "but the Valdor can't get out either."

"We have a pretty good space fleet," Cranius said with some pride, "more advanced than the Valdor. They stole most of our technology."

Kramer nodded. "And apparently there hasn't been much improvement in the centuries since they did steal it."

"We're in inertial attitude," Fred Dexter said.

Stargazer, at the science station, said, "Switch to orbital rate attitude."

"Yes, sir."

Jack Hasta stretched and yawned. "Goddamn. Waiting and waiting and waiting. This reminds me of Orion. Remember that, Stargazer?"

"*Quoi?*"

"Long, long time ago, back on the *Silver Streak*. Remember when President Walden wanted us to get in the middle of that dispute between Orion-1 and Orion-2?"

Stargazer just stared at him.

Jack shrugged. "Ah, maybe you don't remember it. Goddamn, I think you were still on nocturnal shift at the time."

"It does not sound familiar."

"Well, same goddamn thing. Lots of waiting and waiting and waiting and waiting while two civilizations goddamn hang in the balance."

Kramer added, "And while a dumb-ass President wants to get involved in other people's business."

Jack grinned. "Goddamn."

Dexter came to attention. "Uh, something's happening. The Valdor have opened fire. Yeah…TSRs are closing in, opened fire on the Ghost fighters. Vron are returning fire. It's a free-for-all out there."

Kramer stepped up to the empty command chair, tempted to sit in it himself. "Damn it, I'm not going to stand here while a war starts. I want an open frequency to both the Vron and the Valdor."

"All right, we're transmitting," Jack said.

Kramer hit the transmit tab on the command chair's armrest. "Attention Commander Lizette of the Vron and Dugrow of the Valdor. I want the fighting stopped. Both sides are to cease and desist immediately."

Silence reigned on the bridge while the main screen showed the flashes of light of hundreds of energy beam weapons, and bursts of ephemeral flame as ships exploded.

"Not acknowledging, goddammit," Jack said.

"Lizette is probably laughing at you," Cranius said.

Kramer nodded. "And Dugrow probably would be if the Valdor ever laughed."

Stargazer moved to the command chair. "I request permission to launch fighters."

Grudgingly, Kramer said, "Granted. The Triumvirate Council has sided with the Vron, therefore we too will open fire on the Valdor."

"Launch all fighters, Jack."

Jack touched his console and said, "Launch all fighters!"

The ship vibrated as the QV Fighters and Intercore D-4000s hurtled down their launch tubes and into space.

As the fighters streaked into the battle, Kramer fumed. "To lose good pilots because of this *stupid* engagement!"

"Hey, hey, you're not alone, Mr. President," Jack said. "Goddammit, how many battles did we fight with Mordrax because he couldn't give up a goddamn grudge?"

That didn't help as Kramer watched the tactical display on Dexter's console. Three QV Fighters disappeared off the scope, blown to bits along with their pilots, for no reason whatsoever except that two civilizations couldn't get along.

"The *Phoenix* has gone into action too," Dexter said. "She's launched her fighters, also opening fire with her gun turrets. Shall we go in too?"

Stargazer leaned forward in his chair, nibbling his thumbnail. "No, no, hold position here. It would not do anybody any good for us to just jump in. Let us just hold back and observe the battle and coordinate things."

Kramer said, "And let's try to put a stop to this battle as quickly as we can."

Jack Hasta watched his scope. "Well, we're goddamn attacking the Valdor. Best thing to do would be to coerce them into surrendering."

"Well? What do you have in mind?"

"Let's focus on taking out the goddamn TSRs, signal the Vron to divert their superweapons on Klym Valdor with the intention of blowing it up."

Stargazer said, "Jack, you cannot be serious!"

"I don't goddamn mean *actually* blow it up, I mean make the Valdor *think* we're going to blow it up."

"The Vron are just as likely to do it for real," Cranius said.

"They'll do it with or without our permission," Kramer said. "It's a good plan."

Stargazer shrugged. "*Si vous de lites.*"

As he watched the vessels on screen hurl themselves at one another and annihilate one another with superheated beams of death, Kramer found he disliked the plan just as much as Stargazer did.

———

Tobey had no desire to watch SSBC, especially during *Kaisman and Friends*, but it was the only one of the three networks giving continuous coverage of the trial of the Human Power terrorists, so he watched from his command desk in PHC. Jerome Flynn, filling in as second-in-command while DuBois testified, watched with him.

DuBois was the first witness called by prosecutor E. Peter Roche.

"Were you shot as you were being escorted to your pretrial hearing?"

"Yes." DuBois had been advised merely to answer the questions asked, no embellishments, no explanations.

"Did the shot come from a ring of protesters who were surrounding you?"

"Yes."

"Were the protesters chanting?"

"Yes."

"What were they chanting?"

" 'Kill Ebor DuBois'."

At that point, Defense Attorney Edward Foale requested a recess, which Senator Kaminsky granted. As soon as the court recessed, Burt Kaisman held forth.

"Well, the court is in recess. Dr. Ebor DuBois has been testifying. So far most of the questioning has centered around the fact that he was shot, allegedly by a Human Power activist. Of course, there has been no mention so far of the fact that Dr. DuBois was suspected of saving the life of Zach Mortimer, who was convicted and executed as a traitor. I can't wait to hear the cross examination."

Tobey muted the show and said, "They're not going to call me to testify because I'm the Station commander."

"That sounds pretty ridiculous," Flynn said. "Who has more information about this whole thing than you do?"

"Since I'm accused of being this tyrannical overlord, Kaminsky figures that anything I say will automatically be prejudiced."

"I'm a little surprised I wasn't called to testify."

"Probably your history with the rebellion."

Flynn grew morose. "I thought that was long in the past."

Tobey knew better than anyone that one could never really outrun his past. "Might as well get used to the fact that once you've done something, it follows you around for the rest of your life."

———

The battle around Klym Valdor continued to rage. Most of the human fighters were still thousands of kilometers from either the Vron or the Valdor, but both fleets were caught in between the vast artificial world and the incoming TSRs. The Valdor, however, were still unable to launch anything from their artificial world without it being easily picked off.

"Goddamn," Jack said, "got something. It's a message from Klym Valdor."

"Put it on," Stargazer ordered.

There was no image, only the scratchy audio of Dugrow's voice. "This is Dugrow. I would like to ask to surrender."

Kramer hurried over to Jack's station and said, "This is Kramer. We accept your surrender." He put a hand to his ear, and Jack muted the mic. "Put me on SPACEWEB-7."

"Goddamn." Jack switched his settings. "Okay, everybody out there can hear you."

"Attention. Attention all Vron and Valdor ships. This is President Damon Kramer of the Unified Republic. The Valdor have surrendered. Cease all hostilities. The Valdor have surrendered."

It took a while for the battle to end. Pilots pumped up on adrenaline didn't easily stop shooting, nor were combatants eager to stop defending themselves when they were unsure if an enemy would attack them. But all ships received Kramer's message, and slowly they stopped firing and peeled off.

"Yeah, the fighting's stopped," Dexter said. "The Vron are letting the TSRs through."

"How bad is the damage on the Vron side?" Stargazer asked.

"A lot of Vron ships bought it. We weren't getting TM from them, so I can't give you exact numbers."

Cranius said, "Well, a lot of Vron were destroyed, but Klym Valdor is badly damaged."

That was evident at a glance. Even from here, the clouds of debris were visible around gashes in the giant curving hull. Wreckage surrounded the Valdor homeland. It wasn't nearly as bad as the gouge that had been inflicted by a naked starship during the Doomsday War, which had torn out a quarter of the station, but the Valdor would be repairing this damage for a long time.

"Recall all fighters," Stargazer said, "step down to level two."

Jack repeated, "Recall all fighters, step down to level two."

———

Burt Kaisman was invigorated by the trial. He was more animated even than usual as he lectured at the camera. "So far the prosecution's argument has been very one-sided. None of the defendants have yet testified, and I'm sure the courtroom will ring when they reveal the astonishing events which have taken place on Station Post One, which prompted their courageous act of resistance—although I'm sure that even that will not sway this prejudiced jury. And let's return to the trial, where Butch McCrae has been called to testify."

"Was the Human Power movement using authorized sidearms?" Roche asked.

Butch McCrae remained stoic. "They were using sidearms authorized to Station Post One security personnel."

"The sidearm that damaged the exterior skin of the Station, was it fired by one of your people or by one of the Human Power people?"

"The shot definitely came from the opposite direction from where we were, so it was coming from one of the Human Power people."

"Thank you. Your witness, Mr. Foale."

"Thank you." Foale stood and read his questions from his linkpad. "Mr. McCrae, what exactly were your orders during the period of martial law?"

"My orders were to patrol the hallways and ensure that curfew was obeyed."

"And what was the punishment delivered to those who violated curfew?"

"They were to be arrested, taken to the security office, and interrogated."

"What was the period...the acceptable—the outer limit to the period that one of these people could be detained?"

"There was no mandatory period handed down. We were to hold them until we determined that we'd received satisfactory answers to our questions. In most of these cases, the civilians were released to go back to their own lives within twenty-four hours."

"You say *most* of these cases. Under what circumstances were civilians detained indefinitely?"

"I'm not aware of any specific cases."

"You're not aware of any *specific* cases, but you just said in *most* cases."

Butch fidgeted. "Look, fella, I don't know. I can't guarantee one hundred percent that civilians were always released within a twenty-four-hour period, but I'm not aware of any cases where they'd been held longer than that."

"So we can say that the twenty-four-hour period is the longest period that a civilian was detained?"

"I told you I don't know."

"Objection," Roche said, "the witness has answered the question."

"Sustained," Senator Kaminsky said.

"Thank you, I have no further questions," Foale said.

———

There was little objection to holding the peace conference aboard the *Exodus*. A Vron transport and a Valdor TSR docked with the Space Star by pressure snake, and Dugrow and Lizette were met by Stargazer, Jack, Kramer, and Cranius.

"Welcome to the Vron and welcome to the Valdor," Stargazer said. "As Captain of the Space Star *Exodus*, it is my pleasure to introduce the President of the Unified Republic."

Kramer stepped forward to light applause—Dugrow, his claws curled under his carapace, simply stared at him with those luminous red eyes.

"Thank you, Captain Stargazer," Kramer said, "and I too would like to extend a welcome to the Vron and the Valdor, and I'm hoping that this meeting will be a productive one. We have missed the Valdor's presence in our Republic summits and their invaluable support in the war against the Thermians.

"This latest engagement resulted in many losses for the Vron, yet many more for the Valdor. And Dugrow, as you've seen, the Vron are capable of destroying Klym Valdor, and at the present time, they enjoy the support of the Triumvirate Council. Commissioner Dugrow of the Valdor, welcome aboard."

"Thank you," Dugrow said.

"Commander Lizette, welcome aboard."

Lizette took a step toward him and bowed her head. "Thank you." She turned toward Dugrow. "Commissioner Dugrow, these are my terms: the Valdor will immediately surrender all Thermian Destroyers to us and provide our inspectors access to Klym Valdor in order to assure that you possess no more, as well as verify that your computer systems are blanked of all data concerning the construction of the Thermian Destroyer. Refuse and Klym Valdor will be destroyed."

"Unacceptable!" Dugrow waved his claws around wildly. "Unaaceptable!"

"Dugrow," Kramer snapped, "listen! Now, just a minute! Now, listen! The Vron have not been authorized by the Triumvirate Council to dictate the terms of this ceasefire. Now, here are *my* terms: on behalf of the Triumvirate Council, as well as the Congressional Council and the Centralized Committee, I would welcome the Valdor back into the Republic. If Dugrow will agree to stop using the Thermian Destroyer, all the Republic will double down on efforts using the TAD and the P-SAR. And Vron will cease all interference in Valdor affairs. Now, are these terms agreeable to each of you?"

Dugrow hesitated, his crab-face unreadable, but finally he growled, "Very well. On behalf of the Valdor, I agree."

Lizette turned to Kramer and fixed him with the snarl that was a Vron smile. "On behalf of the Vron, I agree."

———

In the rec room after the conference, Jack toasted Stargazer. "Goddamn! Not a bad day's work, huh?"

Stargazer clinked glasses with Jack and drank—hot cocoa, of course, as he and Jack were still bound by their Vow of Perpetual Sobriety. "We have done Captain Cameron proud."

"We sure as goddamn have! The goddamn Valdor are part of the goddamn Republic again, no more use of the goddamn Thermian Destroyer, galactic peace is restored—what's say we hit the goddamn bowling alley?"

"Sorry—the 'bowling alley' is in use tonight. Dr. Robbins is working on Nautabot Seven."

"Goddamn." Jack slumped. "I miss the goddamn *Silver Streak*." He smiled as he thought of the *real* blowing alley, as opposed to the electronics bay that he and Stargazer used here on the *Exodus*. Of the fun times when they were just crew members under Dick's command—of course it hadn't seemed so fun back then, when Jack was always left behind when Dick and Frank went on all the exciting missions...

On his way back to the bridge, he found himself intercepted by Cranius.

"Mr. Hasta? Mr. Hasta?"

"Yo!"

"I've been thinking about it, and I've decided I'd like to accept your offer and transfer to the *Exodus*."

"Oh...goddamn...Cranius, look—I'm *real* goddamn sorry. I talked to Philippe about it, he says there's no place for you here. I'm goddamn sorry for leading you on."

"Oh...that's...that's okay." Cranius's black face and shimmering black eyes were unreadable, but the disappointment in his voice was obvious nevertheless. "That's okay," he said again as he walked off.

———

Cranius went to the guest quarters, shaking off his disappointment along the way. He tried to remind himself that Station Post One wasn't so bad, that all his friends were there, and that the *Exodus* might look nice from a distance but would probably disappoint once he was in it.

He was surprised that the President was there, reclining in a padded chair and reading a book.

"Damon. I wasn't expecting you to be back so soon."

"Well, there's nothing more to take care of. The treaty is signed, the Vron are headed back for Vron, and now we're headed back for Station Post One. Have you made up your mind whether you're going to transfer to the *Exodus* or stay with us on Station Post One?"

"Yes, I've made up my mind. I'm going to stay on Station Post One." He giggled. "I couldn't imagine leaving. Station Post One is my home."

Kramer smiled, obviously relieved. "Well, I'm glad, Cranius. I'd hate to lose you."

Cranius turned away, haunted by memories of the mobs, the shouting, the constant crises, the unending series of complex tasks...he could hear Tobey Dingell's voice...*No more civilians in the hallways for the evening...all civilians are to report back to their privacy pods immediately or you will be placed under fucking arrest!*...Dr. Lazarev treating him after his various beatings...crowds chanting *Kill Ebor DuBois! Kill Ebor DuBois!*...Burt Kaisman warning that *the real threat to Station Post One is the aliens, people like Cranius, who has wormed his way onto our Station through favors*...the battles in the halls, Butch McCrae bellowing, *round everybody up! Round everybody up and take them to the brig!* The endless chants of *No more aliens! No more aliens!*

He saw and heard those things in his dreams that night, and he dreaded returning to Station Post One as though he were scheduled for execution in the morning.

Which, the way things were going, just might be true.

The Seige

Cranius stood near the main elevator on Dock Deck One, watching with conflicting emotions as a vessel from his home world taxied into the hangar bay. The Vron ship was a shuttle, brought here by a cruiser hanging off of Station Post One.

Tobey Dingell's voice sounded over the intercom. "Cranius? You there?"

Cranius stepped up to the wall intercom. "This is Cranius."

"Vron ship has now cleared the red line. It's on Dock Deck One. How are you doing?"

"I'm on Dock Deck One right now. I'm just outside the main elevator. I've been watching."

President Kramer, who had been waiting with him, nudged him aside and said, "Tobey, it's Kramer."

"Hey, Damon, you're not there without Secret Service, are you?"

Kramer chuckled. "On every side of me, and above and below, and a few places I can't even see."

"All right, I hope so, because Human Power isn't too fond of the Vron. Just because all the *known* Human Power members are on trial or in the brig doesn't mean there couldn't be a few malcontents wandering around looking for their lucky shot."

Smiling, Kramer said, "It'll be the luckiest shot they ever had, with all the security we've got here!"

As he spoke, the hatch on the Vron shuttle opened.

"The hatch is opening," Kramer said. "I need to greet the Vron."

"Okay," Tobey replied, "enjoy licking their melchers."

Kramer laughed, though he glanced at Cranius to see if Tobey had given offense. Cranius's expression remained unreadable, as it so often was, but he said, "I wouldn't say that to them if I were you."

"Don't worry."

The Vron delegation emerged from the shuttle. In the lead was the ambassador, whom Kramer recognized by his gold uniform with the red, triangular ambassadorial emblem and religious headdress.

Kramer folded his hands together and cocked his head once to each side. "Ambassador Thobius, welcome aboard Station Post One."

"A pleasure to be here," the Ambassador said in English, though with a thick accent, "and a pleasure to meet you, President Kramer. We have brought the medical professionals you requested. This is Dr. Kos, Dr. Setoris, and nurses Paragrin and Kasaba."

Kramer turned to the four and gave the same folded-hand gesture. "Welcome to all of you."

They replied in kind.

Ambassador Thobius said, "President Kramer, I have been authorized with the authority of President Lyskia to speak on behalf of the Vron on our planet's policy within the Unified Republic."

"And as President of the Unified Republic, I welcome you. Although I'm not empowered to speak on behalf of the Triumvirate Council, I am empowered to speak on behalf of the human race. If you'll come with me, I'll take you up to our Prime Hab, where you'll be guests of honor."

"Thank you."

———

Only one SSBC camera operator had been allowed on Dock Deck One during the arrival of the Vron delegation, but that camera operator, Angela Grisholm, provided Burt Kaisman with just the footage he was looking for. He would have preferred close-ups via nanodrone, but the high-resolution zoom images of the Ambassador's face were distorted and comical enough to look ridiculous—which is what Kaisman wanted.

In fact, he had to quell his own chuckling as his theme music played and he looked into the camera to begin the show.

"Good afternoon, ladies and gentlemen. Welcome to *Kaisman and Friends*. I'm Burt Kaisman here with Derek Winchester and Shellie Hurlburt. And I am now speaking aboard a Station which we share with the Vron."

On his cue, the images of Ambassador Thobius played as he went on.

"Yes, no sooner did 'President' Kramer promise the Human Power movement that the aliens would be leaving the Station, that there would be no more refugee ships, he has invited a delegation of Vron aboard the Station."

The images of Thobius ended, and the red light on the camera came on, indicating that Kaisman was once again on screen.

"And that is not all," he went on. "Very soon, Vron civilians will be arriving to share our Civilian Hab. Yes, even as our civilians are forced to compete for diminished supplies, and as part of the demands for the Civilian Hab are for equal access to food, water, and oxygen, an entire ship of Vron civilians will now be quartered in our Civilian Hab. I wonder who will be put out by this." Kaisman was proud of the carefully measured outrage in his voice.

Discretely reaching under the desk, Kaisman continued, "Perhaps 'President' Kramer would embrace us more if we were more like the Vron." With that, he brought out what he had been concealing. "For that reason, I have made this hat which mimics the headdress of Ambassador Thobius."

While Derek Winchester and Shellie Hurlburt snickered, Kaisman placed the red and purple hat made of construction paper on his head, twirled his fingers in the style of the Ambassador and made a face which mocked the curled lips of a Vron.

"I can't believe you are doing that," Winchester giggled.

"How do I look, Derek?"

"Spectacular!"

Shellie Hurlburt sputtered, "We've really lost it now."

———

Kramer had not watched *Kaisman and Friends*, so he was surprised when Cranius stormed into the Presidential Pod, raving about Kaisman mocking the Ambassador.

"I can't believe Burt Kaisman would do that!"

"Do what?" Kramer was confused. "Don't pay any attention to him."

"I can't help but pay attention to him!" Cranius sounded downright frantic. "The Vron will sure pay attention!"

"To what?"

"To mocking Ambassador Thobius's headdress!" Cranius calmed himself, sat, and explained. "That headdress honors the gods Wushno and Deemu, the gods of Tobias's family. His family is very highly regarded on Vron. So given his position, mocking his family gods is an affront to all Vron."

———

The following day, Kaisman went on the air with no reference to his antics in the previous show. He neither felt nor showed any remorse; as far as he was concerned, it was over, he'd had his fun and garnered his ratings, and now he was on to his new topic: the trial of the Human Power patriots.

His challenge would be to manufacture outrage over a markedly lighter sentence than either he or anyone had expected. In fact, what other commentators were calling an *unreasonably* light sentence.

"The verdict is in. And a reminder, this is a cluster trial, meaning the verdict applies to all defendants. The charge was attempted insurrection, and the verdict is guilty. Since the state of martial law against which they rebelled no longer exists, they have been released on their own recognizance, but they are sentenced to probation and community service. For defending Station Post One against an overreaching government, a tyrannical regime, they are *punished. Two years* of probation and community service! *Two years* of their lives!

"As I said at the beginning, I say once again: the jury was stacked against them. They had no chance of a fair trial. Well, I may not be a Vron, but perhaps I can get in our 'president''s favor by putting on this lovely hat once again!"

Again the hat elicited laughter from Derek Winchester and Shellie Hurlburt, and he defiantly imitated Vron body movements and facial characteristics, silently daring anyone to do anything to stop him.

————

Butch McCrae expected resistance from the Human Power prisoners as he led them into the Rec Pod, so he already had a chip on his shoulder.

"Okay, come on, fellas, we're going to clean the scrubbers today. It's good for everybody on the Station. I don't want to hear any backtalk. Come on, people."

"I'm a civilian this Station!" shouted an idiot taller than Mary Shelley's monster.

"And you've been sentenced to community service," Butch replied sweetly. "This is your community service. Move it!"

Someone else demanded, "Why are we getting punished for exercising our right to free speech?"

A chorus of "yeah"s joined in, along with "I'll bet the Vron wouldn't be doing community service if they did that!" and "Yeah! Get Cranius in here!"

Butch tried to be reasonable. "Look, people, this is what you got instead of a brig sentence. If you'd rather go to the brig, I'd be happy to oblige you!"

————

Burt Kaisman sat in his privacy pod with Meyer on his lap. Deb sat across from him, Meyer's spelling text open on the realscreen. Meyer was in first grade, and Kaisman was concerned that she was behind the other kids in learning the alphabet.

"You learned the letter Q?" he asked.

"Yeah," Meyer said.

"Let me see the letter Q."

He was irritated when a knock on the door interrupted him. He lifted Meyer off his knee and set her in one of the desk chairs. "I'll be right back."

Leaving Deb to help Meyer with her homework, he went to the door and opened it. He was astonished when he saw none other than the President of the Unified Republic. "Well! 'President' Kramer visits my humble privacy pod."

"Could I talk to you for a moment?"

"Of course. We're just having dinner, so I trust you won't keep me too long."

Ignoring the blatant lie, Kramer said, "No, no. The headdress that Ambassador Thobius wears—I wanted to let you know that that represents a tribute to his family gods. It's a matter of great significance to the Vron."

"And this is important?"

"Well, yes, because the way you mock it on your show, the Vron are offended by that. I would appreciate it if you wouldn't do that."

"Really? Well, supposing *I* am offended by the activities of the Vron; would you have a similar conversation with them?"

"I want to do everything I can to normalize relations between us and the Vron."

"And that would involve telling *me*, a member of the free press, how to dress on my show?"

Kramer held on to his patience. "I'm not telling you anything. I'm making a request."

"Really? Make me!"

Kramer clenched his jaw; Kaisman hoped to God that Kramer punched him right then and there. Instead he nodded, smiled, and said, "Well, I tried," and left.

———

Kramer walked side by side with Tobey toward the Presidential Pod.

"You should have known better than to try to reason with Burt Kaisman," Tobey said.

"Yes, I should have."

"So, did you lose your temper?"

They reached the Presidential Pod and Kramer collapsed into his bed. "No, I managed to keep my temper reined in, and it's a good thing, too, because he was probably recording the conversation."

"That is exasperating."

Kramer rubbed his eyes. "It's going to be more exasperating when the rest of the Vron arrive."

Tobey settled into Kramer's easy chair. "Is it really an entirely good idea to have more Vron come on board after you just told the people of Station Post One there would be no more aliens?"

"Well..." Kramer sat up. "...it never even occurred to me that the Human Power people who were on trial would simply be released."

"No, that's not very good. I suppose if martial law hadn't been lifted, that wouldn't have happened."

"No, it wouldn't have. Well, that's freedom. That's the kind of world we're trying to preserve."

"Yeah...for better or for worse, huh?"

Kramer had to agree with that.

———

As soon as he arrived in the Prime Hab Center in the morning, Tobey began watching the clock. The Vron skyplane was scheduled to arrive at 0715, and notification had come during the night that it would be late.

It was 0746 when Jerome Flynn said, "Vron ship just emerged from light speed. Identification beacon matches. They're requesting permission to come on board."

"Give them the okay." Tobey hit the intercom tab. "Dock Deck Three, you set for arrival of Vron skyplane?"

A voice answered, "Dock Deck Three. We're set. Bay One."

"Thank you. Jerry, Dock Deck Three, Bay One."

"Yes, sir." Flynn put an earpiece in his ear, touched an icon on his screen, and said, "Approach Dock Deck Three, Bay One." He hit the intercom tab. "Dock Deck Three, PHC."

"Dock Deck Three."

"Transmit landing beacon from Bay One."

———

The skyplane was a tube about the size of a bus. The engine compartment was a cylindrical projection in the rear. Overall the ship looked like a silver pen with landing gears.

The hatch opened and the Vron began to file out. Tepper stepped forward, a line of security officers behind him. The Vron in the lead approached him, put his palms together, and cocked his head to the side.

"I am Fakrius. I request permission to come aboard your Station." Like Ambassador Thobius, Fakrius spoke with a thick, almost impenetrable accent that left Tepper wishing he would just speak the Vron language and let the translation fibers do their job.

"Granted," Tepper said. "I'm Captain Elmer Tepper, Chief of the Dock Decks. I will conduct you up to the Civilian Hab, where you'll be shown to your privacy pods. Do any of you require any medical attention or any special treatment?"

No one said anything. Fakrius said, "We are all fully prepared for your climate."

"All right, please come with me then."

Tepper led them to the elevator, which took them up to the Civilian Hab. The elevator was crowded with twelve of them, but it was rated for up to twenty. The doors open and Butch met them.

"Hey, Butch," Tepper said, "these are our Vron civilians. You'll take over now?"

"All right." Butch easily slipped into the mantle of gracious host—easily because his manner oozed sarcasm that the Vron would not pick up on. "Ladies and gentlemen, I'm Butch McCrae, head of Civilian Security. I'm going to conduct you to your privacy pods. If you have any difficulties in these first few days that you're here, you just let me know and I'll take care of it for you until we get your security classification straightened out. After that, there will be a member of our Congressional Council responsible for your section. So if you'll follow me?"

The Vron followed Butch, some of them taking pictures with little, red, penlight-shaped cameras.

As they passed the Rec Pod, two Human Power activists paused in their sweeping of the floor. The taller of them said, "Look at all those damn Vron."

"They're everywhere, man," the shorter one said, "they're everywhere. I knew Kramer was going to stick them on us just as soon as we were convicted."

———

Kramer held a press conference in the Press Pod. Reporters crowded into the small room, cameras snapping and microphones extended.

An SSBC reporter asked, "Mr. President, you had promised that the last of the refugee ships had departed and there would be no more aliens on the Station. Wouldn't you say that you're now going back on that promise by quartering Vron civilians here on the Station?"

Kramer answered carefully. "I appreciate that question, Jay, and I'll put it this way: The last of the refugee ships *did* leave. There's going to be no more of that going on here now that we are apparently in a ceasefire with the Darian Empire. However, the situation with Vron has been delicate from the beginning due to their, ah, militant attitude toward the Valdor. This is a subject that even Human Power was concerned about. So in order to prevent any further unpleasantness such as that, we want to gain a tighter and more productive relationship with the Vron. Therefore, I consider it very important that we both quarter their civilians on our Station and in time send our own people to Vron—those who are willing to go, that is."

More questions were shouted at him, but he wanted to finish answering Jay Orcutt's question. "Now, these people are seeking citizenship within the human race. Now, as most of you know, we're seeking to reintegrate nanotech into our civilization. The Vron are masters of nanotech. They've developed it into an art form, and therefore, the presence of Vron scientists on our Station will be instrumental in accomplishing that, in reintegrating nanotech into our technology and doing it without the dangers that we have feared for seventeen hundred years."

———

Burt Kaisman did not see the Vron invasion of the Station the way Kramer did, and he did not hold back during his next show. "People are struggling to make a living in the Civilian Hab, and our Human Power patriots now laboring under community service simply for standing up for what they believe in. Which brings me to the subject of the Vron...as I don my ridiculous Vron hat."

Once again, Derek Winchester and Shellie Hurlburt dissolved into helpless giggles as Kaisman fitted the paper hat over his head.

"Yes, Vron civilians have overrun Station Post One. They are *everywhere!* When I had breakfast in the Rec Pod this morning, I would say at least half of the people there were identifiably Vron. And they were not only identifiably Vron, but they were speaking in the Vron language without the use of any kind of translation device—which, in my opinion, is the height of discourtesy during the time that they are guests on *our* Station."

————

Butch McCrae entered the Presidential Pod, his manner a strange combination of deference and mockery. "Mr. President, this was given to me anonymously to be given to you." He held out a small, flat, black square.

Kramer picked it up from Butch's palm, puzzled. "What is it?"

"It is a message from the Vron, and as Chief of Civilian Security, I would tell you the source, but I don't know it. It was left in my privacy pod with a note to give it to you."

"All right. Cranius, you have a player that can play these things?"

"I do. It's pretty standard. It's in my privacy pod. Want me to get it?"

"Please."

Cranius returned in five minutes, carrying a small handheld device. "Here it is."

"Thanks." Kramer handed him the square. Cranius slipped it into a slot on his device, which instantly read it, selected the program type and file format necessary, and provided a voice. It was a deep voice, obviously altered by a voice disguiser. "I speak on behalf of the Vron. Since our coming here, our culture has been grossly insulted by the *kyb* called Burt Kaisman."

"What's a *kyb*?" Kramer asked.

"A dirty species of vermin on Vron," Cranius said.

The message continued, "His ridicule of Ambassador Thobius's family gods ridicules all of us Vron. This ridicule must now stop or there will be punitive action." The voice stopped.

"Is that all there is to it?" Kramer asked.

Cranius looked at his device. "End of file, yes."

"For now, at least," Butch said, "but trust me, things are getting ugly. So if something isn't done, they're going to follow through on their threat. I guarantee that as a security officer."

"All right, thank you, Butch. I'll do what I can. That's all."

Butch left without saluting.

"Cranius," Kramer said, "humans don't take well to threats."

"I'm very well aware of that." Cranius sat opposite him and said, "Neither do Vron."

"Well, then, it should be known among the Vron that these cryptic messages being sent to me are not going to accomplish the goals they set out to accomplish. I can't stop Burt Kaisman from spreading his filth."

"Well, *I* understand that, and I'll try to explain that to the best of my ability, but frankly, I understand the Vron point of view in this case."

———

Ambassador Thobius shoveled what looked like black, oily spaghetti into his mouth. "This is an excellent approximation of Vron *sephilac*."

"Well, we try to accommodate," Kramer said. "You know we've had Cranius on board for two years."

"You are most accommodating."

"Thank you; we certainly are making every effort we can to make you feel comfortable." As he said it, Kramer looked out the corner of his eye, scanning the Rec Pod for unfriendly looks, listening for disrespectful talk, but people seemed to be behaving themselves.

Thobius said, "I've never gotten used to your human way of...edging around the conversation. Let's cut to the point."

"Yes." Kramer sighed. "Burt Kaisman. I hope that you and the other Vron understand that he does not speak for all humans."

"Then make him stop." The Ambassador controlled his tone, but anger crept into his voice.

Kramer tried patiently to explain. "I can't make him stop. See, we humans have something called freedom of speech. It's one of our most cherished rights. Burt Kaisman can say anything he wants. I can say anything I want. Now, you're perfectly within your rights to appear in any public forum you want and denounce what he's saying, but he has a legal right to speak his mind, no matter how misguided, no matter how offensive."

"We also have free speech," Thobius said, "but we also have a sense of ethics. What is the point of free speech if that right is used for negative, unproductive purposes?"

"The question is, who gets to define 'negative' or 'unproductive'? That could apply to anyone that I might disagree with, or who you might disagree with."

The Ambassador was barely holding on to his temper. "What is he accomplishing with his gratuitous attacks on our culture?"

"That's not the point. If I have the authority to restrict him from speaking his mind on something like this, then I also have the authority to restrict his speech on anything else. That doesn't help anybody. All I'd be doing is aiding his cause."

Thobius was baffled. "What *is* his cause?"

Kramer hesitated before answering. He shrugged. "I've never been exactly sure. I think it's primarily to gain ratings for his news network, though he does have a political agenda. I imagine the presence of the Vron in some way or other places him at a disadvantage or places a politician who's funding him at a disadvantage."

"Isn't his job to tell the truth?"

"He doesn't work for the government. He works for SSBC, a private organization. He can say what he wants. Surely if you have free speech as well, you face similar problems."

"No," Thobius said emphatically. "We don't. We don't! We have a sense of ethics. There is no point to such poisonous speech."

Kramer found that remarkable. "Well, you Vron must be fundamentally better people than we are."

He would come to regret saying that in a crowded Rec Pod.

———

Burt Kaisman beamed as he played the soundbyte on his show.

"Well, you Vron must be fundamentally better people than we are," the recorded voice of the President said.

"Well, there it is, ladies and gentlemen." It was hard for Kaisman to inject the proper tone of outrage into his voice when he was so gleeful at having caught the incriminating statement. "Those words were spoken by 'President' Kramer to Vron Ambassador Thobius. 'You Vron must be fundamentally better people than we are.' There it is. The 'President' is on record with his mission statement. He believes the Vron are better than we are. He said it. I didn't make it up." He picked up the mock Vron headdress and placed it on his head. "I urge all of you to wear these hats in public everywhere you go. Show 'President' Kramer and the Vron that this is *our* Station and we do not accept the President's policy that the Vron are better than we are."

———

"Damon, you've got to be more careful what you say."

Kramer felt stupid enough for having said what he said in public; he couldn't help snapping at Tobey. "Kaisman isn't careful what he says."

"Anything can be used against you—*is* being used against you."

"I have to watch what I say? On my own Station?" Kramer poured two drinks, handed one to Tobey and sat at his desk.

"Like it or not, you accepted a position of power and responsibility that's open to very invasive scrutiny."

"I know." Kramer took a long, slow sip. He swished it, savored it, and swallowed. "You're right. I fumbled the ball on this one."

"Well, it's not irreparable. The Human Power movement is on probation; they can't take any steps without going in the brig."

Kramer was not at all sure of that, but he remained silent. Right now all he wanted was to get drunk—or as drunk as his job permitted—and get some sleep.

———

Fakrius was in the Civilian Rec Pod, waiting for his friend Lysenthol to join him for lunch. He had noticed more and more of the humans wearing those offensive hats, but he tried to ignore them.

But one of the white-skinned creatures approached his table and began taunting him. "Hey, Vron! Hey, Vron! You like my hat?"

"Get that sprogging hat out of my face."

The human laughed. So did his companions. "Hit a nerve, did I? Everybody put your hats on!

A whole group of them donned the hats. Fakrius noticed some of the humans turning away in disgust; he too was disgusted, wondering why they didn't do something if they disapproved. "Get that sprogging hat out of my face," he repeated.

"Come on! Why don't you do something about it, Vron?"

He shot to his feet, swiped the hat off the man's head. "Get it out of my face!"

Laughing, the human and his companions surrounded him. He charged at them, his fists waving. One went down. Two others caught him and held him by the arms. The one he had swiped delivered a punch to the jaw that sent him sprawling over the table. Soon other Vron jumped into the melee, and now the Rec Pod was filled with brawling bodies.

———

"Fight. Civilian Hab Rec Pod." The voice on the intercom sounded tired.

Butch got to his feet. "All right, security alert, condition one. Get twenty guys, I'll be right there."

Butch hurried out of the security office, down the corridor, and up two levels. When he arrived in the Rec Pod, the fight had degenerated largely to shouting and waving arms, but there were some wounded—all Vron, it seemed at first glance.

"All right, everybody!" He fired his sidearm at the ceiling. It was on too low a setting to make an audible crack, but the flash of light grabbed attention. "That's enough! Break it up!"

He shoved people out of the way as he forced his way through to the injured Vron. There were three of them, beaten and oozing blue blood.

———

Butch brought his report to the Presidential Pod.

"Security camera confirmed what eyewitnesses saw. It was the Vron who started the fight—but with plenty of instigation from the humans in the Rec Pod, who have been identified, all of them, as Human Power members."

Cranius turned to Kramer. "Well, I would say that is a violation of their probation. I think they're going back to the brig!"

"Now, just a moment." Kramer got up and walked across the room, hands locked behind his head. "Let's not overreact here."

Butch slammed his report onto the desk. "They were waving their hats in the Vron's faces!"

"And I've already explained to Ambassador Thobius that we have a policy of free speech. The Human Power members were not violating any laws by wearing those hats. The Vron *did* violate the law by physically attacking them."

———

Kramer presided over the hearing to decide whether to put the Human Power activists back in the brig. On one side of the hearing pod were the Human Power activists who had been involved in the fight—many of them sporting casts and bandages—and on the other side were Fakrius and the other Vron who had been there, none of whom wore similar affectations.

"And so although the behavior of the Human Power members in the Rec Pod was reprehensible and was incendiary, they took no *physical* action to provoke the fight. It was the Vron who threw the first punch, it was the Vron who instigated hostilities. Therefore, I find that the Human Power members in the Rec Pod were not in violation of their probation. Yet, in the interests of maintaining good relations with the Vron representatives on board this Station, and considering the mitigating circumstances of the provocative action by the Human Power members, none of the Vron will be confined to the brig as a result."

That brought the expected groans from the Human Power members. Kramer banged the gavel and they wisely shut up.

"However," he said, "until this situation is resolved, the Civilian Hab will be segregated: Vron on one side, humans on the other."

———

Civilian Security had their hands full. Neither the human civilians nor the Vron were pleased with the order. Civilians who had never supported Human Power, who found themselves put out of their privacy pods and told to relocate, found their loyalties shifting.

One of the loudest voices was Fakrius. "I protest this action! We are being discriminated against!"

"Look, I've got my orders," Butch said, "you're moving to that side of the Civilian Hab and that's final! I'm not hearing any more protests!"

Fortunately it was not necessary to discharge any weapons despite the shouts and threats and protests and general resistance. But once it was done, Butch felt that the bad feeling on the Station had only gotten worse.

Once the distasteful duty was finished, Butch reported to the Presidential Pod. For once, Cranius was absent, for which Butch was thankful; he wanted to talk to Kramer alone. "Mr. President, the segregation is complete. I've posted guards along all corridors and junctures that provide access, so there should be no more trouble on that front."

"Thank you," the President said.

"Permission to speak freely?"

"Granted."

"I think it was a mistake to bring the Vron on board."

To Butch's surprise, Kramer said, "I agree with you. I made the decision to bring the Vron on board not realizing that the Human Power members would still be running free. If I had known, I would have had second thoughts. But it's too late now. This isn't just an internal matter. It's an international matter. And expelling the Vron now would be an international insult."

———

Burt Kaisman was giddy. It seemed that every day, Damon Kramer played right into Kaisman's hands. His job was not even a challenge. "So now," he bellowed at the camera, "the Civilian Hab is divided! Humans are only allowed access to one half of *our* Civilian Hab! In other words, our 'President' is allowing the *Vron* to tell us how we are allowed to dress on *our* Station! What next? Will the Vron be allowed to tell us what we are allowed to say? Will they be dictating our international policy? *Or are they already?!*"

Kaisman dropped his voice to a conspiratorial stage whisper. "Our 'President' has already stated that the Vron are 'fundamentally better people' than we are, and now he has stated that we are to dress according to Vron's standards of…conduct…" Kaisman trailed off for a moment as the sounds of commotion from the studio reached his ear. His earpiece rang with a truncated shout from the producer.

Puzzled, Kaisman continued the show. "And…"

But then he made out the distinct smell of ozone and saw the flashes of weapons fire. He removed his earpiece and gave a frantic look to Derek and Shellie, who stared through the glass partition into the master control room. Panic seized him as he saw armed Vron randomly gunning people down. And they were headed this way. As a beam of light sizzled through the booth, he dove under the desk.

———

Butch walked at a brisk pace down the corridor, shouting into his transmitter, "Well, how'd they get out? We had the whole area cordoned!"

The voice of Assistant Security Chief Pereira replied, "I don't know. We haven't had time to figure out where the breach might be. The point is, the SSBC studios are under attack."

"Security alert condition one! All security forces to the SSBC studios!"

As he ran toward the SSBC pod, his transmitter chirped. He activated it and Tobey's voice demanded, "Butch, this is Dingell! What's going on?"

"I don't have all the details yet, but the SSBC studios are under attack!"

As he rounded the bend at the intersection, Tepper ran from the other direction.

"Tepper!"

"Thought you could use the help."

"Yeah, you were right."

Pereira ran out of the SSBC pod, out of breath, and intercepted Butch. Pale, huffing and puffing, he said, "The attackers were Vron. They're gone."

"What's the situation in there?"

"Twelve dead, seven injured."

Butch brushed past him and peered into the studio. It was a scene of horror. Blood spattered the floor. He saw the body of a woman twisted in an unnatural contortion, a man kneeling over her gripping an arm gushing blood. A headless torso sat at a desk. Someone behind a translucent barrier was crying.

Butch answered his beeping transmitter. "McCrae here."

"Sergeant March. They've holed themselves up in the Civilian Rec Pod."

"Anybody else in there?"

"Haven't confirmed yet, but I think there are a few people in there."

Butch looked at Tepper. "Okay, this just turned into a hostage situation." Knowing Tobey was monitoring, he said, "PHC, this is McCrae."

"Dingell here, what's up?"

"We got twelve dead down here, seven injured. We need Lazarev. The perps got away. They're in the Civilian Rec Pod. We have a hostage situation."

"You got any experienced hostage negotiators?"

"I'll check, but I don't think so."

"Well, you're the old word king. Do what you can."

"Right, gotcha." He lowered his transmitter, found himself gagging as the stench of human entrails accosted his nostrils. He gripped Tepper by the shoulder and pulled him out into the hall. "Tepper, would you check and see if you've got any hostage negotiators?"

"Yeah, right on it." Tepper trotted down the hall.

Butch leaned against the wall, nauseous.

Tobey Dingell sat at the command desk in PHC, numb. As the reports of the carnage came in, he said in a trembling voice, "Flynn, all your years as a special agent, you ever negotiated a hostage crisis?"

Flynn shook his head. "No, I climb behind controls, manipulate joysticks, and fire weapons."

"Great." Tobey buried his face in his hands. Then he clenched his fists and pulled himself together. Now was the time he had to show leadership. If he had any to show.

———

Butch stood outside the sealed door of the Civilian Rec Pod, aware that any action he might take could result in the deaths of the hostages. Yet he also knew that hesitation would only empower the terrorists.

A muffled voice—heavily accented, Vron—issued from the other side of the door: "If anyone comes in here, the hostages die!"

"All right, I gotcha," Butch replied. "Now, listen —this is Butch McCrae. I'm the Chief of Civilian Security. Since you are guests on Station Post One, we will not take it upon ourselves to mete out justice. You'll be handed over to the Vron government. So come on out. Nobody's going to hurt you."

"We will not be handed over to anyone!" the defiant voice shouted. "We acted for the good of the Vron, to avenge the shaming of Wushno and Deemu! They are now avenged! The only way we're coming out is if you kill us!"

Butch pulled out his transmitter. "Hey, Tepper."

"Yeah, Butch," Tepper replied at once.

"If you've found a hostage negotiator, I could sure use one."

"Found one. Lieutenant Macri. We're on our way right now."

"Well, make it fast. I'm losing the argument here." He pocketed the transmitter and called through the closed door, "Listen, how long do you plan on staying in there?"

"Until you come in and kill us! We want to die martyrs to Wushno and Deemu!"

———

Tobey entered the SSBC studios and almost gagged as he smelled the guts and gore. He tiptoed between the bodies, trying not to step in blood, and approached

Pereira, who was interviewing survivors. "Everything under control here?"

"Yes, Commander," Pereira said.

He saw Burt Kaisman sitting on a stool, his face covered in blood. Dr. Lazarev knelt next to him, dabbing at his nose and applying cytosealant from a squeeze tube.

Tobey tried not to sound smug as he said, "Mr. Kaisman, they got you too?"

Kaisman's eyes glanced up at Tobey and he winced as Lazarev rubbed some of the sealant against his wounded nose. "No, no. I broke my nose diving under my desk."

"What happened?"

"Well, when I heard the shooting start, I didn't know what was going on, but I tried to stay on the air. Then my producer got shot and I knew that we were under attack, so first I got up and I was going to try to get out through the exit, but then I saw all the shooting going on in there, and I thought I'd better hide under the desk. They were heading my way. So I dove under the desk and hit my nose; blood went everywhere." He chuckled. "I don't know if they saw that and figured I was already dead or if they saw security coming or what, but that was about the time they darted out through the back way that I was going to go out."

"What about your co-hosts, Derek Winchester and Shellie Hurlburt?"

"I didn't see what happened to them. I've been looking for them."

"Okay." Tobey moved off to talk to Pereira; he was uncomfortable with the feeling boiling in his gut, that these assholes had gotten what they deserved. He buried those feelings; he didn't want to be part of the cycle of violence that was ripping the Station apart and causing tragedies like this.

———

Butch had run out of arguments and was just killing time, looking for something, anything to engage the terrorists' attention. He was almost ready to start discussing the basketball scores when Tepper arrived.

"Butch! Macri."

Butch shook hands with Dan Macri. "Glad you're here, Macri. Still don't know who's all in there, but the attackers confirm they have hostages, and they're going to kill them if anybody bursts in there. And they don't want to talk about any terms, and they said they want to die like martyrs."

Macri, to his credit, was unruffled. "Okay, I'll do what I can," he said in a cheerful voice.

Butch pulled Tepper aside. "Tepper, what do you say we circle around the maintenance corridor and we blast in there from behind with K-42 explosives. We've got a damn good chance of gunning them down before they kill the hostages."

Tepper glanced at Macri, who was in earnest talks with the disembodied voice behind the door, and said, "In all the confusion, I'll bet on that."

"Let's give it a try. I'll go get the explosives."

"Okay, while you do that, let me see if I can find us a sharpshooter."

"Kay."

Butch ran back to the security office, opened the hatch to the armory. On the bottom shelf was a box of the explosives he was looking for. He picked it up, noticing the handle was loose on one end. Holding the box with one hand underneath, he hurried back to the Rec Pod.

Down the hall from the Rec Pod was a circular hatch. He put down the box and pulled the hatch open. He picked up the box and stepped through into a cramped, tube-shaped corridor. Bending low, he crept through into an open area where a wooden walkway encircled the outer edge of the Civilian Hab. From here the spherical shapes of the expandable pods could be seen, as well as the exposed pieces of equipment that controlled atmospheric content, temperature, water pressure, electricity, food recycling, and all the other miscellaneous items that made each pod comfortable for human use.

Butch set the box down and pulled out his transmitter. "Tepper, this is Butch."

"Yeah, this is Tepper."

"Service corridor open, and I've got the explosives. Did you find a sniper?"

"Yeah, I've got Kyle Franzik. We'll be there in two minutes."

"Okay." He entered Macri's transmitter code. "Macri?"

"This is Macri."

"This is McCrae. How are things going on your end?

"They're totally closed to talking. I'm not making any progess at all."

"All right, we've got a plan B. Stall them, and if you can, keep them close to your side of the pod."

———

Kramer had followed the attack via the feeds he was receiving from Civilian Security, the Secret Service, and the news coverage. He contacted Tobey, who was on scene at the SSBC Studios.

"We're in a state of full lockdown," Kramer said. "All security forces are concentrated on the Civilian Hab. Have there been any incidents elsewhere on the Station?"

"No, no incidents, just—we've confirmed the identity of the two assassins, Vron civilians Laius and Fabio. Right now they're in the Civilian Rec Pod and I'm not sure what's going on there. Butch and Tepper are in the middle of an op. We'll get a full report on it later. I don't want to bother them."

"All right, fair enough." Kramer was seized by an irrational anger at Cranius; suddenly he hated all Vron, and had to remind himself that he couldn't blame an entire species for the actions of a few.

———

Tepper ducked into the maintenance corridor, followed by a young, helmeted man carrying a plasma rifle.

"Butch, Kyle Franzik, chief of the sharpshooters," Tepper said.

Butch was too busy setting explosives to shake hands. "Okay. Charges are set. When it blows, I want you to take out those assassins as quick as you can."

"All right, let me get in position." Franzik knelt near the explosives, plasma rifle at the ready. He pulled down the helmet's blast shield.

Butch held the remote control detonator in his hand. "All right, this is going to blow the hole *inward*. No debris or shrapnel ought to hit us. There's a chance it'll hit the hostages, but that's just the risk we're going to have to take. Okay. We set?"

"Yeah, ready anytime," Tepper whispered.

"Yeah," Franzik said.

"All right, here we go." Butch stabbed the red button with his thumb.

As designed, the explosives blew against the hull. A circular section exploded into the Rec Pod. Screams followed.

The Vron reacted quickly, firing their weapons toward the explosion, but Franzik was quicker—and more accurate. They had gotten what they wanted: they died as martyrs.

Butch stepped through the smoking hole. "All right, is everybody okay?"

"We've got wounded," a young woman said.

Another woman was crying. "They killed my husband!"

"Most of us are okay," a white-haired man said.

Butch pointed at the dead Vron. "Are those the guys that did it?"

"Yes," a chorus of voices answered.

Franzik stepped into the room, shaking his head. "Lousy shooting. They got off two shots before I got the second one."

Butch pulled out his transmitter. "PHC, this is McCrae."

"PHC, Flynn," the transmitter crackled.

"The bad guys are down, two confirmed kills. We've got at least one dead hostage, two wounded. We need to make a complete inventory here, though."

"Marked, we'll send in a clean-up crew."

———

His nose braced from within and coated with cytosealant, Burt Kaisman went on his air. His tone was subdued, solemn. The show's upbeat theme music had been replaced by a somber tune hastily composed for this tragedy.

"Good afternoon. *Kaisman and Friends* is back on the air. I'm Burt Kaisman. I'm pleased to report that Derek Winchester and Shellie Hurlburt are uninjured and they're here at my side as usual. We stand grief-stricken over the unprovoked murders of twelve of our colleagues, but SSBC is up and running. I would like to express my most heartfelt thanks to the heroes of the hour: Butch McCrae, Elmer Tepper, Daniel Macri, and Kyle Fransik, for taking down the two thugs who perpetrated this inhuman act and rescuing the hostages.

"And we are awaiting right now a brief statement from the President on this tragedy. And we're waiting for him to come out...and here he comes..."

President Kramer emerged in the Press Pod, his expression grave. The press pool was silent.

"Thank you," the President said. "Ladies and gentlemen, yesterday afternoon, the Station Post One offices of the *Silver Streak* Broadcasting Company were ruthlessly attacked by a pair of violent extremists who murdered twelve innocent civilians. I'd like to express my thanks to the extraordinary security forces of Station Post One for very quickly hunting down and killing the two attackers.

"The two attackers were identified, and we presume their motivation was retaliation for the political speech expressed by certain SSBC news anchors. I promise you that I condemn this attack in the strongest possible terms.

"But I also want to point out that this kind of violent extremism does not represent mainstream Vron. I have spoken to Ambassador Thobius and I've communicated with President Lyskia, and Vron stands by us in stern condemnation of this brutal massacre. We must stand together and show all who think it's their right to take innocent lives in the name of political or personal ideology, and show them that they have failed to persuade anyone. And if you inflict pain and suffering on our people, you will be hunted down and brought to justice.

"Thank you; that's all I have to say."

Kramer turned and left, and the camera pointed at Kaisman once again signaled that it was active. In order that he be able to provide an immediate commentary, his reply was already scripted. "Well, I am deeply disappointed," Kaisman said, "deeply disappointed that our 'president' never once referred to these thugs as what they are: Vron. That is what these people are, make no mistake. Vron!"

He took a deep, theatrical breath and let it out again, inserting an emotional tremble. "It will be impossible for us to win a war if we won't admit that it exists. We are at war with the Vron. The Vron culture is based on killing all who don't embrace their culture and their silly religion. And now that the Station is infested with Vron, there will be more attacks. Every human is in danger until all Vron are destroyed.

"I'd like to call upon all Human Power, and any other civilians who may be listening, to wear those hats. Ridicule their religion! Show your defiance of the Vron way, and show them that this is *our* Station!"

––––––––

Crowds clustered in the hall outside Ambassador Thobius's privacy pod, chanting "No more aliens!", in defiance of the segregation of the Civilian Hab. Kramer knew it would be fruitless to try to disperse them without inviting more violence.

The Secret Service formed a human shield around him as he maneuvered through the chanting crowd to the Ambassador's door. When he hit the doorchime, Thobius was reluctant to admit him, but finally, cautiously, opened it manually just wide enough for Kramer to enter.

"Ambassador, I'm assuming you've seen what's going on. Virtually every civilian on this Station is wearing those mock headdresses."

"Yes, I have seen that." Thobius sounded drained. He sat at the foot of his bed, looking utterly defeated. "President Kramer, I'm very sorry about this incident."

"And I'm sorry about the reactions of my people. I'm thinking, for the benefit of all, it might be best if the Vron vacate the Station. We may have made this move too soon."

Thobius gestured toward the door, through which the chants of "No more aliens!" were not only audible, but impossible not to hear. "I am hardly in a position to disagree. But I'm afraid many of my people will feel opposed to human closed-mindedness. They were looking forward to starting a new life."

Kramer looked at the door, regretful. "And I was looking forward to having them here. The timing wasn't good."

"You are an interesting people."

―――――

The Vron ships departed, and as they went to light speed, Kramer's stomach churned. As much as he reviled the attack on SSBC, he also felt that Burt Kaisman and his xenophobia and organized hatred had won. He watched on the realscreen in the Presidential Pod, Cranius at his side.

Once the last of the Vron ships had disappeared into hyperspace, Cranius said, "At least we still have the Vron medical personnel for next time those Human Power sprog-faces beat me up."

Kramer didn't find the comment humorous. "Yes. Cranius...what do you make of all this?"

"Well, I'm with you. I condemn that attack in the strongest possible terms. It was inexcusable, morally reprehensible, and I'm glad those two animals were gunned down." Cranius took a deep breath. "But I am a Vron. And although I don't condone the attack...I understand the emotions that led to it."

The Thousand Light Year Stare

Tobey Dingell was, as usual, furious. He stood at President Kramer's desk in the Presidential Pod, holding forth, red-faced and gesticulating and pointing. "There's no point in putting Human Power on probation if they're continually finding loopholes around it!"

Weary of the argument, Kramer said simply, "If they don't break the law, we can't send them back to the brig."

"Isn't it against the law to harass innocent people?"

"If they're doing so in a public setting, and if they don't inflict physical bodily harm, then yes, it's legal." The desk intercom chirped. Kramer answered it. "President Kramer here."

"This is Dr. Lazarev." Her voice sounded strained, hoarse. "I have the results of your cellular exam."

Kramer cast a sidelong glance at the curious Tobey, then left without saying anything.

When he arrived in the Infirmary, Dr. Lazarev was waiting for him in her office. The results were displayed on her realscreen.

"These are your lab results from your first examination after you got rid of the Thermian in your head." Lazarev paused, allowed Kramer to take in the image and the chemical analysis. Then, with a remote control, she switched to another view. "These are your lab results from your examination last week."

Kramer saw no difference between the two images.

"To put it simply," Lazarev continued, "in over a year you have not aged."

"I thought that might be the case," Kramer said. "When I went to the *Silver Streak* to learn what the Thermians are, Captain Cameron told me as much. How long will I live?"

"That is impossible to say. Your cells have produced an abundance of telomerase and they lack the P53 protein. Without apoptosis, your cells are not dying—but I would think this increases your risk of cancer."

"Of course. A Thermian already gave me a brain tumor. Funny that death and immortality could have the same cause."

"But there is no trace of cancer growth," Lazarev assured him. "Your cells are entirely healthy."

"How could mere exposure to the Thermian universe do that?"

"There's no way I can know."

Kramer signaled the Prime Hab Center. "Is Dr. DuBois there?"

"Negative," Flynn's voice answered, "he's in the Wheel."

"Very well. Please alert him that I'm coming to see him."

He went up to the Wheel, found DuBois in his cubicle. Kramer showed him Lazarev's images and repeated what she had told him. "I want you to keep this information confidential. I want no one to know that I've suddenly become an immortal superman."

"That's a bit of an exaggeration."

"Well, so explain it to me. How did this happen?"

"The Thermian universe is a high-energy universe," DuBois said, "which means high concentrations of radiation. In our universe, exposure to that kind of radiation would spur cancer growth. Maybe there's some kind of radiation in the Thermian universe that has a similar effect."

"But I'm not at all cancerous," Kramer objected. "Neither is Captain Cameron or Frank Johnson."

"It's all speculative. Unless I get some samples from the Thermian universe, I can only speculate."

"So speculate. What could have caused this?"

DuBois looked at the images, the chemical analysis, and scratched his chin, thinking. "How long you're going to live is determined by your DNA—aside from accidents and disease and so forth. DNA is nothing more than a long chain of atoms. Whenever the DNA molecule splits, an enzyme catches molecules and incorporates them into the DNA strand to create the duplicate. Sometimes there are duplication errors. Maybe those enzymes got scrambled by the radiation in the Thermian universe."

"But scrambled in a way that makes me healthier and live longer?"

DuBois shrugged. "Unless it's a sort of intelligent intervention by the Thermians—but often, throughout the history of evolution, there have been random mutations that have proven beneficial to a life form. Why shouldn't this be one of them?"

"Because this so-called 'random mutation' happened to two other people under the same circumstances."

"Well, I'm sure Dr. Lazarev will research it. I have biologists in the Wheel researching it. What I don't understand is why you've chosen to keep this a secret."

"Primarily because of Human Power. I'm already unpopular because of my open relationships with aliens. If *this* became known, they'd probably think of me as an alien myself."

"Can you see distant events?"

"No...I haven't even tried that. But having had Dreb powers, I think I at least know how to try."

———

One of the few people in whom Kramer entrusted his secret was Cranius. They discussed it in private in the Presidential Pod while Kramer once again hoped the room wasn't bugged.

"The Dreb powers come from the Thermian universe, don't they?" Cranius asked.

"Yes," Kramer said.

"What specifically are the powers of the Dreb? You had them; what were they?"

Kramer's brow furrowed as he tried to remember how that confused time had felt. "I had the power to touch other people's minds without any sort of transmission medium. I had the power to instantaneously transport myself from one place to another. I was able to..." He smiled, realizing how melodramatic—how *absurd*—was what he was describing. "...shoot energy beams from my body, create force fields."

"In other words, you did things with your body, with your mind, that ordinarily would be done with electronic tools."

"Yes, I suppose you could put it that way."

"On Vron, most of our leading neurologists believe that on the fundamental level, the activity of the brain is based on quantum operations."

"Yes, our neurologists have suggested that as well. Though most of the operations of the brain are electrical or chemical, certainly involving the atom and larger structures, once neurologists delve down to a particular level, their model of the brain's operations breaks down unless you account for quantum activity. I'm sure the Sev would say that it's that quantum activity that keeps us in communication with the consciousness of the cosmos."

Cranius lowered his voice and said, "Maybe there's something to that. Maybe when you entered the Thermian universe, your brain harnessed whatever..." At a loss for words, Cranius shrugged and said, "...is there. And assimilated a different kind of consciousness."

Kramer held his breath, not wanting to laugh at Cranius's suggestion, but unable to take it seriously. Cautiously, he said, "Well, that sounds more like metaphysics than real science."

Cranius laughed. "Well, sprog. You sound just like one of my professors."

"Seriously. We want to look at what's really going on and determine—"

"No, no, once we get down to the quantum level, science does start to resemble philosophy."

As an astrophysicist, Kramer knew that. But he also knew that the philosophical interpretations were merely human explanations for what was really just simple math.

Cranius continued, "Right now we can't observe the Thermian universe, but whatever the case, you can't argue with the fact that the Dreb powers really exist."

"I can't argue with that," Kramer admitted.

"You haven't tried yet to see distant objects. Why don't you try to do that?"

The notion fightened Kramer—frightened him because he knew it might work. But it was a logical suggestion. "That's fair enough." He closed his eyes and concentrated. "All right, I will."

He didn't know how to do it; no human did. But then no human really gave much thought to how to move an arm or a finger. You just knew how to do it. Doctors and biologists could explain exactly the mechanism by which the brain signaled the muscles to pull the bones and move the limbs, but even they rarely gave that any thought as they went about their daily bodily movements.

And so Kramer didn't know *how* he looked through hyperspace—he just *did* it.

And he saw—and heard—Argo, the Dreb from Derringer-9 whom he had befriended. And Argo saw him! He heard *Argo's voice asking, "Commander Kramer, is that you?" And he* felt *Argo's mind intruding into his own.*

Cranius caught Kramer as he slumped over, moaning. "What is it? Are you all right?"

"Yes, it's me," Kramer said—or did he say it? Was he merely thinking? He wasn't sure.

"Where are you?" Argo asked. "Do you still have Dreb powers?"

"I've been to the Thermian universe. I have some of the powers of the Dreb."

"That's amazing! Would it be all right if I come out there? I might be able to help you!"

"Maybe you can." The thought comforted Kramer, the idea of having a teacher, a trainer, someone who had at least some intuitive understanding of this state of being. *"You're no longer a Dreb. I'll send the* Frontier *to pick you up. Are you still on Derringer-9?"*

"Yes!"

Did any of that happen? Kramer was curled on the floor in the fetal position, gripping his head with both hands. Cranius knelt over him, feeling his pulse.

"Cranius?" he mumbled. Then he began to laugh, on the verge of hysteria. "I think I know what mental telepathy feels like!"

————

Once he had regained control of himself, Kramer went up to the Wheel to report what had happened. Cranius accompanied him, bracing him—and shielding him from passersby who saw him and wanted to make their opinions known.

When they arrived in the Wheel, DuBois listened with his typical stoic impartiality, but his eyes did widen a few times. As Kramer spoke, he turned and looked at his screen, tapping at it to bring up a prerecorded reading.

Once Kramer had finished, DuBois went to work, studying the data on his screen and then listening to his earpiece at something. Then he turned and said, "What you're doing is consistent with quantum relativity. I won't pretend to know exactly how exposure to the Thermian universe did it, but we did register your communication with Argo using SPACEWEB-23."

"That's incredible! You mean you can *hear* us?"

DuBois highlighted a segment of the track on his screen and hit 'play.'

"Commander Kramer, is that you?" It was Argo's voice.

And Kramer's voice answered, "Yes, it's me."

"Where are you?" Argo's voice asked. "Do you still have Dreb powers?"

"I've been to the Thermian universe. I have some of the powers of the Dreb."

"That's amazing! Would it be all right if I come out there? I might be able to help you!"

"Maybe you can. You're no longer a Dreb. I'll send the *Frontier* to pick you up. Are you still on Derringer-9?"

"Yes!"

DuBois hit 'stop' and said, "Is that an accurate record of your conversation?"

That hysterical giggle threatened to overwhelm Kramer again. He held it at bay, but felt himself trembling. "Yes. That was it, exactly. What are you saying, that I've become a transmitter?"

"I'm saying your brain is now capable of some of the functions of our electronic devices. I'd say this would be possible if something in your brain was able to…to 'rotate' a bubble of quantum foam into kinetic activity."

"My brain has become a zero point energy harnesser?"

DuBois started to object, then said, "For lack of a better term, yes—in certain minute quantities; you needn't worry about blowing anything up or anything that dramatic. But if the functions of your brain were able to filter this energy properly, then…yes. You could communicate instantaneously with someone else, you could 'see' distant objects, and given further refinement, you might even be able to do things like…" DuBois smiled. "…shoot beams of energy out of your body. I would think that this would cause great damage to your body if you tried it, but on the other hand, the Dreb have done it."

Cranius said, "Probably by long practice and the ability to direct all the energy away from their bodies rather than absorbing any."

Kramer thought of his own experience, what he had felt, what he had sensed, and said, "Or surrounding themselves with some sort of protective barrier."

"It sounds like a lot," DuBois said, "but given the beginning that you have already demonstrated, it's not much different from how Fleming's invention of the vacuum diode in 1897 led to the networked world of the twenty-third century. Or how the original discovery of tiny black holes in the ancient supercolliders led to today's Gravity Propulsion System."

Kramer was beginning to feel drunk, and he wondered if he had deprived his brain of oxygen during his experiment. "So then *theoretically*, how far could this lead?"

DuBois smiled and shrugged. "Who knows? You may have exhausted its potential already. Or you may have discovered the ability to become some sort of formless, timeless god."

Kramer's mind reeled at the possibilities. "Formless, timeless god," he mouthed. "In other words, this may be exactly the spark given by Rella to people like the inhabitants of Roanoke who became James Wilcox Lowell."

After a long pause, DuBois said, "Possible. Is it all that surprising that there would be a connection between them and the Dreb?"

"No, not surprising at all."

Kramer, having rested up, was feeling much better. It would be a while before he tried another experiment like that again. One he was sure he had regained his equilibrium, he went to Dock Deck Two—flanked by the usual entourage of both visible and concealed Secret Service agents.

When he entered Tepper's office, Tepper got to his feet and saluted. "Yes, Mr. President?"

Kramer returned the salute and said, "Tepper, I want you to fly to Derringer-9 and pick up Argo. He's still living in the Splendid Palace. He'll be expecting you."

"Yes, sir."

———

Tepper powered up the *Frontier* and checked in with the Prime Hab Center. "PHC, *Frontier*. Temp CBC confirms launch clearance granted."

Kramer stood on the command tier of the Prime Hab Center, watching the launch procedures.

"Marked," Flynn replied. "Copy pressure snake retract, power umbilicals retract, mooring cables retract. Go for discretionary maneuver."

"Coordinates are logged in, acceleration at one-eight-two, range four-five-nine when light speed entry to light speed factor nine on trajectory minus four-five mark seven."

Flynn quickly checked the numbers and said, "Marked. Your drive field is seven one three zero two, no leakage, no deviation. Go for departure."

"Marked, now marking horizontal drift at three one one meters per minute, distance is now eleven meters. Now accelerating."

The *Frontier* moved away from the Station. On the main screen in the Prime Hab Center, it faded quickly into total blackness, marked only by its running lights. Flynn continued to run checks with Tepper, and then there was the telltale flash of light denoting the ship's entry into light speed.

With that task attended to, Tobey turned from the command desk and said to Kramer, "You didn't mention to Argo that you wanted your longevity and Dreb powers kept secret, did you?"

"Well, in our brief contact, no…"

"That's good, because it's not a secret."

Kramer was alarmed. "What are you talking about?"

"Argo must have been blathering to somebody, because it's on the Republic newsfeeds."

————

Burt Kaisman had wondered all morning what he was going to do with the breathtaking news of the President's super powers. He wrote down some thoughts, but decided primarily to do what he did best: talk off the cuff.

He sat at his usual anchor desk, though today Derek Winchester and Shellie Hurlburt sat on the other end of the desk, while Kaisman's special guest sat next to him in Winchester's usual seat.

"Good afternoon, everyone. Welcome to *Kaisman and Friends*. I'm Burt Kaisman here with Derek Winchester and Shellie Hurlburt. 'President' Kramer has become a Dreb. Yes, this comes from Republic newsfeeds. Evidently 'President' Kramer was able to contact the former Dreb Priest King Argo on Derringer-9 using nothing but his mind. It's no wonder 'President' Kramer has been so friendly with aliens—when *he* is an alien himself! Reportedly 'President' Kramer is going to live an astoundingly long time—far longer than us ordinary mortals. Joining me here today is prominent businessman and game show host Mort Walker. Welcome to *Kaisman and Friends*, Mort!"

Walker beamed at the camera, showing off his perfectly straight, white teeth marked by the one gold incisor. "Thank you!"

"For many years you hosted *The Silver Streak Game Show* and you run Exodus Entertainment. So from a business and public relations perspective, what do you make of this?"

"Very simply, this proves what many of us have known all along, that Damon Kramer's sympathies are with aliens, and for good reason. This indicates that he is an alien himself."

" 'President' Kramer an alien," Kaisman said, injecting a note of concern in his voice, as if he had never expected Walker to make so provocative an assertion.

"What do we really know about him?" Walker asked. "He rose to prominence rather suddenly during a Hyron attack back in 4091. Largely on the basis of this convenient accomplishment, Captain Cameron had the confidence in him to place him in command of Station Post One when it became operational in 4093. But where did he come from? It is in vain that I find any record of Damon Kramer's existence prior to that Hyron attack."

"Are you suggesting that 'President' Kramer is a Hyron?"

Walker chuckled. "No, I find that unlikely. The fact that Damon Kramer was somehow able to absorb the energy of the Thermian universe to become elevated to Dreb status, and is now going to *apparently* live forever, is not something that human beings are capable of, and the Hyrons, as most of us know, are descendants of human beings who colonized the planet Hyron in the twenty-first century. The earliest example I could find of Damon Kramer's involvement with high-ranking members of the command crew was on the planet Asturias, where Elkahah Edmonds had stranded the Congressional Council and a number of others. Is it possible Asturias had some native form of life? Something compatible with the high energies of the Thermian universe? Something able to absorb them and become this creature? Or is it possible that Damon Kramer had these powers all along and somehow hyponotized President Copenburg into bringing him back to the *Silver Streak*?"

"What a fascinating possibility," Kaisman said in a stage whisper.

"Well, at this point, that's all it is," Walker said, "a possibility. I call upon Damon Kramer to put this speculation to rest by presenting records of his history on board the *Silver Streak* and his birth as a human. Otherwise, under the Republic constitution, his presidency is illegitimate."

———

When Tobey came to the Presidential Pod and told Kramer about Mort Walker's speculation that he was an alien, Kramer couldn't take it seriously. He laughed and said, "Burt Kaisman has totally gone off the deep end now!"

Tobey remained grim. "It *would* be funny if people weren't believing it."

"Oh, please!"

"StationHub is full of gossip about how nobody knows anything about you."

Kramer called up StationHub, Station Post One's communal chatroom, on his realscreen. "Just Human Power people repeating the rhetoric they hear."

"Mort Walker is powerful and influential. Look, Damon, it wouldn't be hard to prove your history as a human, you used to be an astrophysicist on the *Silver Streak*—you even have soil you brought with you from Earth. That could be tested in the Wheel and confirmed. You have vid recordings of—"

"This accusation is so ridiculous, it's beneath my attention," Kramer said.

Tobey's suggestion was reasonable enough; it would be simple to present reams of evidence of his humanity and make Mort Walker and Burt Kaisman look like fools—but he didn't want to dignify their outlandish conspiracy theories with even a public acknowledgement that they existed.

———

The *Frontier* dropped out of light speed. Ahead sat Station Post One. Next to Tepper sat the Dreb Priest King Argo—as always, his expression was intense, but that was just characteristic of the Derringan face.

Though human-like, the Derrigans were taller than humans, stiffer, their skin mottled white and their faces bony and angular. Argo was completely bald, but unfailingly concealed his bare skin under a wide-brimmed fedora. He wore a long, black robe that hid everything else.

Derringer-9 had been the site of one of Butch and Tepper's first missions. Tepper remembered that encounter with the Dreb of that planet, with the Priest King Argo, and the strange chain of events that had led Argo to be on their side against the Thermians.

So much had changed on that planet, yet from orbit the planet looked the same....

Well, the assignment had gone uneventfully, and although Argo's demeanor gave the impression of aloofness and even hostility, Tepper knew him well enough to know that he was actually pleased to be here, and looking forward to his appointment with Kramer.

Tepper hit the transmitter tab. "Station Post One, this is *Frontier*. I've secured from light speed. I'm on approach and I have your aq beac."

Flynn's voice replied, "*Frontier*, this is Station Post One. You are cleared for Dock Deck One, slip one."

"Marked, thank you."

As the expanded Station grew ahead, sprawling with seven Dock Decks and six Habs, Argo remarked, "It's even bigger now than last time I was here."

Tepper grinned. "You ain't seen nothing yet! We're planning a *major* expansion phase now. We'll be adding seven more Habs and six more Dock Decks. We're really working on developing Station Post One into a full-blown artificial world." As he said it, though, the spindly arrangement of loosely connected modules looked awfully flimsy and fragile compared to a true artificial world like Klym Valdor. The human race had a long way to go truly to rebuild from the destruction of the Earth.

———

Kramer had monitored the *Frontier*'s approach and was expecting Argo. He almost tried reaching out to him with his newfound "powers," but the thought frightened him and he recoiled.

But he knew exactly who was at the door when the chime buzzed.

"Come in," he called.

Tepper entered, followed by Argo.

"Mr. President," Tepper said, "Argo."

Kramer extended his hand. "Argo, it's good to see you."

Argo placed his large, bony hand in Kramer's and allowed him to shake it. "*President* Kramer?"

"Yes. Yes, a lot has happened since the last time we saw each other. Thank you, Tepper, that will be all."

"Yes, sir." Tepper turned and left.

Kramer took a bottle off his shelf. "Well, come on, Argo, please have a seat. Can I get you a drink?"

"I would appreciate that."

Kramer knew that Argo had developed a taste for human beverages, and had the bottle ready. He poured two glasses and brought them to the desk. "As I recall, you had a particular affinity for Electron soda."

"I did indeed."

"Well, I kept some on hand, expecting that one day we'd see you again."

"Thank you." Argo lifted his glass, flicked a snakelike tongue at the rim, and drank. "You know I don't have Dreb powers anymore, but I'll do my best to help you."

"I appreciate that."

Argo took another drink. "Delicious. It's been a long trip. I've missed you. I've missed this Station."

Kramer smiled. "Well, we missed having you around. You've always been a valued ally and a good friend, and I certainly wouldn't want you to think we've turned our backs on you just because you're no longer a Dreb."

"Not at all," Argo assured him. "I've been very busy myself reforming Derringer-9. A lot of my people are still loyal to my brother, even this long after his death."

Kramer's expression darkened; he wasn't sure how to discuss Argo's brother. Cercone had been, unlike Argo, loyal to the Thermians, and had even fractured the Dreb off into a civil war. Cercone was dead now, killed by his own misuse of his powers, and Kramer wasn't sure how Argo felt about his late brother. "There's been a little bit about that on Republic newsfeeds. Speaking of which, I didn't mention to you—I wanted my 'powers' to be kept secret."

Argo showed no outward reaction, but after a pause he said, "I apologize."

"Not your fault. It was bound to get out sooner or later. But we have our own internal problems."

"I would imagine. Captain Tepper tells me you have civilians on board now."

"Yes. The level of complication there is something I wouldn't have anticipated."

"Is Cranius still around?"

"Yes, he's still on board. He's my chief of staff, a very useful friend and a contact with the Vron. As a matter of fact, we just added some Vron physicians and nurses to our medical staff."

"I'd very much like to see Cranius again. I really like him."

Kramer remembered that Argo and Cranius had spent a lot of time together when they had been held prisoner on Zoran's Hyron Dreadnought—back when Kramer had a Thermian lodged in his brain. He shuddered at the memory. "Well, I can arrange it. Now, let me explain to you…I do not have Dreb powers. I just somehow had my cells affected by the Thermian universe, and this has, for some reason, increased my longevity by…I don't know how much. And I was able to contact you. If I'm capable of any more, I'm not aware."

Argo listened impassively, neither his expression nor his posture changing. "You had Dreb powers before, when we were on the *Kinetic* with Zoran. This is different?"

"Oh, very different," Kramer said with feeling. "I've lived my life as simply a normal mortal human being ever since I entered the Thermian universe, and that was over a year ago. When I contacted you, that was my first attempt to utilize whatever it is that I'm now endowed with."

"Well, with a little bit of practice, you may discover you have abilities you don't know about. Dreb powers are not like a muscle. They don't increase with use or practice."

"Really? That surprises me."

"Why should it? You had them before and used them most proficiently against Zoran and his Hyrons. I'm not saying it doesn't take practice; I'm saying that I'm not aware of any Dreb who discovered powers that none of us knew were there."

"Well, we're beginning to develop the rudiments of a theory as to where the powers come from and how they work," Kramer said, "but you can teach me to focus them. You weren't just an ordinary Dreb. You were the Priest King."

Argo thought for a minute, then said, "Since what you have is different, I don't know how useful I can be, but I'll do my best."

———

Mort Walker sat across from the desk of Senator Zemora Wiesenthal. The Senator glared at him, his expression unfriendly beneath his black beard, but he did not dare alienate one of his biggest donors.

"Naturally, if Damon Kramer is not human," Walker said, "then he ascended to the office of President of the Unified Republic under false pretenses and is therefore ineligible to hold the office. Wouldn't you agree?"

Wiesenthal drummed his fingers on his desk. "What would you have me do?"

"Open impeachment hearings on that basis."

"That could easily backfire."

"If Damon Kramer is unable to verify his human origin, no one could hold you to task for simply upholding the Constitution. And, of course, I would be very grateful." Walker placed a transfer card on the desk.

Wiesenthal looked at the card, wondering just how much money it contained. Slowly he reached out and took it, closing his fingers around it as if to hide it. "You have been of great value in the past."

Kramer opened Congressional Session and made a brief speech welcoming Argo on board for, as he put it, a "diplomatic dinner" to keep relations open with the Dreb—though every senator here must have an inkling of the real reason.

Before morning business, he said, "Senator Wiesenthal has a motion."

Wiesenthal stood. "Thank you, Mr. President. Esteemed members of the Congressional Council, as you are no doubt aware, some allegations have surfaced in recent days regarding our President's origin. I find that as a member of the Congressional Council and as a representative of my constituents, I cannot ignore these allegations. Since President Kramer has not seen fit to come forward and provide such proof of his human origins, then I stand before you today to propose that we open impeachment proceedings."

Forgetting his presidential decorum, Kramer blurted out, "Oh, for God's sake."

Fortunately his outburst was muffled by the general mumur that swept through the Congress.

Cranius and Tobey urged Kramer to give in to Mort Walker's challenge, and though he still resisted, he could no longer deny that the outlandish charge was resonating with the people—and with the Council.

As galling as it was to give in, he found himself relishing the task of accumulating the overwhelming and conclusive proof of his humanity. It didn't take long, of course, and he had to stop himself from having *too* much information for the press; if he got boring, the viewers would tune out and he would have gained little. He had to remember that Burt Kaisman had succeeded in turning the running of the Station into a ratings game.

So he stood in the Press Pod before the assembled reporters and tried his best to inject some dignity into the most absurd speech he had ever given.

"People of Station Post One. Some time ago, a rumor began that questioned my human origins, suggesting that I had been 'found' on the planet Asturias by President Copenburg, that I somehow hypnotized my way onto the *Silver Streak*, that I am ineligible to hold the position of President.

"I considered this…conjecture…to be so preposterous that it was not worth addressing. Unfortunately, it seems that it has gained so much momentum that it has even surfaced in the Congressional Council.

"Therefore, I have no choice. Main screen please?"

The screen behind him illuminated. He picked up a pointer from the podium and indicated the screen.

"This is my birth certificate."

The place of birth was noted as Dayton, Ohio, the United States of America, Earth.

At a gesture from Kramer the image shifted. "This is my family's certificate of passage on the *Silver Streak*."

The certificate listed Nestor Van Brugh, his stepfather; his sister, Elin; and Amelia Kramer, his mother; along with himself, Damon Ezekiel Kramer. It was dated September 2, 4072, and was signed by Archibald Gleason of the International Selection Committee and President Henry Walden.

The next image was an atomic force microscopic image of DNA.

"This is my DNA structure, certified by Dr. Lazarev to be human."

Next was a vid of a child in a living room, dancing in his pajamas in front of a Christmas tree.

"And here are some videos of my childhood on Earth."

Through the baby face, gangly limbs, and mop of unruly hair were discernible the features of the current President.

Now Kramer reached under the podium and took out a transparent cylinder. He placed it on the podium in view of the eager cameras. "I have brought with me here a sample of Earth's soil that my family brought along on the *Silver Streak*. Dr. DuBois has provided a chemical breakdown of this soil certifying that it could only have come from Earth."

He set the cylinder aside and brought out a folder containing a number of papers.

"Also some copies of forms that I and other members of the *Silver Streak* science staff signed after numerous planetary missions that that vessel undertook." He opened the folder and held the forms up, one by one, so that the press could take atomic resolution pictures.

"I hope this will prove satisfactory to you all, and that we can all go back to normal business."

———

Burt Kaisman eagerly agreed to have Mort Walker back on his show. He would have been happy to have Walker on every day; the show's ratings had jumped twenty points on Walker's previous appearance.

Once again, Derek Winchester and Shellie Hurlburt were relegated to the far end of the desk while Walker took the spotlight.

Kaisman opened the show with the expected headline: " 'President' Kramer finally presents proof of his human origins. I call this a victory. When the people stand up and demand truth, eventually they get the truth. Now, joining me once again is Mort Walker. What is your reaction to this?"

Walker again shot the camera his toothy PR smile, highlighting that one gold tooth that made his face so recognizable and so well-liked. "Well, it is a victory. Clearly Damon Kramer is on the run. But it's not a *total* victory because every scrap of 'proof' that he presented could easily have been faked."

"Now, just a moment, there's no reason to assume that it was faked."

"There's no reason to assume that it was real."

"Mort, Mort, the very basis of your accusation has disintegrated."

"But it hasn't," Walker insisted. "After so many years, and with the Earth gone, who can really be sure?"

"Well, by that reasoning, who can be sure of any of us?"

Walker chuckled. "I'm sorry, but I'm still not convinced that Damon Kramer is human, not so long as he has these mysterious powers and is going to live forever."

———

Kramer and Tobey had a drink together in the Presidential Pod, watching Mort Walker make a fool of himself on *Kaisman and Friends*. As it was evident that even Kaisman had lost faith in the charismatic game show host, Kramer knew he had won—at least for now.

"Well, you dodged that sidearm," Tobey said. "Mort Walker and Senator Wiesenthal have lost all credibility except for a handful of wingnuts."

Kramer raised his cup in a toast. "Evidence is hard to ignore, even by Human Power."

Tobey toasted that.

———

After their truncated celebration, Kramer and Tobey went to the Infirmary, where Dr. Lazarev had been studying Kramer's genes—from samples taken both before and after his exposure to the Thermian universe.

"We do not know what exactly were the influences in the Thermian universe that gave you this enormous longevity," Lazarev said, "but by examining your cells, we can see that you are receiving a total refresh of your own DNA with each cell division, and so I believe a study of your cells could lead to an elixir of life."

Kramer took that in. He looked at Tobey, whose wide-eyed expression spoke of his horror.

"You mean that you can manufacture a drug that will give everyone this longevity?"

"I am not a pharmacist, but I believe our scientists can do it."

"Well. Then that's something I'll definitely have to discuss with Dr. DuBois. Send this data to him, will you?"

"I already have."

———

Tobey visited DuBois in the Wheel, found him poring over genetic information.

"Ebor? Can I assume you're looking at Dr. Lazarev's information on Damon's cells?"

DuBois nodded. "Lots here to go through."

"Do you agree with Dr. Lazarev? Is this the elixir of life?

"There's no such thing as the elixir of life." DuBois saved the data and stretched. "Tobey, I reject the idea that Kramer's going to live 'forever.' I hear people saying that, and it's just not true. It's clear that he *could* live for a very long time, but we don't know how long it will take for this genetic rejuvenation to break down. There are also other factors we're not considering, like how long the human organism can really live—"

"But we know that Richard Cameron *did* live for two hundred years in a parallel universe."

DuBois shook his head, his expression one of disgust. "No…we do not *know* that. All we know is that he *says* that. We have no direct evidence to examine."

"No, no, the *Silver Streak* Infirmary has verified his age."

DuBois was silent a moment. "Well...okay, I'll allow that. But we don't know the conditions in that other universe. Granted, it's simply an alternate timeline of our own spacetime, but there may be other differences. There may be other factors that contributed to his longevity. There may be peculiarities in his cells that Kramer doesn't share. And even two hundred years is hardly 'forever.' But the important thing to remember is that Kramer has not been endowed with immortality; his DNA has been mutated in a way that favors fewer random mutations."

"But the end result *is* great longevity, and people will be clamoring for that."

"I know. And I won't deny that there is great promise in this research. We already have a way of giving people Dreb powers—I hate that word 'powers'—and so it's entirely feasible that we could manufacture essentially a vaccine against death. Or at least a vaccine against death occurring during the theoretical limits of the human lifespan."

And so Tobey made a public statement using those words.

———

Kaisman and Friends was coming to an end. Mort Walker had left, and Derek and Shellie had taken up their normal places next to Kaisman. Conversation had been unusually subdued in the aftermath of Walker's stubborn refusal to accept the evidence of Kramer's humanity.

Kaisman himself would have been happy to embrace Walker's theory—he had, after all, led the campaign to convince the Station that Butch McCrae and Elmer Tepper had faked their journey to the Andromeda Galaxy, a theory he still espoused—but he didn't want to risk casting doubt on his own humanity, or that of anyone in SSBC. Walker's assertions could be ammunition against anyone. Before slinging mud at anyone, Kaisman always wanted to be sure it wouldn't come slinging back at him.

And so he moved on from that particular conspiracy theory, though he did flounder a bit during this show in search of a new slant.

"And now it's time for 'Burt's Corner,' that part of the show when I give you my opinion. And my subject today is Dr. Ebor DuBois' statement that by studying 'President' Kramer's cells, he may be able to manufacture a vaccine against death. That's right! A vaccine that would allow us to live virtually forever! This is a terrifying possibility. Bad enough that 'President' Kramer is going to live for centuries, but can you imagine a world in which we *all* live forever?

"Even as it is, it is Republic official policy that planets are not safe for colonization because of the Thermians (who we are no longer able to fight, which is a subject for another discussion), the point is that we are confined to space stations, very limited spaces. *Imagine* a civilization of people who live *forever!* The population would quickly grow beyond control. It is not a sustainable environment.

"Further, if the same generation lived forever, that inevitably leads to stagnation. What would human life be without progress, without new inventions, new discoveries, new ideas?

"And without the imminent danger that our death is only a few decades away, what motivation will there be to accomplish anything? Why rush to achieve your life goals when you have centuries ahead of you?"

———

Butch and Tepper sat in the Rec Pod. They had finished their dinner and had settled in to an evening's drinking and conversation. And the topic of their conversation was that which had swept every corner of the Station.

Butch held his glass of wine and swirled it. "Immortality," he mused. "What do you think of this, Tepper? What do you think of living forever?"

Tepper slugged the rest of his drink and said, "Well, usually, when you ask me what I think, you just want me to say something so you can leap in and tell me what *you* think."

"No, no, I want to know what you think."

Tepper stared into his now empty glass, wondering whether to have another or to switch to something harder. "I'm against it."

"Why?" Butch asked. "This is the greatest—"

"You see? You're doing it already. You don't want to know what I think."

"All right, all right—I'm asking you why. Why are you against it?"

"If you'd *shut up*, I was about to tell you!"

"All right, shutting up."

Tepper paused to compose his thoughts, taking the chance of Butch running his mouth again. Slowly he explained. "If you never die, you never get to Heaven."

Butch scoffed. "Well, that's a chance I'm willing to take. Look, you want to go to Heaven, so you're striving for immortality anyway. What's the difference?"

Tepper gestured around at the cluttered, noisy environment of the Rec Pod. "Look around you. You call this eternal paradise?"

"Yeah, well, what if you don't make it? What if you go to the Other Place?"

Tepper shrugged. "I believe God gave us seventy years. That's time enough. What about your boy Shakespeare? I mean, so many of his plays deal with death and...and the fragility of life. If we all live forever, how can we appreciate those plays?"

Butch finished his drink and said, "Like I said to you before, I can't appreciate them much anymore."

Tepper laughed. "Well, naturally. You and Ophelia *lived Romeo and Juliet!*"

Butch smiled. "Well, yeah, now that you say it, yeah."

"Look, what gives you the right to live forever?"

Having encountered that question before, Butch had a ready answer. "What did I do that merits the death penalty?

Tepper shrugged. "You're Butch. Isn't that enough?"

———

Cranius had overheard some of the debates in the Rec Pod, the Prime Hab Center, and the Intercore offices. He had not participated—partially because he didn't want to risk being beaten up again. But when he joined Kramer at the end of the day for their evening retrospective, he brought the subject up.

"I don't understand why extending your lifespan is such a hot debate among so many of you people. I mean, who wants to die?"

"Some people do want to die," Kramer said. "Living forever would be a wonderful thing—if life is pleasant. But for some, it represents eternal suffering."

"As long as you're alive, the possibilities are limitless." Realizing he was growing unreasonably angry, Cranius lowered his voice and continued, "If you're dead, you're dead; that's it. You have no more possibilities."

"I understand concerns about societal stagnation," Kramer said. "Old people tend to become fixed in their views."

"Oh, I don't agree with that." Cranius realized most of his experience was with Vron, who were in many ways different from humans, but he nevertheless felt he had been around humans long enough to have an idea of their psychology. "Old people are inflexible because death is getting closer. Their bodies are failing. The younger generations are reinventing the world and forcing the older generations out as unwelcome. Why adapt yourself to a changing world when your days are numbered anyway? Eternal life means eternal childhood."

"Well, perhaps we'll find out who's right."

———

In order to complete maintenance and repairs on Dock Deck Three, the Space Star *Phoenix* was moved to Dock Deck Four. The layman might have thought this would be a simple procedure that would take minutes, but it was a delicate operation, maneuvering the huge ship among the cluster of pressurized modules that comprised Station Post One. Furthermore, it was a lot more complicated to moor the giant starship than it was a small scoutship such as the *Frontier* and the *Saviour*. Dozens of mooring cables and pressure snakes had to be disconnected, and new ones erected. Further, flexible booms with shock pads on the ends, called space stops, had to be extended to prevent the ship from drifting into a collision.

The whole operation took over three hours.

Flynn sat next to Tobey and coordinated, though this consisted mostly of simply acknowledging reports. Finally Dock Deck Four signaled, "Mooring completed, pressure snakes extended, space stops are locked and sealed."

"Marked, Dock Deck Four." Flynn turned toward the command desk. "*Phoenix* has been moved from Dock Deck Three to Dock Deck Four."

"Thank you," Tobey said.

With the delicate work completed, PHC had some much needed down time. Flynn sat back and rubbed his eyes, then said, "Commander, can I ask you a question?"

"Sure." Tobey did not sound enthusiastic.

"Would you want to live forever?"

"My fucking life? Hell no!"

Flynn turned back to his console. He had little to do, but Tobey's reaction did not invite conversation.

But after a moment, Tobey asked, "What about you?"

"Don't know. I'm still thinking about it. Just don't know."

———

In the morning, Kramer had his daily briefing with Cranius and, satisfied that no urgent interstellar crisis required his attention, he went to Argo's guest pod to begin his training. DuBois was already there, holding a petabyte drive containing his latest information.

Cranius joined them, curious himself about the potential of the "elixir of life." After all, since Vron's evolution was doomed, it would be just as well for the Vron to have a ticket to immortality.

With Argo's permission, DuBois used the realscreen on the desk to show his data on the holographic screen.

"If I'm right, your 'powers'—I hate that term, but I don't know what else to use—have to do with quantum entanglement."

That made sense to Kramer. "Captain Cameron intimated that he could 'see' distant occurrences and objects through tiny wormholes."

"Yes, and most modern scientific thought agrees that entanglement is impossible without the use of tiny wormholes. If you have conscious control over the quantum operations of the brain, you in effect have a part of the brain that none of the rest of us have. That's how you are able to communicate with Argo over long distances. You said you're not a transmitter, but in effect, you are. Your communication with Argo was over SPACEWEB-23."

Kramer turned to Argo. "Argo, can we communicate on other quantum frequencies?"

"I don't know," Argo said stiffly. "I've never had a scientific interpretation of these powers. But you succeeded in contacting me. That was on your initiative, not mine."

"Yes, I know." It made sense to Kramer that the communication had occurred on SPACEWEB-23; it had to be on a technologically aided medium, because quantum entanglement by itself was not sufficient to communicate instantaneously faster than the speed of light. Yes, entanglement was instantaneous, but the ability to *observe* that instantaneous communication required a cheat, and that was the decoder in the communications computer which matched the configuration of the communications code with light years-distant quantum ripples in the zero point field which were measureable by a probability algorithm. Theoretically a human brain was physically capable of the same cheat, but Kramer could not believe his own brain had developed the ability to do that.

"Were you able to see Argo during your contact?" DuBois asked.

Kramer frowned, trying to remember that brief, disorienting, and painful contact. "Yes," he said, though his memory was less certain than his words. "Not visually, but I was able to picture him very precisely." He looked at Argo. "Maybe it was my imagination filling in the gaps, but I have the impression that I was actually imaging what you were saying and doing."

"Yes," Argo agreed, "and I visualized you in your privacy pod."

"When you had your powers, did it give you a headache to do that?"

"No."

"Didn't give me a headache when I had Dreb powers, but it sure did this time."

DuBois said, "Well, obviously this is different from Dreb powers."

"But I wonder in what way."

DuBois thought for a moment. "Probably in that no Thermian endowed you with the powers. You simply were in the Thermian universe, and its properties modified your cells—or I should use the term mutated."

"Try it again," Argo suggested. "See if you can focus on something. Somewhere, someone on this Station is thinking about you or talking about you. Just close your eyes, forget what's around you—don't concentrate! Don't concentrate; just let yourself drift."

Kramer found that a rather confusing instruction, but he tried. He closed his eyes and, without too much concentration, tried to "feel" if someone was touching his mind.

Argo said, "I always found it helpful to think about my favorite food."

Kramer's brow furrowed. "Wait, I'm getting something."

"*...spine needle...virtually undetectable by medical instrumentation.*"

Who was that? Kramer heard the voice, vaguely saw a face, but didn't recognize her.

"*Excellent.*" That was Mort Walker! "*At 1215 this afternoon, Kramer will be entering the Council Chamber. You wait just outside the door posing as a lobbyist, and as he walks by, just a quick puncture to the spine.*"

"*It'll take a while to kill him; I hope that's okay.*"

Kramer opened his eyes. "It's Mort Walker! He's planning to assassinate me!"

"Are you sure?" Cranius asked.

"Sure enough!" He hit the intercom tab. "Civilian Security, this is President Kramer."

"Civilian Security," Butch's voice answered. "This is McCrae."

"Get to Mort Walker's privacy pod *immediately!* He's planning an assassination."

"Right on it! Donnelly, McNabb, let's go!"

———

Mort Walker's privacy pod was not far from the Civilian Security office. Butch led Dutch Donnelly and Michael McNabb around the corridor to the door to Walker's room. He used his security override key to open it without knocking.

The door opened to a young woman in the red overalls of a civilian electronics technician on her way out the door. Butch drew his sidearm.

"Stop there! Stop there! Civilian Security!"

The startled woman raised her hands, but kept her composure.

As Donnelly and McNabb kept their sidearms trained on her, Butch backed up to the intercom on the other side of the hall. "Mr. President, we caught a young woman leaving Mr. Walker's privacy pod. I don't know her."

"Search her for a spine needle," Kramer's voice ordered.

"Sir." Butch trained his pistol on the woman's forehead. "Turn around. Turn around!"

She turned around.

McNabb scanned her with a portable Friskotron. It beeped steadily, then screeched. "Right, microwave sidearm, spine needle."

Butch turned back to the intercom. "Mr. President, we got our perp."

"Walker's in on it too," Kramer replied.

Walker had appeared in the open door. "What's going on here?"

Holding the sidearm on the woman, Butch pointed his finger at Walker. "You're under arrest!"

"On what charge?"

"Plotting the assassination of the President!"

Walker crossed his arms, smiled smugly, showing off his golden tooth. "I take it you can prove this?"

Butch gestured with his head at the young woman. "Your girl here had a microwave sidearm and a spine needle, and I'm dying to see what you have in your privacy pod."

"You have a search warrant, I take it?"

"I will. Meanwhile, you'll both come with me. You have the right to remain silent. Anything you say can be held against you. You have the right to legal representation. You have the right to challenge this arrest through the Command Section or through Civilian Security. You have the right to a supervised communication with anyone on the outside. Do you understand these rights?"

Walker and the woman replied simultaneously, "I do."

"Let's move it!" Butch marched the two prisoners down the hall, anxious to learn more not only about Walker, but about the young woman.

———

Butch arrived in the Civilian Hab conference pod with a digifile containing the information he had dug up. Kramer sat at the head of the table, next to Tobey, Tepper, DuBois, Lazarev, and Flynn.

"Well, you wouldn't believe the stuff that we found in Walker's privacy pod," Butch said.

DuBois frowned. "Found? You had a search warrant?"

"Yes, the President issued a warrant. Walker had not only stockpiled weapons, but he had a detailed plan for *your* assassination—" Butch pointed at Kramer. "—and his takeover of the Station."

Kramer cocked his head. "Why would he need to? He's already got Senator Wiesenthal in his back pocket."

"More than Wiesenthal!" Butch leaned across the table and said, "He's funded half the Congressional Council!"

Kramer's eyes widened. He'd had no idea.

"The guy's a big shareholder in Intercore, you know," Butch continued.

DuBois said, "But the question is, will any of these charges stick?"

"It's bulletproof!" Butch was confident. "Look, if you're worried about the legality of the search, I told you, I got a warrant."

"You got a warrant, yes, from the President. How did we know about this whole thing? From the President' illegal surveillance of Walker's privacy pod."

Kramer raised an eyebrow. "Illegal surveillance? I'm not sure the law covers Dreb powers."

"However you did it, you monitored his privacy pod without permission and that's how you learned of this. Was he doing bad? Definitely. But I don't know if, legally speaking, it will hold up in court."

"It's an unusual way to catch a criminal," Butch admitted. "Would have been better if I'd taken him dead than alive."

"Well, it will certainly complicate our law books," DuBois said. "We now have to account for hyperspatial spying."

"Oh, no we don't," Kramer said. "We don't. That gave me such a headache, I don't think that we have to worry about my using this ability for a long time."

DuBois frowned. "Well…I'm sure it will stop hurting as you get used to it."

"Captain Cameron has been at it for two hundred years and it still hurts him. Looks like we've found a major Achilles heel in this newfound power. I think for now the longevity is enough."

Butch nodded. "Enough for me. I don't need to peep into people's closets. Give me a thousand years of life and I'm happy!"

But from the expressions on the faces around him, Butch knew that he was alone in his unqualified enthusiasm for immortality.

Carly

Dr. Carly Miselle was a biologist who had been assigned to study President Kramer's cellular mutation, but her real passion was marine biology. She had transferred to Station Post One on the realization that the *Silver Streak*'s life was winding down, and that the Thermians had ruled out the colonization of planets. In her spare time, she had been composing a paper proposing that an Aquarium Hab be added during a future expansion phase.

As it was, some sections of the Agrihab had been petitioned off for fish, but Carly wanted to study marine mammals. She had long worked on understanding whales, though the only samples on the *Silver Streak* were fetusus held in cryogenic suspension for eventual release on colony planets (now on indefinite hold), but now she had a new subject of fascination—a subject she kept to herself for numerous reasons.

She had discovered the Sev.

Although she longed to pursue her passion, she was grateful for the daily assignment of studying Kramer; it gave her a distraction—and it was quite an interesting study.

It was almost lunch time, and she decided she was satisfied with this draft of her latest study. She wrapped up the report and brought it to Dr. DuBois' cubicle.

Handing him a petabyte drive, she said, "This is the breakdown of the enzymes in the President's cells."

"Thank you, Dr. Miselle." DuBois plugged the petabyte drive into his console and looked at the holographic display. "Very good work."

"Thank you."

"You put this together pretty quickly."

"Well, I know how important it is."

DuBois turned and regarded her. "Well, you're pretty important yourself." He smiled. "Say, I'd like to treat you to a drink after shift and thank you properly."

Carly blushed. So it had finally happened. She knew Dr. DuBois had a reputation as a ladies' man. It was hard to believe this awkward, hunched, round little man who looked like a turtle had once been a handsome young player. She had to admit he could be charming, but she had no physical or romantic interest in him; she had learned early in life that her sexual interests lay with members of her own sex. "Uuummmm…I don't think that would be appropriate."

DuBois jerked, waved his hands, and covered for himself. "Nothing, nothing like that, just a drink."

"I don't think so."

"Okay. Sorry. I didn't mean to make you uncomfortable."

"No, no, it's okay." Truth be told, she was flattered by the attention, and she truly did feel comfortable in DuBois' presence. When she had first come aboard six months ago, he had seemed aloof, cold, even a little mean. But she had quickly learned that was only a first impression; as soon as she had worked one-on-one with him, she had found him to be kind, charming, and very helpful. She had come to think of him as sort of an uncle. "Dr. DuBois? Can I tell you something?"

He looked into her eyes and said in a friendly tone, "Sure."

"Well…I guess the reason I shot you down is…"

"You don't have to explain."

"No, I mean…I have a bit of a problem."

"What is it?"

"Well…I'm in love."

DuBois smiled. "Oh? Who's the lucky guy?"

Ever since the destruction of Earth, homosexuality had been frowned upon, and the default assumption was that everyone was heterosexual. "Well…it's not a guy," she said, blushing. "It's a girl."

"Oh." DuBois fidgeted. "Sorry. I didn't know. Who is she?"

She hesitated, not sure she wanted to confide in him after all. But she was sure he would understand, so she took a deep breath and finally said it out loud:

"Fweery."

DuBois raised his eyebrows. "Oh."

She blushed. "Does that sound strange to you?"

He chuckled. "I've seen so much in the time I've worked on this Station, *nothing* seems strange to me anymore. But I am fascinated by the Sev, and I never shared other people's fear of them."

Carly breathed a sigh of relief. "I'm glad. Then maybe you can understand."

"I can try to."

"Okay." Carly took some deep breaths to calm herself, and quietly explained. "During the time that the Sev were on the Station, I met and got to know one of the Sev: Margot McDowell. Did you know her?"

DuBois pursed his lips and then shook his head. "I don't think so. The name isn't familiar."

"Well…as I said, I'm a lesbian…is *that* strange?"

DuBois laughed. "In the post-Earth world, it's unusual, but there's nothing strange about it. Go on."

"Well, I was very attracted to Miss McDowell. But it got deeper than that as we talked. And as I learned more about the Sev way of life, I became very enamored of it, and I began to realize that the part of Margot that I really loved…" She shrugged. "…was the part that was Fweery."

"I see. I think I can probably understand that. Fweery is a whole different personality that embeds itself in the human brain, and eventually fuses with it."

Carly nodded. "Right. But I came to decide that I want that. But I'm not infected with the Sev gene."

"I can understand that. I'm not sure any sexual intercourse with Margot would infect you. If I understood what Zach Mortimer said, the gene is only passed through heterosexual intercourse."

"It's possible two vaginas might mix enough fluid to pass the Sev gene...but if I have to have sex with a man...well, I'll suffer a lot to have Oneness with Fweery."

"I think I understand. You want me to try to arrange passage to Fantasia for you."

"Well...yes..." She held up a finger. "*But*...I want to continue my work on Station Post One. I believe in what I do here. It's important work. And if I succeed in persuading Commander Dingell to install an Aquatic Pod, it's very important to me to continue my studies of whales and dolphins."

DuBois laughed. "You'll kind of have the ultimate study if you've got Fweery in you!"

"Not the same thing. The Sev are entirely different from our marine mammals. And like us, they're one disaster from extinction. My work with them is so important."

"I appreciate that, and that comes through in your work. But will you still feel that way once you're infected?"

"I've considered that, and my answer is yes. The Sev are still individuals. Their lives changed, yes, but many of them continue to do things related to what they did before. Well, to give an example of a man you knew personally, Zach Mortimer continued as CEO of Intercore for quite some time."

"Yes, until he left to start the Sev religion on Fantasia."

Carly had no good answer to that. "I still want to try."

DuBois sighed. "Okay. So you want to go to Fantasia, get infected by the Sev gene, and come back here to continue as a member of our crew. I've got to tell you, that'll be a hard sell. Commander Dingell doesn't like or trust the Sev."

Carly turned away from DuBois and looked at the floor. "It's not fair."

"No...it's not."

"Isn't there a way to arrange a trip there without telling him why?"

"In order to sign out the *Frontier* or the *Saviour*, we'd have to log the ship's destination and file a flight plan, and there'd be no disguising the fact that you're on board. And there is absolutely no valid reason for you to go to Fantasia."

"Suppose I just want to go there? Take some vacation time and spend a weekend there?"

DuBois laughed. "If only it were that easy! But no. Commander Dingell is far too suspicious of the Sev, and you are a member of our science staff. He'll want to know why."

They both fell silent. Then Carly asked in a small voice, "Will you try?"

"I'll try." DuBois stood. "Don't get your hopes up, but I'll try."

"Thank you, Dr. DuBois."

He patted her hand. "You're one of my best scientists. I'll do my best."

———

Tobey did not react well to DuBois' account of Carly's story.

"God, this gets creepier and creepier!"

"She's not infected by any kind of alien intelligence. She's simply a normal human who's having a normal emotional reaction."

"There's nothing *normal* about the Sev or anybody's reaction to the Sev!"

"Well...what Dr. Miselle wants is very simple: she would like to go to Fantasia, become infected with the Sev gene, and come back here to work on Station Post One."

Tobey's face scrunched up. "What are you *talking* about?! Once she becomes infected with the Sev gene, she's going to want to live in their weird hippy commune."

"Not according to her. It's not like individual Sev don't have any free will. She likes her job on Station

Post One and would like to continue working here. She just wants to undergo the Oneness."

"Do you realize how goddamned crazy you sound?"

Actually, DuBois thought, *you're the one who sounds crazy right now.* "I'm just trying to help a friend out."

"What you're trying to do is get in a friend's pants!"

DuBois was offended by the accusation—true though it might be.

"This is absolutely—" Tobey shook his head emphatically. "No! Absolutely not! When she comes back here, she's going to want to spread that Sev gene all over the damn place. We just got rid of that problem! I'm not bringing it back. Absolutely not!"

———

Carly was studying a blood sample from Argo when Dr. DuBois returned.

"Hi, Carly."

She didn't look up from her microscope. "Oh…hi, Dr. DuBois."

"I need to talk to you when you have a minute."

"Just a second, I just want to note…okay, the purine to pyramidine bond under the A to T hydrogen bond…it's pretty normal…okay." She sat down and put down her linkpad. "Yes?"

"I talked to Commander Dingell; I won't keep you in suspense. He said no. A most emphatic no."

She had told herself not to get her hopes up, but she nevertheless felt her spirits fall. "So no chance he'll change his mind?"

"Carly, if you knew him the way I do…no. No chance he'll change his mind. I should have warned you ahead of time it was a forlorn hope."

"What about President Kramer? He usually carefully weighs things and doesn't have kneejerk reactions—"

"Well, first of all, yes he does. He's gotten a lot more level-headed in the past few years, but I've seen him jump down people's throats like a diver into a swimming pool. Besides, he doesn't run the Station; Commander Dingell does."

"But still—"

"No, Carly…I can't bother the President with this. And I'd advise you not to either."

She turned back to her work. "Okay. Thank you for trying."

"My pleasure. I'm sorry it didn't work out."

But Carly was not prepared to take no for an answer. During her lunch break she pulled out her linkpad and looked up information on how to make an appointment with the President.

It was surprisingly easy; it turned out all she had to do was send him a direct message and ask for an appointment—but she would likely be turned down unless she had a very good reason, or was such an interesting person that he couldn't turn her down. And so she hit the CONTACT THE PRESIDENT icon and recorded a message.

"Mr. President, my name is Dr. Carly Miselle. I'm a biologist assigned to Station Post One six months ago. If you'll check with Dr. DuBois, you'll find that he has a very high opinion of me. I am currently studying your own Dreb mutation and the structure of Argo's blood and brain. But what I would like to talk to you about is the Sev. I had close contact with a Sev and I am interested in studying them much more closely. I have a request to make of you, and I would appreciate a chance to discuss it in detail. May I have the honor of making an appointment to speak to you?"

She finished her lunch, not hopeful that her message would yield any results.

But when she went back on shift, her terminal lit with a red icon signaling a high priority message. The sender was the President!

She opened the message; it was a text message.

Dr. Miselle:

The President will meet with you in the Presidential Pod at 1630 hours this afternoon. Report to Civilian Security five minutes prior to your appointment and you will be escorted to the Presidential Pod.

Cranius
Chief of Staff

She stared at the message, her heart thundering. It had been as easy as that.

The question was, would he listen to reason?

———

Kramer had just gotten back from Session and was trying to get some sleep before his conference with the Valdor when his doorchime rang. He got up with a sigh; the President was never off duty. "Come in!"

Butch McCrae entered. "Mr. President, I've got a Dr. Carly Miselle here who says that she's got an appointment with you."

Kramer looked at the clock, then at his appointment calendar. Damn, he had forgotten. "Yes, Butch, bring her in."

"Right in here." Butch escorted a pretty young blonde in. At the sight of her, Kramer instantly thought of Kiani Fulquist, his lost love who now lay in a coma in the *Silver Streak*'s Infirmary, savagely beaten by an abusive boyfriend. Carly looked much like her.

That was the real reason he had agreed to see her; after receiving her message, he had looked up her profile, and the photo of her tugged at his heartstrings.

By coincidence, Tobey had mentioned her during his daily lunchtime rant, and so Kramer knew—or guessed—what this meeting was about. "That will be all, Butch."

Butch grunted a reply and left.

"Mr. President," Carly squeaked nervously.

Even her voice was the same. The way she held her hands in a praying position as she spoke. But having spoken to Tobey, he knew he had no chance with her. Besides, he still hoped Kiani might recover.

"Come in, Dr. Miselle."

"Thank you for seeing me."

"Don't mention it. Please sit down."

She sat across from him, her face a grimace of nervousness. "See—I have a problem."

"I know. I'm already familiar with it."

Her eyes widened. There was a stark difference in the eyes; Kiani's eyes were hazel, Carly's were blue. The chin was different too, a little more square. The face was more oval as opposed to Kiani's heart-shaped face. The sandy blonde hair was straighter. But the resemblance was nevertheless so close that they might well have been sisters. Same nose, same smile, same complexion, same eye shape, same striking sunshine-colored hair.

"So you know that Commander Dingell said no?" she asked, crestfallen.

"Yes, I do."

"Well...I know he's your friend, but I just can't understand why he would just shut me down like that. I mean, who am I hurting?"

"All right," Kramer said, trying to calm her by speaking in a gentle, soothing voice. "Just...try for a minute to understand his position. He's responsible for the safety of the Station."

Carly also had Kiani's fiery personality. "How does my personal choice affect—"

"Please, let me finish. The Sev seek to spread their 'seed.' Commander Dingell is afraid that once you're infected, you'll be driven to infect everyone on the Station."

"That won't happen."

He smiled. "And why not?"

He could see that Carly was fighting to remain in control. Again he tried to sooth her with a gentle and understanding smile.

"For one thing," she said, pacing her words carefully, "Fweery learned her lesson. She's promised not to infect anyone against their will. Anyone who becomes infected now does so voluntarily. Secondly, I'm a professional. Remember, I won't *become* Fweery, I'll just…just be One with her. I'll still be in here. I won't run off and sleep with everyone I see. I'll be no threat. Please. You can't keep me from what I want so badly."

Kramer was touched by the abandon of her plea, but he still had political realities to deal with. "Dr. Miselle…"

"Mr. President, the Sev Oneness has often been compared to marriage. All I'm asking for is the right to marry who I choose to marry."

"I understand your point," Kramer said. "I can't directly countermand Commander Dingell's orders without going to the Council, but I'll talk to him."

Her relief was so palpable that she seemed to crumple before him. "Thank you!"

"That doesn't mean I can promise to change his mind, you understand. He is *very* strong-willed about things like this."

"But…you're on my side?"

Again he gave her that gentle smile. "Yes. I'm on your side. I'll do my best."

———

Kramer wasn't sure whether he genuinely agreed with Carly Miselle's points or if he was simply swayed by her sincere emotion and her resemblance to Kiani. He had to admit that Tobey had a point; the Sev, deliberately or not, had proved dangerous. Danny Diseker had died as a direct result of his Sev infection. If someone committed a murder, he wasn't let off the hook if he apologized and promised not to do it again.

But Kramer also couldn't see his way clear to denying Carly the chance to, as she put it, marry whomever she wished.

He met Tobey in the Prime Hab rec pod after shift and tried to explain Carly's point of view.

But Tobey would hear nothing of it. "I can't understand your liberal attitude toward the Sev. You actually want to permit this?"

"I think it wouldn't do any harm."

"Wouldn't do any harm?! Look what happened last time the Sev were here! Have you forgotten about Danny Diseker?"

Kramer wished Tobey would lower his voice; there was no telling who was listening, or monitoring the conversation.

"A Sev tricked him into having sex with her," Tobey continued, "he was infected with the Sev gene, and he killed himself rather than face it."

"Carly won't allow that to happen."

"Carly can promise anything, but once Fweery is in her, we're talking about a whole new ballgame."

"The Sev mandate is to spread their gene, yes," Kramer said, pointedly lowering his voice. "I grant you that. They are doing that on Fantasia."

Tobey did not get the hint; he shouted, "Their mandate is to spread their seed *everywhere!* Station Post One is included in 'everywhere'!"

"Carly won't be able to trick anyone into sleeping with her. The whole Station knows about this."

"I'm not going to allow it!"

Kramer tried not to sound challenging as he said in a soft, reasonable tone, "I can take it to the Congressional Council and override you."

"I know you can do that."

"That last thing I want is to be at loggerheads with you over this—or anything else."

Tobey finally lowered his voice. "I don't want that either. But I just don't think we're going to see eye-to-eye on this. I will not risk contaminating this Station."

Kramer nodded, understanding Tobey's point of view. "And *I* won't risk eroding people's individual rights."

"So where does that leave us?"

Kramer shrugged. "I have no choice. Don't take it personally, Tobey, but I'm taking it to the Council and I'm going to attempt to override your decision."

Tobey clenched his jaw, gave a slight nod, and said, "Let's change the fucking subject. You going to watch the Stompers game tonight?"

———

Kramer opened the following day's Session with a motion to dispense with morning business and put a motion on the table. Eighteen senators voted in the affirmative.

"Ladies and gentlemen, we have a petition here from a member of our science staff. Dr. Carly Miselle has asked for transportation to the planet Fantasia, where she wishes to be infected with the Sev gene and return to Station Post One and go back to her job." Kramer paused, looked over the faces of the senators to see any reaction; some looked disgusted, others simply attentive.

He continued, "Commander Dingell has refused permission because he fears contamination of the Station by the Sev gene."

There were now a number of nods and murmurs of assent.

Kramer went on. "Dr. Miselle has come to me personally to ask for my help. I told her I would give it. Now, I think everyone here can understand Commander Dingell's reticence to bring the Sev gene aboard the Station."

There was a distinct "yep" from someone at the table, along with other mumbled affirmatives.

"But we have Dr. Miselle's assurance that she will not spread that gene on the Station. Further, we have the word of Fweery herself, who has assured us that no further infection will occur unless a person volunteers. That being the case, this is a harmless request. We're talking about a citizen of the human race who wishes to marry—yes, marry—the person of her choice. In my opinion, this is not a request that we can turn down. I therefore ask the Council to vote to overturn Commander Dingell's decision and provide Dr. Miselle with transportation to and from Fantasia. Thank you."

Kramer sat, feeling the negativity from the assembled senators. He felt he knew what the vote would be; he had wasted his time.

———

Burt Kaisman appeared on *Kaisman and Friends* in a new suit with alternating red and black cummerbands. He felt good—he liked his new look, and he liked the subject matter of today's show.

"Good afternoon, everyone. Welcome to *Kaisman and Friends*. I'm Burt Kaisman, here with Derek Winchester and Shellie Hurlburt. And today's subject: the Sev Army is back! We have one aboard this Station: Doctor Carly Miselle." Kaisman chuckled as he said, "She has *fallen in love* with Fweery."

Derek Winchester and Shellie Hurlburt joined in the derisive laughter.

"Yes, apparently unable to find a date here on Station Post One, she now wants to go to Fantasia and have sex with one of the Sev, implant herself with the Sev gene, and *return to our Station*, carrying that gene with her, to live, what, a normal life? Well, ladies and gentlemen, I don't even know where to begin with this one. First of all, there are plenty of men on the Station for her—"

"She's a lesbian," Derek and Shellie interrupted.

"Oh, she's a lesbian? All right, well, there are plenty of *women* on the Station for her to marry, but no, she wants to go and marry Fweery the Sev. What's your take, Derek?"

Winchester laughed and said, "Well, I don't know what's going on with all these interspecies relationships on the Station, Burt. We already have Butch McCrae shacked up with an Etuknip—who is not even a native of our *universe!* And now this Dr. Miselle has literally fallen in love with Fweery, a strange oceangoing organism from the planet Zelnor!"

That brought fresh laughter from all three of them.

"Thank you, Derek," Kaisman said, "a sparkling and hilarious commentary as always. And Shellie, you appear to be bursting to weigh in. What is your view?"

"It's disgusting!" Shellie shrieked. "It's disgusting! It makes me sick to my stomach! It's like the animal porn I used to see on some of the sick corners of the Solarnet! I don't know what's becoming of the human race! But this is something we cannot allow!"

"Very well put, Shellie," Kaisman said, "erudite as always. Yes, ladies and gentlemen, once there is one Sev on the Station, there will be more! If this Carly Miselle gets her way, this represents a fundamental change in our way of life—the *human* way of life."

"Right!" Shellie shrieked. "Too many of our people have been seduced by the Sev way! The entire planet Fantasia has been given over to them! I'd say that's quite enough!"

Derek put in, "And Commander Dingell has already refused this request."

"Yes, yes," Kaisman said, "whether his refusal was sincere or merely for show..." He winked at the camera. "...*you* can decide. But 'President' Kramer is now taking it up with the Congressional Council to overturn his decision. I certainly hope the Council will show a little sanity and turn down this bizarre request from our 'president' and not let the Sev on our human Station."

Now that her request was general knowledge, Carly found it very difficult to work. Not only could she not concentrate—because she was so angry—but she was constantly distracted by the scrutiny of her co-workers, and of others who happened to be passing through the Wheel.

And on her way back to her privacy pod after shift, she found herself accosted by several journalists, including Burt Kaisman, who asked, "What's wrong with the human women on our own Station that you can't find a lover here? What do you have against humans?"

On reaching her privacy pod, she found a backlog of messages from total strangers weighing in on her personal life. Some were supportive, some were rude, all were intrusive. Then she saw the recap on the evening news, including clips from *Kaisman and Friends* of their fiery ridicule of her personal life.

She had trouble sleeping that night, and she worried what the next day would be like.

As she left her privacy pod in the morning, a civilian walking by called some angry comment at her that she didn't make out. And soon the reporters appeared. Once again Burt Kaisman was among them, shouting, "Dr. Miselle, as a biologist, you must surely know the evils of beastiality. How can you participate in interspecies sex knowing how unnatural it is?"

She ignored him. To the other reporters she kept saying, "No comment."

It was difficult; she had made a career of sharing information with the press and with the public. She considered herself an open and friendly person, and it went against her nature to be rude. But she was also angry, and she knew that she owed these people nothing. Her personal affairs were nobody's business but her own.

When she reached her work station, she was already so frazzled that she wanted to quit for the day. But where would she go? She didn't dare go to the Rec Pod—and the thought of walking that gauntlet back to her privacy pod was too much to bear.

Her distress must have been evident, for DuBois approached her and asked, with alarm on his face, "Are you all right?"

She knew she should just deny that anything was wrong and get to work, but her frustration poured out. "I resent this! Why are my personal life choices now a subject of public debate?"

DuBois sat next to her; it was unnecessary to ask what she was talking about. "I'm sorry it's come to this."

"I can't even come to work now without people jeering at me and jerks like Burt Kaisman asking obnoxious questions and sticking a microphone in my face."

DuBois nodded sympathetically. He looked away from her and said hesitantly, "Please don't misinterpret this, but you're welcome to stay in my privacy pod until this blows over."

The offer irritated her; she wasn't sure whether he had made it in good faith or if he was still hoping to get her into bed, or at least to catch a glimpse of her naked body, but she said gently but firmly, "Dr. DuBois—no. Thank you, no."

He nodded. "All right." He got up, squeezed her shoulder, and left.

All right, back to work. She hoped that burying herself in lines of genetic code would distract her from the hell that her life had become.

———

Kramer had hoped for a vote the same day as his request, but the Council had moved on to other business. He planned to raise the request again today, but as it turned out he didn't need to.

Senator Manchester asked to be recognized. Kramer recognized him.

Manchester stood. "Members of the Congressional Council, I would like to speak in response to the President's request that we overturn Commander Dingell's decision to refuse Carly Miselle permission to go to Fantasia, become infected with the Sev gene, and return here. As most of you are probably aware, there's a growing sense of concern among the civilians in my section regarding some of the nonhuman relationships which have been…sprouting in recent years—the first, of course, being Zach Mortimer's relationship with the Sev Fweery on Zelnor, which directly led to the situation we now face. This was not merely the expression of mental Oneness that we see in the other Sev; this was a literal sexual mating between a human and a nonhuman life form on Zelnor.

"Similarly, we now have the representative of the Etuknip Hegemony, known as Ophelia, living in communion with the Chief of Civilian Security, Rand McCrae.

"Now, I need not tell you that these are unnatural conditions. Simply on the surface, the scientific fact is that a human and a nonhuman cannot breed—at least not without extensive artificial genetic recombination. But further than that, should the government of Station Post One condone relationships which can only be described as beastiality?

"I would like to forward a bill which would prohibit physical mating or marriage between humans and nonhumans. Thank you."

———

The news of Senator Manchester's bill broke immediately, and SSBC broke into *Kaisman and Friends* with live coverage of the Congressional Council.

When Manchester was finished speaking, the camera signaled that Kaisman was back on. Quickly he ad-libbed his reaction.

"I congratulate Senator Manchester for addressing this issue, but there is no need for another law. We already have laws against beastiality. Why not enforce the laws we already have?"

Derek Winchester cut in, "It is a shame we even have to address this issue, Burt. It should be so common sense."

"Yes," Kaisman agreed with a laugh.

Winchester continued, "But some people see mating with other *intelligent* nonhumans as not counting as bestiality."

Shellie Hurlburt shrieked, "Arbitrarily!"

"But why create *another* law," Kaisman pressed, "when we already have—"

"The definition of beastiality may be in dispute," Winchester said. "Maybe what we should do instead is to put a law on the books defining marriage as a union between two humans."

————

Kramer had often suspected that certain senators had a much closer relationship with SSBC than others. Some senators—such as Arthur Manchester and Zemora Wiesenthal—even appeared as SSBC "contributors." Now it seemed that certain SSBC journalists were having a direct influence on policy.

So it was when Kramer picked up Manchester's modified bill, which now fell into direct accord with Burt Kaisman's suggestion of the previous day.

"Senate Bill SB10256595541," Kramer read, "a bill to be entitled the Human Relations Bill, specifying that the legal definition of marriage is a union between two human beings of either sex or gender, in order to remain consistent with Article 196 prohibiting the practice of beastiality. Put simply, this bill would make illegal any sexual relations or marriage between humans and nonhumans. Is there public debate on the bill? Is there public debate on the bill? Senator Fontenot, you are recognized."

Senator Maureen Fontenot stood and said, "Mr. President, Senator Manchester, I rise today to object to the bill. This bill is unnecessary in that we already have Article 196, and it risks infringing on people's personal rights. Mr. President, ever since we joined the Community, relations with alien civilizations have become closer, and we can expect that interspecies relationships will become more common. As long as these relationships are between two consenting intelligent life forms, then it's not the place of the government to regulate their personal lives. The laws against beastiality are intended to protect animals from nonconsensual and potentially harmful sexual abuse. Laws are intended to protect people's rights, not restrict them. I intend to vote no on this bill, and I urge my fellow senators to do the same. Thank you, Mr. President, I yield."

"The Senator yields. Is there further debate? Further debate? Senator Shields, you are recognized."

Senator Declan Shields stood. "Mr. President, I rise in support of SB10256595541. My good friend Senator Fontenot has argued that this bill infringes on people's personal rights, but Article 196 already restricts sexual relations to same-species. No right to any interspecies sexual contact has ever been granted by this Congress. All this bill does is clarify the meaning of marriage. In the future, if relations between humans and intelligent nonhumans does become more common, this Congress may propose legislation defining another form of union than marriage which would grant the same rights and privileges, but would not infringe on the sanctity of human marriage. I urge my fellow senators to vote yes on this bill. Thank you, Mr. President. With that I yield."

"Thank you, Senator Shields. Senator Dallas, you are recognized."

Senator Gilbert Dallas lifted his pudgy body and drawled, "Mr. President, fellow senators, I think there's an issue that we haven't been considering, and I think it's about time somebody bring it to the table. Now, the place of government may be to protect people's rights, as Senator Fontenot said, but it's also our place to stand as an example of moral virtue in order to lead our people to a prosperous and ethical future. A few of my friends here today have pointed out that interspecies relationships are becoming more common in the galaxy. Well, my friends, that, I submit, is the problem. That is an aberration and a corruption of the human body, which was designed, I believe, by a creator higher than any of us, to serve a purpose loftier than to fulfill carnal lusts. My friends, SB10256595541 is not merely an extension of legal precedent, it is an expression of our moral being. I plan to vote in favor of the bill, and I call on all of you, my good friends, to do the same. For if we stand by and permit the mingling of our species with the bodies of aliens for the purposes of sexual gratification, then not only those who partake of such acts, but we on this Congress will, I believe, have to stand one day before the Almighty and justify what we did. I thank you, Mr. President, and I yield."

———

Butch McCrae was following the Council Session closely. Ophelia caught him sitting on the edge of their bed, avidly watching C-SPONE's continuous coverage of the Congressional Council.

She sat behind him, framing his waist with her legs and massaging his neck. "Yourself calm."

"Can't," he said, his fury rising. "These assholes are prepared to obstruct everything you and I have been trying to build."

"The bill has not yet law become," she reminded him.

"Yeah...but I'm seeing more and more of these self-important, sanctimonious animals standing in support of it."

"What can do we?"

"I don't know. I just don't know. All I know is I'm not going to stand for it." He turned off the monitor, unable to tolerate any more. "I've left the Station before for your sake and I'll do it again if I have to. Nobody's going to keep us apart, Ophelia, not after all we've gone through to be together. Nobody!"

She smiled. "Yes, Butch. Believe I you. But do not overreact before something is there to react to."

She could feel him relaxing under her touch.

"Yeah, you're right," he said with a sigh. "I guess I'm getting all steamed up before there's really anything to get steamed up about." He paused, a thought hitting him like a thunderclap. "Wait a minute, wait a minute—there *is* something we can do!"

"What?"

He turned and grinned at her. "We can get married before they have a chance to pass this law!"

She stared at him, not sure whether he was proposing something dangerous or not. "Allowed this is?"

"First of all, I don't give a damn if it's allowed or not, and secondly, that's my point—let's do it while it *is* allowed!"

She smiled. "Klay!" She took his hands. "Happy will be I marry you to!"

He leaned forward and kissed her; she kissed back, an intimate human custom she enjoyed and appreciated. Their mouths, unlike their sexual organs, were compatible.

———

After making love to Ophelia—a challenging affair that involved some creative postures and judicious thrusting into body cavities not designed for human use—Butch went to Dr. Carly Miselle's privacy pod. Finding a group of protesters clustered around her door chanting "No more aliens!", he snapped at them, "Get a life!"

Recognizing him as Chief of Civilian Security, they dispersed, albeit with a few grumbles. But evidently they were in no mood for a violent confrontation—and nor was Butch.

He rang the doorchime.

"Who is it!" rang the voice from inside.

"Butch McCrae, Chief of Civilian Security."

The door opened, and he entered. Dr. Miselle was out of uniform, in a shear white sleeveless blouse, relaxing in an easy chair in the corner, a large hardback book in her lap, her bare feet propped up on the bed. "Hi," Butch said. "Dr. Carly Miselle?" He recognized her, of course, from her picture on the news, but wanted to put her at ease. "Don't get up, please."

She put the book down on the armrest. "Yes."

"Listen, I know what's going on with you—"

"Who doesn't?" she snapped. Then she smiled. "Sorry."

"Hey, that's okay, that's okay. You have every right to be mad. That's why I'm here. I want to help you."

She cocked her head. "How?"

"By taking you to Fantasia."

She grimaced and shook her head. "Thank you, but you don't understand. I like my job here. I want to stay—"

"Yeah, yeah, I know you do. So I'll take you there, you do your thing, and I'll bring you back."

She was silent a moment. She shifted, putting her book on the bed and drawing her legs under her. "Won't you get in trouble for that?"

He shrugged. "Ah, I'm always in trouble. What do you say?"

"Why? Why would you do this for me?"

He felt his face reddening. "Well...aside from the fact that injustice always pisses me off...I'm in the same position as you. I want to marry Ophelia. You must be aware of that." He grinned. "I guess we downtrodden have to help each other out."

"I was under the impression you had as negative a view of the Sev as everyone else does."

That gave him pause; she was right about that, and it surprised him that he hadn't even thought about that. "Well. Okay. You want to know something? I hate broccoli. Can't even stand the smell of it. I hate the way if it's even *part* of your meal you can't avoid it because it comes apart and gets into everything. But other people like broccoli, and I will defend to the death their right to eat it. If being infected by the Sev doesn't bother you, and it's what you want, then the fact that it's creepy to me is my own goddamn problem, not yours. I'll move the heavens to give you the ability to at least try the life you want."

She got up, walked over to him, and took his hands in hers. Smiling, she said, "All right! Why not?"

He nodded. "Meet me on Dock Deck One after yellow shift. You know where slip three is?"

She put a finger to her chin and thought. "Ummm…between slips two and four?"

He laughed. "Sharp. That's where the *Frontier* is."

"I'll be there."

"Great. See you then."

"Wait…is there anything I can do for you? You say we downtrodden have to help each other—"

"Don't worry about it. My services in this particular case are free of charge. I don't like it when politicians or anyone else stand in the way of people pursuing their dreams. I don't like it."

"Well…thank you. I'm in your debt."

"You're not. We're on the same side. See you tonight."

He left, feeling no doubts that he was doing the right thing, nor any trepidation about the trouble he would be in.

———

Butch had selected the best people on the Station to serve as his staff. His assistant was Demitrio Pereira, a former detective and profiler. As soon as Butch had come on duty in the morning, Pereira felt something was amiss. He couldn't define it, but he watched Butch carefully. Gradually the picture came together; Butch's obsessive watching of C-SPONE during his break, his angry outbursts at "the damned politicians," his general distraction. It wasn't hard to guess the reason; Pereira knew that Butch wanted to marry Ophelia, and he quickly put together that the new bill bothered Butch because it would forbid that.

Knowing Butch's history, Pereira's mind began to run through scenarios; he did it unconsciously. By the time he had finished his dinner, he had come to the conclusion that Butch would likely try to help Carly Miselle. Butch's history of leaving the Station without permission led Pereira to a growing certainty that Butch would try to smuggle Carly to Fantasia. And so he alerted Tepper.

"You want me to watch Butch? What are you talking about?"

"It's just a feeling, Mr. Tepper, but I just think you need to keep an eye on the *Frontier* and the *Saviour*. I'm not saying anything's going to happen; I just think it would be a good idea to watch out."

"Well, okay, if you think so, but Butch is my friend and I think you're jumping at shadows."

"I hope so, sir."

But as soon as Elmer Tepper was done talking to Pereira, his faith in Butch wavered and quickly turned into the certainty that Pereira was right; it would be so like Butch to play the hero and try to spirit Carly away. So he posted a guard in the *Saviour*, and he himself went to the *Frontier*—knowing that Butch would most likely try to steal his favorite ship.

———

Carly peeked out of the elevator into the darkened Dock Deck One. She saw no one. She knew that technicians continued to work during blue shift, but since she saw no one and heard no tools, she presumed they must all be in offices right now. All the office doors off to the side of the Dock Deck were closed, so she felt secure enough to leave the elevator and cross the hangar.

The Dock Deck was subdivided into multiple sections, and fighters and shuttlecraft were parked in the various berths, so there were a lot of places to hide, especially in the dark. But no one burst from a hiding place to challenge her.

Despite her joke, she wasn't sure where slip three was. She knew, of course, that the slips were out at the rim, the big subdivided berths that led directly to the launch tubes, but their numbering was not obvious. In the dim nocturnal lights, she squinted to see the markings over the berths.

CAUTION, KEEP CLEAR OF PLASMA BLAST; THIS AREA FOR CLASS-C SPACECRAFT OR SMALLER; BOOSTER CLEARANCE 19 METERS; ATTACH TOW LINES HERE—she looked above the slips, below, on the floor, and saw no markings delineating their numbers. Then she realized she was standing on a huge number 2. She looked ahead of her and saw a huge number 3. They had been hiding in plain sight.

Next to the big tunnel leading to the exit—too small for a craft as large as the *Frontier*—was an airlock. It was open, and beyond she saw a pressure snake dimly lit from the far end. The *Frontier* was on the other end of that pressure snake, powered up and fully lit. She peered into it. "Mr. McCrae?" On the other end of the pressure snake she saw a rectangular light: the *Frontier*'s outer lock. She stepped into the pressure snake, feeling herself lose some of her weight as she stepped beyond the confines of Station Post One's artificial gravity field. "Mr. McCrae?"

Butch appeared in the doorway. "Yeah. All set. You ready?"

"I'm ready." As she crossed the pressure snake, she lost more weight—and then she had a moment of weightlessness as the passed the equigravipoint (or "vomit point"), where she was precisely between Station Post One's gravity field and the *Frontier*'s. "I don't need anything, do I?"

"Just your libido, if I know the way the Sev operate. Get in the ship while I disconnect the power umbilicals."

"Okay." She stepped past him into the *Frontier*. It was the first time she had been on board the famous scoutship. The lounge, with its two bunks, game table, desk, and various pieces of wall art, was cluttered, dirty, and smelled bad, but there was a hominess to it and she could easily imagine Butch McCrae and Elmer Tepper on long voyages.

Butch ducked into the ship and began to work at a piece of equipment next to the airlock—when Elmer Tepper stepped from a closet, holding a sidearm. "I don't think so. Hold it, both of you."

Carly stood still, too frightened to move. Butch stood slowly, hands raised. "Tepper."

Tepper gestured at Carly with the sidearm. "Put your hands up."

She obeyed.

Five security guards—Command Section Security, not Civilian Security—tromped into the ship and frisked both of them. One of them pulled a sidearm from the inside of Butch's jacket and handed it to Tepper. "Standard issue security plasma sidearm."

"Thank you," Tepper said, taking the gun.

Butch stood against the wall, hands and legs spread. "Tepper, listen to me. What's going on here is wrong."

"Stealing the *Frontier* and defying the commander's orders by taking her to Fantasia?" Tepper asked. "Yeah, that's wrong."

"Just turn around and pretend you didn't see this."

Tepper's tone softened. "I can't do that, Butch. Come on, both of you."

Butch slowly lowered his hands and followed Tepper to the pressure snake, pausing to look over his shoulder and say, "Sorry, Carly."

"Thanks for trying," she replied. "That means the universe to me. I don't really think I believed we'd get away with it."

"You have the right to remain silent," Tepper said. "You have the right to an attorney. You have the right to challenge this arrest. You have the right to a supervised communication with anyone on the outside. Do you both understand these rights?"

"That's a blithering stupid question," Butch said.

"I understand," Carly said.

"Then move it."

———

As Tepper escorted them through the Station, word inevitably reached the news media. The nocturnal dispatcher at SSBC spotted the flashing light on the newswires and casually glanced at the incoming notification: BUTCH MCCRAE AND DR. CARLY MISELLE ARRESTED. "Holy cats," the dispatcher breathed. He hesitated as he reached for the intercom, decided Burt Kaisman may maim him for waking him up, but would *kill* him if he didn't.

———

As Burt Kaisman and a news crew accosted them on the way to the brig, Butch asked, "Kaisman, do you have an antenna?"

Ignoring the comment, Kaisman shoved his microphone in Carly's face. "Miss Miselle? Miss Miselle? Burt Kaisman, SSBC."

"That's *Doctor* Miselle," Butch snarled.

Again Kaisman ignored him. "You're an attractive young woman. Have you even *attempted* to find a human mate on the Station?"

"No comment," Carly snapped.

"Are you aware that human and Sev body parts are completely incompatible?"

"Leave me alone!"

Seeing he would have no luck with her, Kaisman directed his attention at Butch. "Mr. McCrae, why would you put your career at risk to satisfy this pervert's desires?"

"No comment!" Butch shouted. Then he reconsidered. "Wait, wait, I've got a comment." He glanced at Tepper, who nodded and signaled his men to stop.

Butch looked into Kaisman's camera and said clearly into the mic shoved into his face, "Because I love Ophelia. I've gone through a lot to save her life and be together with her, and *nobody* is stopping me from marrying her. Now, I'm not too fond of the Sev myself, but I know the position that Carly is in. Maybe I don't understand her tastes, but maybe she doesn't understand mine. All I know is whether I understand her or not, I'm going to defend her."

Tepper broke in. "All right, that's enough. Come on. Let's move it along."

Kaisman, having gotten his soundbyte, was satisfied and backed off.

Butch continued on his way toward the brig, not needing anyone to show him the way. Tepper, following close behind, tried to hide his smile.

———

The first news Tobey got when he arrived in PHC in the morning was the written report from Tepper about Butch's shenanigans. Furious, he left Flynn in command and stormed down to the Rec Pod for a much-needed coffee. Then he notifed Flynn he would be a while, and he took off across the Manway to the Civilian Hab, rounded the corridor to the Presidential Pod, and rang the doorchime.

"Come in," Kramer called.

Tobey found Kramer in the middle of his morning intelligence briefing with Cranius. "Sorry to interrupt."

"It's okay," Kramer said. "Mostly recaps. Nothing much has changed since yesterday."

"One thing has."

Perceiving Tobey's anger, Kramer asked, "What's happened this time?"

"Butch McCrae's at it again. He tried to smuggle Carly Miselle off the Station last night."

"Yes, Cranius told me about it and I read the report."

Cranius held up his linkpad. "We got a copy of Tepper's report."

Of course. Tobey realized he had seen that the President's office had been copied in the report. "The guy's unstable. We can't trust him."

Kramer smiled softly. "Kind of reminds me of a younger Damon Kramer."

Tobey shook his head. "You were a troublemaker?"

"I wasn't exactly obeying orders when I boarded the Hyron Galactic Cruiser *Odyssey* to rescue President Copenburg."

"I gave an order and he disobeyed."

"Cranius, will you excuse us?"

"We're not done yet," Cranius said.

"I know. I'll call you when I'm done here and we can finish."

Cranius sighed and left.

"Sit down," Kramer said.

Tobey made an exasperated sound and sat across from Kramer. "Damon, if you're going to give me one of your long and thoughtful—"

"How often have you wished you disobeyed the orders of Elkanah Edmonds?"

Tobey stared at Kramer. "Wait a minute! Are you comparing *me* to *Edmonds?!*"

"Butch McCrae is Chief of Civilian Security. He's duty-bound to maintain security in the Civilian Hab. But he has a larger calling—to battle injustice. And he saw injustice here."

Tobey shook his head, sighing. "Don't get high-minded on me. He disobeyed orders and that requires disciplinary action."

"Well, he's in the brig."

"I'm recommending he be discharged. I'm going to make the same recommendation about Carly Miselle. The situation has escalated to the point that it's intolerable."

Kramer looked down at the desk and said, "Well…you do what you feel you must. Of course, Civilian Security is not technically under the umbrella of the Command Section. Butch is a civilian, and I intend to retain him as Chief of Civilian Security. And Carly Miselle, as a scientist, is also free to continue to work in the Wheel."

Tobey crossed his arms. He had never imagined Damon Kramer as an adversary. "You're really not going to make this easy for me."

"Tobey, I think we both need to accept that you and I are not on the same side in this."

Dropping the subject of Butch McCrae, Tobey leaned forward and asked the question that was really on this mind. "Why would you want the Sev on the Station?"

"I want every individual on the Station to be able to live their personal lives as they see fit."

"Are you really that blind to the danger?"

"Look at the danger we already have," Kramer said. "Human Power and their dangerous ideas; the Station's been thrown into turmoil because of those people. Yet we continue to defend their rights."

"Not by any choice of mine!" Tobey snapped.

"My point is, they're a lot more dangerous than Carly Miselle even if she does have a Oneness with the Sev. If she steps outside the bounds, if she starts spreading that Sev gene, then we take action. Until then, her life is her life."

Tobey slammed his palm on the desk. "Damn it, Damon, you always want to wait until it's too late. I want to prevent a crisis from occurring in the first place. You want to attend to the crisis after lives have already been lost! Ever hear the expression 'a milligram of prevention is worth a kilogram of cure'?"

Kramer smiled. "Spoken like a true commander. Your priorities are in the right place, but my priority is the defense of liberty."

Tobey stood. "No one endangers the Station I'm responsible for." He turned and left, fuming. He was totally unable to reach Kramer nowadays; did the office of President unavoidably have a corrupting influence?

But a little voice in his head reminded him that he hadn't been a paragon of virtue since assuming command. He shoved that voice aside; he knew that in this case he was right.

———

Butch felt a little awkward sharing a cell with Carly. Although he was aware she was a lesbian, he couldn't help responding to her beauty. He was committed to Ophelia, he loved her as he had never loved anyone else, but he was nevertheless a man, and his body reacted to the presence of feminine beauty whether he wanted it to or not. He didn't do anything as overt, or as intentional, as making moves on her, but he did find himself talking to her in a more soothing and affectionate tone than he would a male cell mate.

"Well…sorry," he said when no guards were around. "Guess this didn't go so well."

"I thought Elmer Tepper was your friend," Carly said bitterly.

Butch bit back a plethora of sarcastic replies to that and said simply, "Don't hold it against him. He's just doing his job."

And it was true; Butch didn't hold anything against Tepper. In the past, Butch had done the same thing when Tepper had tried to go rogue. *On the other hand*, he thought, *when Tepper wanted to steal the* Frontier *to release the Ognom that DuBois was studying, I risked everything to help him.* Still, in helping Carly he had known and accepted that he was taking a risk. He wasn't angry at Tepper; he was angry at himself for being so easily caught. It was embarrassing.

"So," he said conversationally, "how'd you get so into the Sev?"

Her face softened. In a quiet voice, she said, "Do you remember Margot McDowell?"

Butch recognized the name. "She was one of the Sev that was on the Station, right?"

Carly nodded.

"I never got to know her," Butch said. "Just know the name. Couldn't put a face to it."

"She was beautiful…inside and out." Carly smiled as she said it, her eyes lighting up at the memory. "Before everything blew up, she spent time with me in the Wheel and she described the Sev way of life." She pulled her legs up against her torso and hugged them, smiling, looking like a teenager in love. "It was Fweery. She told me about gliding through the waves on Zelnor, about the infinite peace of Oneness and of living without fear. She was so…mysterious, but at the same time completely inaccessible."

Butch recognized the feelings and the words. Carly was describing exactly the way he felt about

Ophelia. He wondered if perhaps he was wrong about the Sev. But no…he thought of Danny Diseker, of Mortimer's weird euphoria, of all the trouble that had erupted on the Station due to the Sev's presence. He sympathized with Carly, but he could never accept the Sev.

Gently, he asked, "Did you and Margot…make love?"

"No," Carly said sadly. "Margot was heterosexual, and even if she wasn't, the transfer of the Sev gene doesn't work that way. But it's been very painful for me to hear the way you all make fun of the Sev. You just…you just condemn without trying to understand."

"I guess you're right. Yeah, I've done that. Sorry about that. I was out of line."

"They're beautiful people, and I want to be part of that without sacrificing my life here."

Butch nodded. It was a perfectly understandable and reasonable desire, and what a person should expect in a civilized society.

———

"Come in," Kramer called to the sound of the doorchime. He knew who it was and had been expecting this confrontation.

Tobey tromped in, linkpad in hand, and swatted it down on the desk. "Damon, I just came across this on the wires. You're taking it upon yourself to drop all charges against both McCrae and Miselle?"

"Yes. Butch is a civilian, and you already stated your intention of discharging Dr. Miselle, so you can't court-martial them. It therefore becomes a civilian affair. I'm dropping the charges."

"Jesus…okay, and supposing that I decide to keep them on in the Command Section?"

"In that case, you have the freedom to exercise disciplinary action, as they are both members of the Station Post One crew. Although it seems to me that their offense is not something that would warrant significant brig time or execution or anything like that.

So the only punishment would be discharge. At that point, as I said, I will retain Butch as head of Civilian Security and I will reinstate Dr. Miselle to her position in the Wheel in a civilian capacity."

Tobey's face was turning red. "Do you realize that you are completely undermining my authority?"

"Tobey, I'm sorry about that. I hope that you and I can get around this little disagreement that we're having and continue to work together and...and preserve our friendship."

"I'm not going to do anything to jeopardize our friendship, Damon. I just don't understand why you're trying so damn hard to stab me in the back!"

"I'm just going to ask you once again not to take it personally."

"How else can I take it?"

"Don't you think Carly takes it personally?"

Tobey hissed at that and paced across the room. "Damon, I'm sick to fuck's end of hearing about Carly!"

"I can't change your mind," Kramer said, "you can't change my mind. So where persuasion fails, I simply have to use all the powers at my disposal to do what I feel is right."

Tobey came back to the desk and sat, looking drained. "Damon...do you realize that this is turning into a great big cliché? The Commander and the President of the Congressional Council involved in endless, pointless, resolutionless arguments?"

Kramer laughed. "Yes, I see your point."

Tobey leaned across the desk and asked, "What's going to make you happy?"

"All right." Kramer considered. "Maybe we can compromise. I'd still like to drop the charges. But I will concede that Chief McCrae disobeyed your orders. So the basis of dropping the charges will be extenuating circumstances."

"*What* extenuating circumstances?" Tobey demanded.

"The fact that Chief McCrae finds himself in a personal situation very similar to Carly's. They're both fighting for the freedom to marry whom they choose."

Tobey grunted. "You know I don't see it that way."

"Well, the point us, Butch does."

"I don't grant him the latitude to disobey orders any time he sees fit!"

Kramer understood Tobey's dilemma; when he had been commander of Station Post One, he himself had had numerous problems reining Butch McCrae in, even denying him permission to land on one occasion. He knew Butch could be insubordinate, erratic, unpredictable, and sometimes a downright menace. But on this occasion Kramer understood him, and although he couldn't say so too loudly, agreed with him. "I'm trying to compromise with you here, Tobey."

Tobey shook his head, sat fuming for a moment, then shrugged. "Okay. All right. What the fuck. But I'm still not letting Carly go to Fantasia and get herself infected with a Sev. That's final!"

Kramer nodded. "Arrivals and departures on the Station are your responsibility. That's your choice."

———

Butch arrived in the Prime Hab Center in Civilian Security dress uniform, uncharacteristically nervous. He wasn't used to being let off the hook with no questions asked. He wasn't comfortable with it. Naturally he didn't want to be punished, but he was also trained in an unshakeable system of consequences and discipline.

He stepped up to the command desk and stood at attention. "Commander."

Tobey did not look up. "What is it, Butch?"

"Well, uh, first of all I'd like to apologize for disobeying orders and present myself for any punishment that you decree."

Tobey still didn't look up. "I had a long talk with the President about it. We're going to let it go this time."

Butch let out a sigh of relief and relaxed, putting his hands behind his back. "Thank you."

Now Tobey looked at him, pointed a finger at him. "But let me just say for myself, this is becoming a pattern with you, and it has to stop! You're not going to get off the hook next time."

Butch believed him. "I understand that."

"Was there anything else?"

This was probably not the best time to ask, but Butch had come here for a specific purpose and he had nothing to lose by asking. "Yeah. The Human Relations Bill hasn't been passed yet, so I'd like to get a jump on it. I…I would like you to preside over Ophelia's and my wedding."

Tobey looked away, his jaw clenched, and shook his head. "I don't know. With everything that's been going on—"

"Ophelia is not a Sev. There's no way that this could possibly endanger the Station."

"It could," Tobey said, "by enflaming Human Power and other people who don't like all these interspecies relationships."

"Aren't you the one that's been saying we need to never, ever accede to the demands of terrorists? Besides, what can they do? They're on probation. Look, I can go get the chaplain to do it, but I'd rather you do it because you know I don't believe in all that stuff."

Tobey sat silently, staring at his console, and Butch wondered if he was going to answer. But finally he nodded once and said, "All right, Butch, I'll do it."

Butch's heart swelled, but he remained stoic. "Thank you, Commander."

———

Burt Kaisman was delighted. It seemed that every day the goings-on on Station Post One provided him with fresh fodder to spice up the show, work the viewers into a frenzy, and boost his ratings. He mugged at the camera and said, "Have you received your invitation to the wedding?"

Derek Winchester and Shellie Hurlburt laughingly denied their receipt of anything.

"Those of us here at SSBC are unlikely to receive invitations. You see, while the Human Relations Bill is up for debate, Rand McCrae is rather cheekily marrying his Etuknip girlfriend known as Ophelia. Commander Dingell has already agreed to perform the ceremony—in direct defiance of the will of the people of Station Post One. But, of course, if the Human Relations Bill becomes law, Station Post One will be under no obligation to recognize this marriage, and naturally Chief McCrae can be arrested for consummating this marriage, since Article 196 prohibits bestiality. But unfortunately, he would have to be caught in the act, and I don't think anyone would want to."

Derek and Shellie laughed.

"But I urge all viewers to protest this 'wedding.' They can defy the will of the people right now, if not yet the law, but we can make our voices and our wishes known. Well, Derek, I know you have a lot to say. Do you agree with my assessment?"

"Absolutely, Burt," Winchester said. "Rand McCrae is just flaunting his perversion in front of everyone on the Station to draw attention to the issue. His timing of this joke of a wedding speaks for itself. This isn't about love or romance—which is self-evident since his 'bride' isn't even human—it's about making a point and defying the will of the people by getting this marriage in just before the bill becomes law. It's the most transparent and cynical political statement, and ultimately it serves no purpose, because this marriage will be invalidated as soon as the Human Relations Act is passed."

"Derek, you speak wisdom as always. Shellie, you have a lot to say on the subject too."

"Yes!" Shellie Hurlburt shrieked. "Rand McCrae is parading his sickness in front of everyone! This is after he already defied orders in order to steal the *Frontier* and smuggle Carly Miselle to Fantasia! Damon Kramer let them both off the hook for that! Just let them off the hook! That's an impeachable offense! And now Commander Dingell is going to preside over this illegitimate 'wedding,' which is the most hypocritical thing I've ever seen in my life! He ordered that Carly Miselle not be allowed to leave the Station, and now's he's presiding over the phony wedding of the man who defied his orders!"

"My, my, Shellie, you are really worked up today!"

"I am! This is sick, Burt! I don't understand what's happening to our people! There's no sense of decency anymore! People like Rand McCrae not only have no sense of ethics—"

"Oh, we knew that," Kaisman interrupted. "We've known that ever since Rand McCrae and Elmer Tepper faked their trip to the Andromeda Galaxy."

"Well—and the thing is, they don't even hide it! This kind of perversion ought to be at least kept in his privacy pod! But he's parading it in front of everyone! It's disgusting!"

"It is unnatural," Kaisman agreed. "I believe Senator Dallas. Our government should be the moral leaders of our society, and if they don't protect the basic morality of marriage, then of what use are they?"

———

Crowds gathered outside the chapel pod, carrying placards and chanting "No more aliens!" Their voices carried through the closed door, but Butch ignored them. Today was the happiest day of his life, and their ignorant protests only highlighted the rightness of what he was doing. If they hated it so much, it must be the right thing to do.

He had heard of cold feet, of wedding day jitters, but he experienced none of this. He was positive that he wanted to marry Ophelia. He had gone through a lot to be with her, and now that the moment was here…

…Now that the moment was here, suddenly it dawned on him that this was it. He was about to be *married*. To an alien. To a nonhuman. To a creature to whom he could never have normal sex. Who could never bear him children. Who would always be *different*. And he would be closed forever to other women, to *human* women.

He shook his head, smiled to himself. Okay, so he was prone to normal human emotions. But it didn't matter; he was still certain.

The wedding march struck up, and Ophelia entered, escorted by Ebor DuBois. He couldn't help smiling as he watched her; thanks to Dr. Lazarev, she had been garbed in a wedding gown after all. Not a very extravagant one, but an attractive white dress. Her blue hair was styled in a thick, wavy pattern that was puffier on one side than the other and fell upon her chest. She carried a bouquet of, unfortunately, artificial flowers, since none of the plants in the Agrihab could be spared for anything frivolous. But outshining all was her beautiful face. Her dark eyes were wide and moist, and she wore a joyful smile such as he had never seen on her.

He wondered if those chanting clowns outside had ever seen or known such happiness, or ever would.

Dr. Lazarev followed Ophelia as maid of honor, looking radiant in her own right; Butch had never before seen her out of uniform.

His eyes scanned the pews. There was Kramer; a camera drone the size of a bee hovered near him, the one concession the President had made to the press. And Cranius, Flynn, Pereira, Carly, Clio Steele, Lorne Michaels, a few others from Civilian Security, some of the pilots and Dock Deck personnel from his old days as Chief of the Dock Decks.

Lazarev and DuBois stepped aside, and Ophelia stood facing Butch. Next to Butch was Tepper, standing as best man.

Tobey gestured for everyone to be seated. Opening the paper command manual to a marked page, he began. "Marriage is a sacred trust. A union entered into throughout time, sealing the love and commitment between two people who have chosen to live out their lives together."

Butch swallowed, feeling unwelcome tears welling in his eyes as he gazed upon Ophelia's beautiful face.

Tobey went on, "Marriage is an expression of love and the creation of a new family. We, the family of Station Post One, represent yet another family: the endangered family of the human race. Today marks a new beginning for Randal and Ophelia, and also a new beginning for all of us, as this marks the first marriage between a human and an extraterrestrial nonhuman."

Butch hadn't been sure about that line. Yes, he wanted the distinction of being the first human to marry an alien, but he had wondered, for Carly's sake, if Zach Mortimer's fusion with Fweery shouldn't count. But Tobey had persuaded him that this was different—and as he stood here in front of his friends with his beautiful bride, he had to agree that it was not the same as when Mortimer had stood here marrying…himself.

Tobey continued, "Yet it may not be as novel as some of us pretend. It's been brought to my attention that as long ago as the twenty-first century, some people were marrying virtual people in computer programs. And by the twenty-second century, some nations, such as Greece, Monaco, Malta, and Honduras, recognized marriages between humans and marine mammals not at all unlike the Sev.

"And so I am going to ask that we put aside the novelty and controversy of this union, and instead recognize the opportunity for cultural understanding and togetherness. With Earth destroyed, we are creatures of the cosmos, and we must embrace the cosmos. Randal and Ophelia are doing this in the most literal way.

"And so we are gathered here today to join Randal and Ophelia in the bonds of matrimony. Can I have the ring?"

Tepper handed him the ring—a piece of copper hastily fashioned by Flynn in Intercore's engineering pod. Tobey held it before Butch and said, "Randal, take this ring and place it on Ophelia's…finger, I guess."

Butch took the ring and slipped it onto the end of Ophelia's smooth, blue, nailless finger.

Tobey said, "Do you, Randal Elian McCrae, take…" He slipped a finger into his pocket and touched the play icon on a digifile, which played Ophelia's Etuknip name, a whistle followed by a series of clicks and another whistle. "…to be your lawfully wedded wife, to have, to hold, and to cherish, in good times and in bad, in sickness and in health, forsaking all others, for as long as you both shall live?"

"I do," Butch said with enthusiasm.

"And do you…" Again Tobey played back Ophelia's real name. "…take Randal to be your lawfully wedded husband, to have, to hold, and to cherish, in good times and in bad, in sickness and in health, forsaking all others, for as long as you both shall live?"

"Do I," Ophelia replied, her smile never wavering.

"Then by the powers invested in me as Commander of Station Post One, and duly appointed representative of the Unified Republic, I do hereby appoint you husband and wife. You may kiss the bride."

Butch kissed her to the applause of his friends.

Ophelia threw the bouquet; Carly Miselle caught it! (Actually they had planned it that way.)

As they stepped into the hall, the joyful atmosphere of the chapel was obliterated by the hate of the chanting crowds. Signs and shirts reading "No more aliens!" and vicious faces spewing spittle as they screamed epithets mobbed them as they tried to make their way to their privacy pod.

"Will you leave us *alone?!*" Butch demanded. "Do you people have jobs to go to or anything?"

Civilian security moved in front of them and parted the crowd. It was funny; there really weren't that many protesters, but somehow their shouts and their threats made them seem more numerous than they were.

Finally they reached their privacy pod, and as the door closed, Butch laughed in triumphant glee. "We did it, we did it, can you believe we did it?"

"Did we." Ophelia's smile had not faded since she had walked down the aisle. She wrapped her arms around him and kissed him. "Love you I, Butch."

"And I love you. And there's nothing those white-robed dead-heads can do to stop us."

"Try they will."

He kissed her again. "And I'll knock their heads. We'll leave if we have to, Ophelia."

She shook her head, her eyelids fluttering and a ringing issuing from her throat—the Etuknip version of a laugh. "Not again!"

"Yeah, again. They won't stand in our way. My life here is important to me, but you're more important."

He took her in his arms, picked her up, and carried her to the bed, resolved to show her just *how* important.

———

The ceremony had been beautiful, deeply touching and inspiring, and Kramer hoped the whole Station, including SSBC's viewers, had seen it. The protesters and the SSBC commentators had tried to turn something wonderful, something joyous, that should bring everyone together, into something hateful and ugly. They had failed.

He wondered how many would see that, and how many would cling to their parochial prejudices.

Up to now he had been unsure how to approach the situation with Marly Miselle and the Human Relations Bill; he had felt passive and ineffective, not even sure which side he was on. But the wedding had made up his mind.

The doorchime rang. "Come in," he called.

Pereira escorted Carly in.

Carly stepped toward him, uncertain. "You sent for me, he said."

"Yes," Kramer said.

"What is it?"

"That'll be all, Mr. Pereira."

Pereira saluted and left.

"Please have a seat."

Carly sat facing him.

Kramer folded his hands on the desk and said, "The Human Relations Bill passed."

She closed her eyes and took a trembling breath.

Kramer held up a finger. "But with caveats—and there's one very large loophole. Specifically, although marrying a nonhuman is illegal aboard the Station, should a human and nonhuman marriage take place outside the jurisdiction of the Congressional Council, it must be recognized on Station Post One should such a couple come on board. And, of course, any such marriages that took place before the bill was passed will also be recognized; therefore Butch and Ophelia are safe.

"However, Commander Dingell is absolutely unwilling to reverse his decision. He is not allowing you off the Station. And frankly, with everything that's going on—Human Power, the protests, the whole cultural environment—you could never live here safely as a Sev."

"That's not acceptable!" Carly caught herself, lowered her voice, and added, "Mr. President."

Kramer smiled. "Agreed. But here's what I propose. As President of the Unified Republic, I have it within my power to send you to Fantasia in secret in one of the alien ships that docks here. You can mate with a Sev there, you can become infected with the Sev gene, and I will arrange your return to Station Post One."

Relief and gratitude washed over Carly's face, but before she could speak, Kramer added, "But upon your return, the presence of the Sev gene within you must remain secret. If you tell anyone, there's very grave danger that you will, at best, lose your position in the Wheel—and at worst, be exiled from Station Post One. That's out of my hands. So if you are willing to live a Sev life in secret, I can arrange it. Is that agreeable to you?"

Her face had fallen as he spoke. "I don't know," she said, the frustration beginning to boil again. "I don't want my life to be a secret."

"I know." Kramer looked at her with sympathy and wondered, *How can I be the leader of a whole civilization and be so helpless?* "I don't know what else I can do for you. I'm the President, not the king."

"I know." She looked off to the side, her expression so much like Kiani Fulquist in her moments of deep thought, then she nodded. "All right. If that's the only way, all right. I accept your offer."

"Good." He reached across the table and she shook his hand. "You know—in time, we may change their minds."

"I hope so," Carly said, her voice trembling. "I feel so lost—it's the first time in my life I've ever actually felt disciminated against."

"I'm sorry about that. But we'll set it right someday. Meanwhile, you'll have what you seek."

She smiled, looked off beyond him as if she could see through the fabric of the pods and into space. "And peace. I'll have the peace of the Sev."

Change of Heart

Cranius was assaulted again.

As always, there were crowds of protesters swarming the halls with their chant of "No more aliens!"

For most of the morning, Cranius had been consumed with debugging a new software update in the Intercore office, and now he was on his way to the Presidential Pod to help Kramer prepare for his daily press briefing. As he passed through the Manway he could hear them, like a reverberation shuddering through the Manway with each incantation: "No more aliens! No more aliens! No more aliens!" He almost felt there was a drumbeat to it, though there was not.

Then he found himself being jostled as he pushed his way round the corridor through the shouting, chanting crowd.

"Hey!" shouted a drunken man with a black beard and sweat on his forehead. "Where do you think you're going?"

"To the Presidential Pod," Cranius answered calmly. "I have a report for him on Vron spacecraft movements—if it's any of your business."

The man seized his arm and spun him around. "You better damn well believe it's my business! I'm a civilian on this Station, and this is a representative government! And I don't like the idea of aliens whispering in my President's ear!"

"Well, I'm sorry about that, but I have my orders." Cranius tried to shove past him. "Now, stand aside."

The man blocked his way. "What'd you say to me?"

Cranius almost choked on the man's breath; how much had he imbibed at only 1000 hours? "I said stand aside!"

The man called over his shoulder, "Did you hear that?"

"I heard that," said another man, a scraggly-looking blond man wearing a NO MORE ALIENS shirt.

"Did you hear this alien give me an order?!"

Others started shouting; Cranius distinctly heard someone say, "Yeah, why don't you punch him?"

The bearded man grabbed him by the collar. "I don't know where you Vron keep your melchers, but how about a little of this medicine?" Now came the inevitable punch to the gut.

Cranius was prepared for it, had stiffened his stomach muscles, and didn't have the wind knocked out of him. But the force of the blow sent him staggering backward; he landed in the hands of three other protesters.

"Well done!" shouted a blonde woman with a shrill voice.

"Come on," someone said, "let's get him!"

"Take a little bit of that!" The blond man in the NO MORE ALIENS shirt locked his fists together and delivered a powerful blow across Cranius's jaw. That knocked him on his back. He fell sideways against the floor, and he knew what was coming next because he had been through it too many times before. As they began kicking him, punching him, spitting on him, and pummeling him with projectiles, all he could do was protect himself as best he could by curling into a ball and waiting for it to be over.

He didn't know how long he had suffered the unrelenting abuse before Butch McCrae's sharp voice cut through the noise—and the fog of his pain. "All right, that's enough here! Everybody disperse!"

"You're the one that married an alien!" someone replied. "Let's get him, boys!"

"Now hold it back or I fire!"

Cranius saw the flash of a sidearm, heard the grunt of a man being hit.

Next came the drunken voice of the bearded man who had started this whole thing. "Come on, he can't get us all!"

"Maybe not," Butch replied, "but you get it first!" Rather than shooting Beard, Butch punched him.

"I'm gonna pay you back for that," the drunken man said. "Alien-lover!"

Cranius heard a scuffle, saw prancing feet around him, and then the voice of the blond man in the NO MORE ALIENS shirt boasting, "I got his sidearm! I'm gonna fry him!"

"Now, wait a minute, wait a minute," said another voice, one that Cranius didn't recall hearing before, "we're still on probation! We don't need a murder charge."

That seemed to quiet the crowd. Their shouts died to a murmur. Cranius didn't know what had happened to Butch, but he heard his voice no more. He thought he lost consciousness. The next thing he was aware of was Dr. Lazarev kneeling next to him; he couldn't be sure if he was still lying in the corridor or if he had been moved somewhere. The surface under him was soft, the smells around him medicinal, so he must be in the Infirmary.

"Call Dr. Sitaris and Nurse Paragrin," Lazarev said. "Tell them Cranius is in room three."

"Yes, Doctor," someone said.

Cranius opened his eyes. Yes, this was the Infirmary. One of the intensive care pods. He saw Dr. Lazarev step out the door. He looked down at his arm, saw that it was attached to some piece of equipment. Looking up, he saw an orderly adjusting settings on something that had a sort of antenna pointed at the device on his arm.

He closed his eyes. He had been through all this before. Lazarev would take care of him. And then the protesters would face the Wrath of Damon Kramer.

———

Butch McCrae felt dizzy and nauseous, but he wasn't about to admit that; his pilot's instincts had been honed to so fear the ultimate humiliation, being grounded, that the revulsion to admitting to any illness was second nature to him.

He looked around, puzzled for a moment as to where he was—it was familiar—oh, yes. The Infirmary. Orderlies pushed him through the central pod past the examining pods, brought him to a stop in front of Dr. Lazarev. He tried to grin at her, wasn't sure he succeeded. She held up her hand and asked, "Butch, can you see my hand clearly?"

"Yeah, yeah," he snapped, realizing that his voice was slurred and guttural. He sounded groggy, though he didn't feel it. "Where's Ophelia?"

"How many fingers do you see?"

The image of her hand was blurred, but he was pretty sure he saw two fingers. "Two," he mumbled, trying to sound incomprehensible in case he'd gotten the answer wrong. "Where's Ophelia?"

"She will be here shortly. Pupils dilated, pulse rapid, blood pressure one twenty over ninety. Take him to room one."

They were moving him again. He closed his eyes, enjoying the ride.

———

As soon as Kramer heard about the assault, he wanted to rush to the Infirmary to see Cranius, but he had to attend the morning press briefing. There were only two questions about the attack on Butch McCrae and Cranius; the rest were about relations with the Valdor and the Vron, and whether more aliens would be permitted on the Station. He answered as concisely and as patiently as he could despite his outrage at the lack of interest in yet another incident of violence perpetrated by Human Power.

Afterwards he returned to the Presidential Pod to prepare for today's Congressional Session, was not surprised to find a message from Tobey Dingell requesting a conference. He approved it, sat down, and waited.

Tobey was, as usual, furious. He thrust Dr. Lazarev's medical report on Cranius onto the desk and recounted the details of the attack three times, then ranted, "This is a clear violation of their probation! Assault on two of our highly placed officers resulting in injuries severe enough for confinement to the Infirmary! Clearly Cranius was targeted because he was a Vron, and Butch was called, and I quote, 'alien-lover'! These are hate crimes, Damon! These people need to be locked up and confined!"

Kramer agreed completely. In fact he was sorely tempted to hunt down the lunatics who had done this and gun them down himself. "I warn you, Tobey, we just don't have the resources to confine people to the brig indefinitely. If we truly are interested in meting out justice, as distasteful as the prospect is, it may be necessary to impose the death penalty for minor infractions."

Tobey turned away, chagrined. He paced, nibbling on his thumbnail. "No, no," he muttered. Then, louder, "No, no, no…I never…I never want to put someone to death again."

"You just called these hate crimes. They're endangering the safety of our Station."

"I'm not putting anyone to death again. I have never lived down spacing Vin Jenboch or shooting down my own pilots. Even though I was absolved of any wrongdoing, I've never lived it down."

"What's the alternative, then?" Kramer asked. "Turn this into a prison station?"

"You know…I can't tell if you're serious or not. Do you actually advocate putting people to death?"

Yes, Kramer thought to himself. "No…no, I don't. That's the last thing I want to do. But I also don't want this kind of discord on the Station. I don't want assaults going on in the halls!" His rage finally took hold of him and he pounded his fist on the desk. "Everything we have done has failed! If I go to the Council and pass some sort of measure that will impose the death penalty for assaults and other activities that endanger lives or the structural integrity of the Station, maybe that threat of death alone could be enough to quiet these lunatics."

———

Assistant Security Chief Pereira wished Butch was here; he and the rest of Civilian Security were perfectly capable of herding the angry mob to the brig, but he would rather have Butch's guiding hand. He didn't like being in charge.

"All right, move it!" he shouted, waving his sidearm at the shouting mob.

Civilians emerged from their privacy pods, curious, some holding the hands of little children, some in various stages of undress.

"Into your privacy pods," Pereira ordered. "Go on! Go on! Everybody in your privacy pods!"

The people slowly backed off into their privacy pods, no doubt to open up the StationNet to find out what was happening.

The sidearms had cowed the Human Power mob somewhat, but they still shouted and waved their arms, but finally they entered the brig, and at last the halls were clear of discord.

———

Butch heard bare footsteps approaching. It nauseated him to open his eyes, but he couldn't imagine who would be walking barefoot in the Infirmary but Ophelia. Cautiously he opened his eyes, and sure enough, there she was, her black eyes gazing at him with that liquid love of which only she was capable. He looked at her blue face and smiled, though the action brought on a fresh wave of nausea.

"Butch," she said, her voice ringing with concern. "Okay you are?"

"Sure, fine, no sweat." He was fully aware that she would know what a blatant lie that was, but he couldn't help projecting an image of strength, no matter how preposterous. It was as ingrained into him as faking good health for the doctors. "You okay?" he asked.

"A little scared I am," she confessed, "but fine."

Gingerly he moved his hand and took her slender blue fingers in his. "It's going to be all right. Butch is here."

———

Kramer entered the Infirmary, dreading what he would see. He was, by now, used to seeing Cranius beaten up by mobs of bigots, but he nevertheless dreaded every time he had to sit by his friend's bed.

Dr. Lazarev was in her office. He peeked his head in. "Dr. Lazarev?"

Lazarev was the only one on the Station who was never intimidated by the presence of the President; indeed, he was more intimidated by her. "Yes, Mr. President?" she asked in a tone that served well to convey that she was overloaded with work and this had better be important.

"I was wondering how Cranius is."

"That depends on which piece of him you are talking about," she snapped.

"Please."

Her face softened. "He will be all right."

He sighed with relief and smiled. "That's good. Every time this happens I worry that this time he's not going to pull through."

"Someday he won't. Something must be done to stop this."

"I know. –Can I see him?"

She stood up. "Briefly. He is in room three. This way."

Kramer knew where room three was; Station Post One's Infirmary wasn't very big, but he let her lead the way.

Cranius lay under a white blanket, his jet-black face pinched and his eyes closed. His stump-like arms which protruded from his chest lay over the blanket, his stunted black fingers twitching.

"He awake?" Kramer asked.

At the sound of Kramer's voice, Cranius's eyes opened. "Hi, Damon."

"There is your answer," Lazarev said. She turned to leave, paused and whispered, *"Briefly,"* and went back to her office.

Kramer entered Cranius's room and sat by the bed. "Cranius. How are you feeling?"

"Physically, uh—well, I'm in pain. Emotionally, I am getting really tired of getting beaten up."

"I'm really sorry about this. I'm going to be taking drastic steps to make sure this doesn't happen again."

"Like imposing martial law again?" Cranius' tone was disapproving.

"Not quite that far, but similar."

Cranius closed his eyes and sighed. "Maybe it would be best for all concerned if I were to leave."

Kramer clenched his jaw at the thought. He didn't want Cranius to leave; he couldn't imagine handling the complexities and the stress of being President without his reliable alien friend at his side. "That would be putting a band-aid on the wound. We need to find the source of all this violence and discord and root it out and destroy it."

Cranius opened his eyes to slits and looked at him. "May I say something that you may not want to hear?"

"I always value your advice."

"I think the root cause of it is human nature. I've watched your people since I came aboard. I'm not going to say that we Vron are perfect; we are certainly not. But one thing I have observed about humans is that at the base level, you are very violent people."

Kramer couldn't argue there, but he chuckled and pointed out, "Vron seem to be rather narrow-minded and intolerant people. We all have our flaws."

"I know." Cranius closed his eyes, and for a moment Kramer thought he was asleep. But then he opened his eyes and said, "You're right about the Vron.

We're very bigoted. We're always right about everything. It just seems to me that your people are not willing to live in harmony with other cultures. I don't know why you pretend that's what you want."

Kramer patted Cranius on the arm. "You judge us too harshly. When you're better, I think you'll see things a little more clearly."

Yet as he walked the corridors, back toward the Congressional Pod, Cranius's words haunted him. Could it be that humans only pretended to want harmony with others? Was *he* a hypocrite for reaching out in friendship with the Valdor, the Vron, and others? Could he look himself in the mirror and *truly* claim that he understood other cultures? Or did he, in his heart of hearts, wish other civilizations would change their cultures into something with which he was comfortable?

His thoughts were still churning when he arrived at the Congressional Pod—five minutes late—and took his position at the head of the table. Normal emotions replaced his roiling inner turmoil as he pounded the gavel and declared the Congressional Council in Session.

"I would like to open with a prepared statement to be followed by a motion." He pulled out his linkpad, thumbed the screen to the premarked page, and said, "Esteemed members of the Council, too often in the past year, we have had incidents of violence and assault here on Station Post One, most of them originating with the Human Power movement."

He saw some expressions of disgust; Senator Dallas rolled his eyes.

Kramer looked right at him as he said, "Regardless of anyone's political opinions regarding the presence of aliens on Station Post One, I think we're all in agreement that such violence in the halls of our Station is intolerable."

Dallas remained impassive; Kramer decided to assume he agreed.

"Yet every attempt to curb this tide of violence has failed. We obviously cannot confine a large percentage of our population in the brig. Even if we desired for Station Post One to be a floating prison, we lack the resources to maintain a large population of prisoners for a long period of time. Another solution must be found."

He was relieved to see more than a few nods around the table.

He took a deep breath and continued, "Therefore, I would like to propose that we amend our laws to permit the administry of capital punishment for any crime in which one person deliberately and maliciously injures another or inflicts damage upon the physical structure of our Station."

———

Although Burt Kaisman was positive that the Congressional Council would vote down President Kramer's ridiculous proposition, it was only common sense that he devote his entire show to it. The President slaughtering his own people; that was even better than the recent period of martial law!

"Good afternoon, everyone. Welcome to *Kaisman and Friends*. I'm Burt Kaisman, here as usual with Derek Winchester and Shellie Hurlburt. And today, extraordinary news: 'President' Kramer moves to abolish free speech! Yes, one of our oldest and dearest human rights, dating all the way back to the United States of America, the *original* United States of America. The absolute abolition of the government's ability to restrict what we can say in an open society. Yes, 'President' Kramer has now moved that free speech is punishable by death!

"Since the thirty-sixth century, the death penalty has been reserved for only the most extraordinary cases. When a person has not only committed the most heinous and lethal crimes, but has proven to be impossible to rehabilitate and will always be a continuing danger to society.

"But now, if I speak against our 'president,' I could be put to death! Well, 'President' Kramer doesn't scare me. Let them try to come after me. Let them try to march on my civil rights. No one should be afraid of their government. It should be the other way around; the government should be afraid of the people!"

———

The truth of the matter was, Kramer *was* afraid of the people. He had never seen such a groundswell of irrationality, of hate, of needless anger and violence. And he didn't understand where it was coming from. He had done his best to govern justly, to defend the rights and freedoms of the people and to maintain the peace of the galaxy; and before that, to command Station Post One with level-headedness, logic, and compassion. The mindless hatred and intolerance of anyone and anything nonhuman recalled the bigotry of millennia past, when the human race had divided itself into races. He had thought such primitive impulses had been left far in the past.

Perhaps Cranius was right. Perhaps humans were inherently violent and intolerant. Perhaps it was an unavoidable primate trait, a vestige of their ape ancestry that could never be shaken so long as they retained their organic form.

And yet the alternative was to discard their bodies, to become data incorporated into the structure of the universe—which would create Thermians.

The only remaining option was extinction. For the first time in his life, he began to wonder if that would be for the best.

———

Butch had been, as Tepper put it, in "bubble land" ever since his wedding to Ophelia, but his mood grew darker each day as he saw the hatred continuing to infect the Civilian Hab. The conversations he overheard, many of which repeated verbatim the vitriol spewed by Burt Kaisman, ruined his breakfast, and the security monitors showed far too many people wearing the HP armbands.

When he went down to the Rec Pod for lunch, he found a middle-aged man standing in the doorway with a stack of paper printouts.

"Human Power rally in the Civilian Rec Pod, seven o'clock tomorrow evening. Here, take your brochure. Here, have a brochure, sir."

"No, no, I don't want to come to that," a passing woman said.

"Human Power rally in the Civilian Rec Pod, seven o'clock tomorrow. Here's your brochure, sir."

"No, thank you," said another man.

"Have a brochure."

"Okay, I'll take one," a young guy said, taking one.

"Show your support for the human race. Show your support for the human race. Human Power rally in the Rec Pod tomorrow at seven o'clock."

Butch shoved past the people filing in and demanded, "What is this?!"

"Human Power fundraising rally," the man said in a gentle and friendly tone, "Rec Pod, Civilian Rec Pod, tomorrow at seven o'clock. Have a brochure."

"All right, give me one!" Butch took a brochure, then marched his way down the hall, across the Manway, into the Prime Hab, and up to PHC.

"Here, take a look at this," he said, thrusting the brochure at Commander Dingell. "Human Power fundraising rally tomorrow in the Civilian Rec Pod."

Tobey opened the brochure and looked at it. It was professionally put together, but had a lot of misspellings.

TIED OF THE ALIEN INVESION OF STATION POST ONE?
TIRED OF ALIENS ALWAYS GETTING PREFERENCE WHILE YOUR FORGOTTEN?
WANT TO TAKE A STAND AGAINST AN OPRESIVE GOVERNMENT?

COME TO THE HUMAN POWER FUNDRAISING RALLY IN THE CIVILIAN REC POD AT 7:00 PM ON SATURDAY, DECEMBER 5.

There followed several paragraphs of the usual propaganda floated every day by Burt Kaisman.

"Yeah," Tobey muttered as he looked through it. "Well, nothing we can do about it."

"Well, we ought to keep an eye on it."

"No, leave them alone."

Butch stared at Tobey, uncomprehending. Thinking primarily of Ophelia's safety, he said, "Could lead to trouble."

"I said leave them alone," Tobey snapped. "They have a right to practice their beliefs."

In order to make his point, Butch admitted to something he never would have otherwise. "Yeah, well, I'm still recovering from injuries those thugs inflicted on me!"

"I'm sorry to hear that; just stay away from them. Let them have their rally."

Butch could see he was getting nowhere. He turned and left, furious and confused; up to now, Tobey Dingell had fought against President Kramer's permissive attitude. Butch wondered what had changed, and if there was anything he could do about it.

———

Human Power leader Fabian Marshall was disappointed, and angry, at the small size of the crowd at the fund-raising event. He blamed the news media; SSBC was the only news organization that gave Human Power fair coverage. C-SPONE, Exodus, Starnet, and the others were outrageously biased toward Damon Kramer and his extremist authoritarian policies. Despite his handing out brochures, the word just hadn't gotten out—or people had been poisoned against Human Power by all the alien-loving propaganda.

Nevertheless he resolved not to let on. Burt Kaisman had often said that the secret to public speaking was never to show your anger. Smile and roll with the unexpected. So he smiled and injected good cheer into his voice as he welcomed those who had come.

"Well, I thank you all for coming. I think we'll all have a good time tonight. It's good to see a bunch of smiling human faces there in the audience, and let's hope that Station Post One stays that way."

There was a sprinkling of applause from the pathetically small group, far from the thunderous noise he had hoped would rock the Station.

"Now, we've come a long way. There's no more refugee ships coming through and we've got the Vron civilians off the Station."

That met with gratifying applause—not as loud as he had wished for, but spontaneous and heartfelt.

"But," he said over the applause, "but—but our work's not done. We still have six aliens on the Station."

The small crowd booed—the boos were louder than the applause.

"We still have a president whose loyalties are distinctly alien. We've got a lot of civilians on the Station who still have alien-friendly ideas. The chief of security is married to an alien."

The crowd laughed at that.

"So we have a long way to go. What we need to do is spread our movement, spread our message, and the best way to do that is with money. So that's why we're here tonight."

Some applauded, others brandished their e-cards, ready to donate.

"Now, may I turn things over to one of our most dedicated and influential leaders, the man who negotiated a great victory for our cause with Commander Dingell, Mr. Ti-Hua Chin."

Chin, who was sitting in the first row, got up and came to the podium amid the crowd's applause.

"Thank you, Fabian," he said, grinning broadly. "And thank all of you for coming. It's going to be a great night."

His charismatic speaking brought louder applause than Marshall had managed. Marshall was gratified to see an SSBC journalist in the back of the room recording the event.

"We're going to have a lot of fun," Chin went on, "and I think that's really all we're fighting for. We're human beings, we've survived the destruction of our world, we're fighting a war against the beings who destroyed it, and we'd like to have a little fun in between crises. That's fair, isn't it?"

A chorus of "yeah"s and enthusiastic applause answered him.

"Damon Kramer and his followers are calling us a hate group. My friends, we are not a hate group. They want the civilian population to think that of us because they want to stamp out our free speech. But we are a *love* group. We do this because we love human beings, we love one another, and we want to protect one another from the influence of aliens."

Murmurs of "good point" and "yeah" and "amen" followed that.

"Now, we have nothing against aliens. We love aliens as much as we love humans. We just don't want our spaces, our home, our Station to be given over to them. We don't want our life support, our food supply, our water supply to be cut in order to sustain aliens. We don't want our culture, which is hanging on by a thread since the end of our world, to be contaminated by other ways of living and thinking. And it's already happening. We've seen it with the Sev, who are literally taking over the minds of our brothers and sisters on Fantasia."

Enthusiastic nods and murmurs of agreement and applause rippled through the audience.

"No, my friends, we don't hate aliens. We are not hateful people. We love humans and we love our life here and we are fighting to protect it from those who want to sell us out to aliens!"

Enthusiastic applause. Now Marshall produced his creditron and began walking down the aisle. "Slip your e-cards in here, please."

Every single attendee inserted his or her card, though most tapped in a donation of a dollar or ten dollars; one woman gave thirty. It wasn't much. But the evening was young; there was a lot of time to coax more out of the small and stingy group.

———

Like Butch McCrae, Ebor DuBois was surprised at Tobey's decision to do nothing about the Human Power rally.

He sat next to Tobey in the Prime Hab Center and phrased his concerns with great care. "I don't mean to question, I'm just a little confused about your change of heart about Human Power."

Tobey did not meet DuBois' eye; he stared at his screen as he said, "Well, what Burt Kaisman said yesterday made a lot of sense. People shouldn't be afraid of the government, the government should be afraid of the people. Okay, I'm accommodating the people."

———

Tepper was reading the status reports on spacecraft maintenance when Commander Dingell entered his office without knocking.

"Tepper, what are the arrivals for the next three days?"

Startled—and irritated at the interruption—Tepper minimized the report he was looking at and called up the schedule. "Uh, well, let's see…We've got the Valdor tomorrow, arriving at twelve-twenty hours. The Bala tomorrow at seventeen hundred hours. The Seers are due to arrive Wednesday aboard a Derringan cruiser at eighteen thirty hours. And we've got the Darian delegation Thursday at eighteen hundred hours. Everything after that's still up in the air."

"Cancel all of those," Tobey said abruptly.

Tepper looked up at him, not sure if he had heard or understood correctly. "*All* of them?"

"I'm closing the Station to all aliens." Without further elaboration, Tobey left, leaving Tepper's mind reeling. Well, orders were orders. After all, Tobey was the one who would have to explain his decision to their affronted allies. Tepper obeyed and cleared the arrivals from the schedule.

———

Cranius was in the Prime Hab Center, filing some of the communications from other Republic worlds—one of his duties as file clerk for Intercore—when the message from Vron arrived. Sometimes his work for Intercore and his duties as the President's Chief of Staff overlapped.

He heard the doors open, turned to see Commander Dingell. He got up and approached the commander. "Commander Dingell—Commander Dingell, I've been contacted by my government. I understand that you've shut down the Station to all visits, and the Vron delegation will not be welcome."

"That's correct," Tobey said brusquely.

"Well, um, President Lyskia is going to want to know why."

"It's my decision and the decision's made," Tobey snapped.

Cranius was mystified; he knew Tobey Dingell could be cantankerous, temperamental, and unpredictable, but this decision simply made no sense.

As he sat down at the command desk, Tobey turned to glare at him. "And by the way, you have no business in PHC! Ebor, get security up here."

DuBois started. "*Security?!*" He sounded as appalled as Cranius felt.

"That's what I said, security!" Tobey shouted. "I want all aliens on the Station placed under house arrest!"

Cranius had been placed in protective custody before, which for all intents and purposes was the same as house arrest, but he couldn't understand why Tobey was doing this. It was plain, though, that he would get no answers, so he stood by and awaited security. Maybe Damon could clear this up later.

———

Butch sat in his privacy pod, listening to Tobey's announcement over the intercom. He was livid. Ophelia massaged his shoulders, but even she couldn't think of any words of comfort for him. Fortunately the order would not require her to be confined to the brig, but the injustice of it boiled his blood.

The doorchime sounded. Well, that was quick. Without getting up from his desk, he shouted, "Come in!"

Tepper entered. "Hey, Butch." He was alone. No vanguard of security, no branished sidearm; maybe this visit wasn't about Ophelia.

Butch slowly stood. "Tepper? What can I do for you?"

"Actually I need to talk to Ophelia."

"What want do you?" Ophelia asked.

"I'm sorry. I'm under orders to place you under house arrest."

"But why?"

"The hell you are," Butch said.

"Butch, it's not my decision."

"What the hell's the charge?"

"I'm just following orders to place Ophelia and all the Vron under house arrest."

"But what for?" Butch pressed.

"I don't know. Talk to Commander Dingell."

"I think I will."

"Butch," Ophelia protested, but he was already charging from the room, and it was clear to both Tepper and Ophelia that there was no stopping him.

Tepper turned to Ophelia and said calmly, "Ophelia, let me explain how this works. You won't be taken to the brig, you'll just be required to remain in your privacy pod. If you leave your privacy pod and are caught, well, then you'll be taken to the brig—but I trust you'll be more sensible than your bullheaded husband."

"Will I be," she said, "but under protest do submit I to your arrest. This unjustified is."

"You don't have to tell me. I know it. But I've got my orders."

———

Butch barged into the Prime Hab Center at full throttle, his jaw set, his fists clenched, his head tucked between his shoulders. Everyone who knew him could see he was on the warpath and stayed out of his way.

Tobey Dingell was in the Trench, standing over the communications console and talking to Clio Steele. "Tell them the Station is closed to all outside traffic and that's the end of it."

Butch stormed into the Trench and injected his head between Tobey and Clio. "Commander!"

"The Leezy are wondering about continuing P-SAR delivery," Clio said.

"Tell them to take it up with the Valdor," Tobey snapped, turning his back.

Butch followed him up to the command tier. "Commander? Commander, could I have a word?"

"What do you want, Butch?" Tobey sat down at his command desk, not looking at him.

"Tepper just came to my privacy pod and placed my wife under house arrest."

"I know that. On my orders."

Reining in his anger, Butch asked through clenched teeth, "May I ask why?"

"This is a human station; I don't want aliens running around. It's for her protection as well as to satisfy our own civilians."

Butch was momentarily at a loss for words. He couldn't believe such sentiments could come from Tobey Dingell. "Uh…with all due respect, it sounds like you're caving to Human Power!"

Now Tobey did look at him, his eyes flashing. "I don't have to explain my decisions to you, Butch! The decision's made! Live with it or quit!"

The words stung. As indignant as he was, as sincere as he was about quitting rather than letting Ophelia be tormented, he was sensitive about his reputation as a quitter. He didn't want to be known as a quitter. He still considered himself a man of service, even though he had betrayed that service for personal reasons. His shoulders sagged and he said, "Yes, sir."

He turned and slunk out of PHC, feeling worse than he had before. He wanted to defend his wife and he wanted to do his duty, but he couldn't do both. There was no way out of this situation without feeling lower than a worm. And on top of it all, he had blinked; he had slunk away from Tobey Dingell with his tail between his legs. As the doors closed behind him, he whirled and punched the wall with his fist. It hurt, and as he pulled his fist away he saw that he had cracked the ceramic wall. And the corridor was monitored; they would know he had done it. Damn. So on top of everything else, he would have to pay for the repair.

He headed for the Manway, then changed his mind, turned around, and stormed toward the elevator. He rode it to Dock Deck One, crossed the hangar, and suddenly realized he should have checked to find out if Tepper was here. Well, he had come all this way, might as well just knock on the door and find out.

He came to Tepper's office, found the door open. Tepper was at his desk. He rapped on the doorframe. "Tepper?"

Tepper looked up, rolled his eyes. "Butch, before you say anything, I was just following orders—"

"I know that, I know that. I just want to talk to you."

"Okay, come in. Close that door."

Butch stepped into the office, touched the tab that closed the door. For a moment he felt a wash of nostalgia for his old job; this was *his* office, and he noted with distaste that Tepper had changed things—most egregiously, the picture of Beethoven on the wall had been replaced by a 3D moving photo of Lupo McGrease. Blasphemy! But no time for that now. "Look, I think you and I can agree that Ophelia is harmless."

"Of course she is, but I had my orders."

"Right, right, but why did Tobey give you those orders?"

"How the hell should I know? Ask him!"

"I did. I swear to you, Tepper, he's catering to Human Power."

Tepper shook his head. "That makes no sense. He's been one of the loudest voices against Human Power."

"I know that. That's why this is so bizarre. But that's what he told me, that this is for Ophelia's protection and to satisfy our own civilians—'our own civilians,' he said, but it's obvious what civilians he's talking about."

Tepper shrugged. "Well? I mean, that's a point. She'll be safer locked in her privacy pod than wandering out among those wackos."

"So why lock her up rather than these violent lunatics who are tearing our Station apart? And lower your defense screens, Tepper, I'm not blaming you. I'm trying to bring to your attention that our commander might be unbalanced."

Tepper grew silent. He stared at the desk, drummed his fingers.

Butch broke the silence. "Well, you're not saying anything, so at the very least you're not arguing with me about it."

"Yes I am. When Kramer assumed command of this Station, he selected Dingell as his second-in-command. I've had some issues with Kramer, but he's smart enough not to select someone who's mentally unstable."

"Sure, I agree with you, and I think Tobey's been stable and likeable—until now. I really think the strain of command and Human Power and being blamed for all our problems has just caused him to crack."

Again Tepper grew silent, then let out a long sigh. "Shit. I wish I could disagree with you. He has gotten, I don't know—well, he's changed. Same thing happened to Kramer a couple years ago, but he pulled himself out of it. Tobey seems to be…God. Just a wild man sometimes."

"So what do we do about it?"

"Nothing," Tepper said firmly. "I am an officer of Station Post One and I don't throw that away. I follow my commander's orders even if he seems like a nut case."

"Yeah. I guess that's the difference between us. I'm a quitter."

"You're not a quitter, Butch, you just…"

"I'm a quitter." Butch sighed. "It feels good to be part of something again. Chief of Civilian Security isn't where I want to be; I want to be back behind the controls of a high-performance spacecraft, but—aw, that's besides the point. Look, I'm not suggesting we mutiny or anything, but why don't we at least take our concerns to DuBois? Who knows? Maybe he can set our minds at ease. Maybe there's something going on we don't know about."

"Dangerous. Just bringing it up to the Station's second-in-command could be construed as mutiny."

"Yeah, it could be, but DuBois won't go there. He's a reasonable guy."

Tepper nodded. "Yeah. Well, I guess I would like to get some answers. Fine. But not now. Let's visit him in his privacy pod after shift."

Butch looked up at the wall clock. Still six hours to go. "Damn. Okay. Yeah, that makes sense. I'll meet you here at four bells."

"I'll be here."

Butch left, simultaneously feeling better about himself and worse. At least he was *doing* something—but what he was doing could prove to be disastrous, not only for himself but for Tepper.

———

Ebor DuBois retired to his privacy pod after shift. Tobey had said nothing about going over the daily reports, and since DuBois had no desire to spend an hour alone with Tobey Dingell right now, he did not propose to broach the subject himself.

He sat at the foot of his bed and turned on the entertainment monitor. A *John and Jake* movie was on; he had seen this one: *The Devil-Worshipers*, the most comedic of the pair's outings. He was just getting to the hilarious scene in which John and Jake find themselves in a sewage treatment plant named POOP CENTER (the humor could be crude, but was funny in context) when the doorchime rang. Damn. Some good outrageous fun was what he really needed right now, and he was sure his visitor was Tobey Dingell.

He shut off the entertainment screen and called, "Come in!"

To his relief (sort of), his visitors were Butch McCrae and Elmer Tepper. "Dr. DuBois," Butch said.

Less belligerent than his volatile friend, Tepper said mildly, "Sorry to disturb you at this hour."

"That's all right," DuBois said, not quite accurately. "What's the matter?"

"Ummm," Butch hummed, blushing, "we'd…like to talk to you in strict confidence."

DuBois settled into his seat at his desk, watching them warily. "All right, this is all off the record."

Tepper said, "Butch and I are very concerned about the attitude that Commander Dingell has taken toward Human Power."

"Locking down the Station," Butch said, "placing all the aliens on board under arrest—I mean, it's hardly a way to cultivate a meaningful relationship with our colleagues in the Unified Republic."

Coldly, DuBois asked, "And what are you suggesting I do about it?"

Butch and Tepper looked at each other, abashed. Finally Tepper said, "Well, you're the second. You work more closely with Commander Dingell than any of the rest of us. Can you lay our fears to rest?"

DuBois eyed them each in turn, considering his reply. Slowly he said, "If the commander is acting in a manner that we consider atypical or abnormal, we must consider the possibility that he is acting on information that we don't have."

"That's what we were hoping was the case," Tepper said, "and that's why we're talking to you, because if there's information we don't have, it's probably information he would have shared with you."

"Yeah," Butch agreed. "Has he shared anything with you? Would you mind telling us?"

After a long pause, DuBois said firmly, "Anything Commander Dingell says to me is in confidence."

"I understand that. But as Chief of Civilian Security, I'm awfully worried about the way we're treating our alien guests."

"Including your wife," DuBois pointed out.

"I admit I've got a conflict of interest."

Tepper chimed in, "And because of that conflict of interest, it was up to me to place her under house arrest. I really didn't like doing that."

"Well, thank you for bringing your concerns to my attention," DuBois said. "You both have your duties to perform, and I promise you that no one will learn of this conversation."

It was clear from the way Tepper stiffened that he had made his point: that their actions here amounted to conspiracy to mutiny.

But Butch was not so keen to take the hint. "So…that's it?"

"That's all I have to say. Thank you."

Tepper gripped Butch's arm. "Come on, Butch. Let's get out of here."

As Tepper tugged him toward the door, Butch squirmed loose. "Look, I just want to know, is this some sort of way to try to—"

"Butch, we tried. Come on, let's go." Tepper grabbed Butch's arm again and pulled.

"Dismissed!" DuBois snapped.

Butch again fought free of Tepper's grasp. "All right! All right." He gave DuBois an acid glare as he followed Tepper out.

DuBois went back to the love seat and turned *The Devil Worshipers* back on. He was surprised how long the confrontation with Butch and Tepper had taken; it was already the climactic ending when the Devil Worshipers had incarnated Satan in the form of a giant Charlie McCarthy dummy who stomped through the city thundering "YEAH, YEAH, YEAH!" and breathing fire. DuBois could no longer find it in himself to laugh.

He waited until the end of the movie, just to be sure Butch and Tepper were well and truly gone. As John and Jake turned to each other, gave each other the thumbs-up and gave their trademark "*Nuuuu!*" and the screen faded to black, DuBois got up, turned the screen off, and headed over to Tobey's privacy pod.

Hoping Tobey hadn't already gone to bed—he was irritable enough when not awakened from deep sleep—DuBois sounded the doorchime.

"Who is it?" Tobey's irritated voice called.

"DuBois."

"Come in."

DuBois entered, found Tobey lying in bed with a book. Curious, DuBois squinted to read the title: THE QV FIGHTER: THE EPIC STORY OF THE TROUBLED DESIGN AND CONSTRUCTION OF THE SPACECRAFT THAT CHANGED EVERYTHING by Fernando Sanchez.

"I thought I asked not to be disturbed," Tobey said.

"I needed to talk to you in private."

Tobey set the book aside and sat up. "All right, what is it?"

DuBois crossed the room and sat in the divan at the foot of the bed. He stared at Tobey, firmed himself, and asked bluntly, "Have you been bought off by Human Power?"

For a moment Tobey did not answer; he merely stared in disbelief at DuBois. Then he asked, "What the hell kind of a question is that?"

"A fair one, I think, considering the strange decisions you've been making."

"Like safeguarding the safety of the Vron and Ophelia by placing them under house arrest?"

"And closing off the Station to our allies in the Unified Republic."

"Do you want more riots on the Station? More beatings?"

DuBois considered how to answer. "Is that how we operate now? Surrender to criminals?"

"No! We operate by obeying the Commander's orders! Thank you. That's all." Tobey lay down again and picked up his book.

DuBois knew it was fruitless to pursue this further—at least with Tobey. He got up and left. He started toward his privacy pod, stopped, and pondered whether to take this matter further.

Considering Tobey's weird, unpredictable behavior, and the fact that he had already been approached by Butch and Tepper, he decided the situation had escalated to the point that he should at least bring it to Kramer's attention.

He reached the Presidential Pod at 2310 hours; he hoped the President wasn't asleep. He rang the doorchime.

"Who is it?" Kramer's voice called.

He didn't sound groggy; good. "Dr. DuBois."

"Oh. Come in."

DuBois entered; the President was at his desk as usual; DuBois almost smiled as he imagined Kramer growing roots into the chair. "Mr. President, I'm sorry for coming to see you so late—"

"You're always welcome, Ebor. What is it? Is there a problem?"

"I don't know. But I wanted to talk to you about Commander Dingell." He described his meeting with Butch and Tepper, though he left out their names, and he told of his own meeting with Tobey.

Kramer chuckled. "Tobey Dingell would never take a bribe."

"Then how do you explain the weird decisions that he's making?"

"Ebor..." Kramer got up and paced, frowning. "You weren't in command of Station Post One for very long—probably less than a day. How did you like it?"

DuBois answered honestly: "I didn't like it at all."

"I commanded Station Post One for three years. It's a rough job. You have to make all kinds of difficult decisions."

"I just feel that Butch and Tepper have a point—" DuBois quickly realized he had slipped; he hadn't meant to mention them by name. No matter; it had been clear that Kramer had guessed who he was talking about. He went on in hopes that Kramer had missed, or would ignore, his slip. "We're alienating our allies in the Republic—and especially by placing our Vron guests under house arrest—"

"Ebor, Tobey is the commander."

DuBois was cowed by the anger in Kramer's voice; he hadn't expected that from the usually mild and understanding President. "I have full faith and confidence in him. This conversation is over."

Startled, surprised, and hurt, DuBois slowly stood. "Well, thank you for your time."

"My pleasure." Kramer's more typical mild tone was back, but DuBois was nevertheless put in his place. He left, his anger growing.

———

Burt Kaisman was not feeling well. He had felt weak and nauseous all night, and this morning he had had trouble urinating. He was tired and confused.

Meyer was at school, and Deb had gotten up and gone to work while he was still sweating and suffering in bed, and so no one advised him against going to work today. Still, he was running late, which was very unusual for him. He usually showed up at 0900 to prep for the show; it was 1015 by the time he arrived, his hair unkept and his suit crooked.

As they did his makeup, he surprised everyone by getting up and rushing to the bathroom to throw up. When he returned he felt better.

When he entered the broadcast booth, he began to cough—a hacking, wracking cough that he was afraid would bring up his breakfast. But he regained control of himself and directed his attention and his energy to doing the show. His body usually kept its weaknesses at bay when the cameras were rolling.

"You okay, Burt?" Derek Winchester asked.

"I'm all right," Kaisman lied.

"You don't look so good."

"Probably something I had for breakfast. Let's go on the air."

The director, seated behind the glass partition behind them, spoke, his voice sounding in Kaisman's earpiece, "And in five...four...three..." He mouthed "two" and "one," and the theme music began.

Kaisman felt flushed and disoriented and looked at the wrong camera as the show started. "Good afternoon, everyone. This is Burt Kaisman, and welcome to *Kaisman and Friends*. I'm here with Derek Winchester and Shellie Hurlburt. And today we're talking about the mysterious and fascinating change of heart by Commander Dingell." Kaisman said the words, but his usual passion was absent. "Yes, it would—ah—seem that Commander Dingell has placed all aliens on the Station under house arrest and closed the Station off to all alien visitors. This is a fascinating development, for it seems Commander Dingell has acceded to all of the people's demands, everything we might have asked of him. But is this change of heart genuine, or is he doing this for some mysterious political reason? It is hard to imagine what political advange he may gain by completely flipping around and alienating his dear friend President Kramer, but perhaps he has finally listened to the people and has determined to give the people what they want. What do you think of this, Derek?"

Winchester had watched him with concern, but when Kaisman threw to him, he carried on as if all was normal. "I think it's most likely that he's just giving in to popular demand. He does represent the people, whether he likes it or not." Noticing Kaisman's pallid features, Winchester lost his train of thought and filled the silence with nervous laughter. "Well, why don't we go to a break and hear from our sponsor?" He turned toward the director. "Let's go to a break, what do you say?"

"Let's go to break," the director agreed, signaling the producer.

"We're in a five-minute break," the producer replied.

"Is he all right?" Shellie Hurlburt asked.

Winchester leaned over. "Burt, are you sure you're all right?"

Kaisman waved him aside. "I'm just not feeling well."

Winchester's eyes widened as he studied Kaisman's face. "Burt, you're yellow!"

"Uh…it's come and goes. Let's just wait for it to pass. I'll be fine."

"Burt, I'm not kidding! You're yellow! I think you'd better go to the Infirmary."

Kaisman got up, feeling sick again. "I think I'd better just get to the bathroom." He rushed urgently from the booth.

As he vomited his guts out, breathing deeply, his chest hurt. He hated to admit it, but Derek was right; there was no way he could get through a three-hour show. Slowly, he got up, flushed the toilet, and headed back into the studio.

The station manager accosted him on the way out. "Hey, Burt?"

"Mr. Cromwell?"

"Hey, we've been watching and we've been talking about it back in the control room, and we think you'd better sit it out today. Go to the Infirmary."

"I'm feeling a lot better now."

"Hey, Derek was right, man. You really are yellow. You're trembling, you're barely holding it together. But yellow skin, that's a sign of a serious condition. I think you'd better get to the Infirmary right now. Derek will handle the rest of the show for you."

Well, there was no arguing with the station manager. And he had to admit, he did feel awful. The gravity of Cromwell's tone chilled Kaisman. "All right. All right."

As he left the studio and faced the long, winding journey to the Infirmary, he wondered just how smart this was. He wished Station Post One had some sort of internal transport vehicles—something to bring up in a future show. He staggered down the hall, thankful for the intermittent public restrooms.

He felt vertiginous as he went through the Manway; the small tube felt as though it were swaying back and forth and in circles as he navigated through it—but when he stepped through on the other end in the Prime Hab, he didn't feel much better.

Finally he reached the Infirmary, and the attendant immediately saw his distress and ran to catch him. "Sir, right over here, right over here."

He was escorted into an examining room and lay down gratefully on the bed.

Dr. Lazarev arrived within minutes. "Mr. Kaisman." She smiled. "Well. Having a bad day, are we? Well, we will get you fixed up." She scanned him with a whirring instrument. "Have you been feeling ill?"

"It's been happening on and off for a couple weeks, but I didn't make anything of it because it always got better. But this morning it's just been constant."

Lazarev turned to the nurse who had escorted him in here. "I need a blood sample and a urine sample."

"Right away," the nurse said. He leaned over Kaisman and felt his back. "Let's just ease over into the restroom. Think you can pee for me?"

"I'll certainly try."

"Have you been having trouble peeing?" Lazarev asked.

Kaisman nodded, embarrassed at the discussion.

"Is it pain or is it just not coming?"

"Just not coming."

"Well, let's just see what you can give us."

Once the bathroom door was closed, and he found himself standing alone in a stall the size of his closet, he was surprised that he was indeed able to provide half a cup. He placed the cup in the cabinet next to him and shut the door, then left into the arms of the nurse.

"All come out good?" the nurse asked.

"Well…it came out."

The nurse laughed. "Well, let's get you back to bed and take a quick little blood sample. Won't hurt a bit."

Kaisman had to admit he felt a little better to be in the care of medical professionals.

———

DuBois was in his cubicle in the Wheel. He didn't really have anything in particular to do, but he was avoiding working alongside Tobey Dingell in PHC. There was always something to study; a supernova had been detected in the Triangulum Galaxy, and he was curious if there were Thermians there.

He heard a throat clear. He looked up and was surprised to see Dr. Marfida Lazarev. "May I speak to you, Dr. DuBois?"

"Certainly."

"I have a new patient: Burt Kaisman."

"Oh. Did someone finally shoot him?"

Lazarev looked disgusted. "No!"

"Sorry, sorry. So what's the matter with him?"

"Severe liver damage from overindulgence in alcohol. He will need a transplant."

"You've typed him, I assume?"

"Yes, of course! But I do not have a compatible liver on hand."

"Oh."

"So I was hoping you could see if you have any good cadavers lying around with good livers."

As far as DuBois could recall, no one on the Station had died recently, but there could easily have been some incident, or a death by natural causes, that hadn't come to his attention. "Well, I'll check and see what we've got."

"Thank you."

DuBois checked his records; the last deaths in the log were three weeks ago, when the SSBC Studios had been attacked by Vron terrorists who had then gone on and killed a hostage in the Rec Pod. The bodies of all the victims had already been buried in space or recycled.

"No, we haven't had any recent casualties. But I find it hard to believe that after all the battles and wars we've fought in the past several years that you don't have a really good, solid organ bank with everything you could imagine!"

"Organs are perishable," Lazarev explained.

DuBois sighed. "Then what else is there?"

"Not much…unless we have someone with a terminal disease with a compatible liver who'd be willing to donate."

"Well, do we?"

Lazarev shook her head. "Not on the Station."

"Well, the Republic worlds can't help; they're all aliens. Even when they have equivalent organs—"

"What about nearby colonies? Or the *Silver Streak* or one of our other ships?"

"All right, I'll contact the *Silver Streak* and the *Exodus*, see if they've got anything for us."

Lazarev left. DuBois saved his data, got up, and went up to the Prime Hab Center. He spotted Tobey at the command desk and sat next to him. "Commander, we've got a problem with Burt Kaisman."

"Ebor! Damn it, you said you'd be in the Wheel for the next three hours!"

"Well, yes, but I need to talk to you."

"You're my second-in-command. You need to be where I can find you in case I need you!"

"Well…here I am. If you need me—"

"All right, skip it. What about Burt Kaisman?"

DuBois explained the situation.

"Okay," Tobey said, "we'll contact the *Silver Streak*, the *Exodus*, the *Phoenix*, and any colonies in a few days' light speed range." He frowned. "In the meantime, we still…we've got a lot of people on board who support the incursion of aliens on our Station. Yeah, we can screen them."

DuBois was confused. "What are you talking about?"

"Starting with Butch McCrae. He's an alien-lover; he married an alien."

"I don't follow you."

"Those are expendable members of our population. We can take their liver if we need to."

DuBois gaped at Tobey; surely he could not be suggesting what it sounded like he was suggesting! "You're not serious!"

"A man's life is at stake, a highly valuable man." Tobey spoke without conviction, but with firmness.

"Tobey," DuBois stammered. He was at a loss for words. Surely this was a farce. "Hasn't this gone a little far?"

"I'll handle it."

DuBois sputtered nonsense words, flabbergasted, before managing to form a coherent sentence. "I have to discourage this." A ridiculously low-key response, but DuBois didn't know what else to say to his commanding officer.

"I'll handle it!" Tobey raged. "That's all! Dismissed!"

DuBois stared at him. He was now convinced that Butch and Tepper were right: Tobey had lost his mind. But what could he do about it? The crew members in the Trench were glancing his way; he couldn't make a scene in front of them. He needed time to think. He muttered, "Yes, sir," and hurried out.

He knew he should go to the Wheel, because that was where Tobey would expect to find him, but instead he went down to Dock Deck One. He hoped Tepper would be in his office.

He was. "Tepper?"

Tepper looked up. "Dr. DuBois!"

"Please don't get up." DuBois entered. "We need to talk." He told him about his meeting with Tobey.

Tepper gaped. "He wants to force Butch to donate his liver?!"

DuBois nodded. "That's what he said."

"He can't be serious."

"He sounded serious to me."

"Look..." Tepper looked around the room at nothing in particular, fumbling for words. "I don't know what Commander Dingell's been up to lately, but *that*...not only is it illegal, but it's downright insane!"

"I agree with you. And you know I'm committing a serious breach of regulations by talking to you about this."

Tepper got up and started to pace. "What's going on with him? This goes beyond being bought off by Human Power. The man's got to have lost his mind! Have you considered something like...like mind control from some sort of radio transmitter or something?"

In point of fact, DuBois had considered it, but as a scientist had dismissed it. "There's no evidence of such a thing, and we shouldn't go leaping to outlandish conclusions."

"Outlandish conclusions! This is already pretty outlandish!"

DuBois couldn't argue with that. It wouldn't make sense for this to be a manifestation of insanity, because Tobey's new attitude was profoundly opposite everything he had believed in until now. If Tobey had indeed been driven over the edge by the stress, he would more likely be ordering the execution of Human Power members, not suddenly aligning himself with them. But mind control? Who would have the capability of doing that?

Well, SSBC was a broadcasting station; it wasn't beyond the realm of scientific possibility for them to have some sort of subliminal transmitter—but what would be the receiving mechanism? How would it transmit into Tobey's brain? That would only work if someone had implanted something into Tobey—but who would have done that? And when? No, that was adding too many improbable variables to an already unsupported hypothesis. The explanation must lie elsewhere.

————

Butch took the news rather well. In fact, Tepper was puzzled when Butch actually broke down in laughter.

"Gee," Tepper said, "I hope I find it as funny when the commander of the Station comes after my life."

"Sorry, sorry, it's not funny, it's not funny at all. It's just that this thing has gotten so ridiculous it's turned into a comedy."

"I fail to see how."

"If they'd made an immie about this, I'd scoff at it and say it can't happen in real life."

"Well, it can happen and it's happening. I don't know what to tell you to do, but you can't sit there and take it."

"It's not going to happen," Butch said with certainty. "I mean, Tobey doesn't have the authority to order me to donate my liver. If he tries to, I'll just say no. What's he going to do? Have security grab me and take me to the Infirmary? And then what? Is Dr. Lazarev going to do that without my signing a consent form? Hell, would she do it even if I did sign a consent form? No. I'm not worried about this actually happening. What I'm worried about is that Tobey's gone so off his rocker that he would even say such a thing."

"So what do we do?"

"I don't know." Butch looked at Ophelia, who stood in the corner wearing an expression of concern. "What do you think?"

"Confused am I," she said. "This unlike Tobey Dingell is. Must there be something going on unaware of are we."

"Must be," Butch agreed. "I don't know what the explanation is, but there's got to be one—some other explanation than that Tobey's gone off the rails insane. And I'm going to find out what it is if I have to turn the Station upside-down." He opened a cabinet and pulled out a deerstalker hat and gourd Calabash pipe. "Always wanted to wear this." He put on the hat and put the pipe in his mouth. "When you eliminate the impossible, dear Watson, whatever remains, however improbable, must be the truth."

"What the hell are you doing?" Tepper asked.

"I'm commencing the investigation."

———

As long as Tobey intended on killing him, Butch figured he had nothing to lose by visiting him and confronting him. He marched up to the Commander's privacy pod and rang the doorchime.

"Come in," Tobey called.

Butch found Tobey at his entertainment center, watching SSBC's evening show, *The Naked Truth With Henrietta Malodora*, who was yelling and screaming about Damon Kramer's conspiracy to poison all the food with nanotech germs lethal to humans but beneficial to aliens.

"Commander," Butch said.

Tobey turned off the program. "The woman makes some good points. Jesus, I never realized what Damon was capable of."

Butch chose not to weigh in on that non sequitur. "Can I talk to you a minute?"

"Yeah, Butch, what can I do for you?" Tobey made no comment about Butch's unusual attire, which now included a nineteeth century overcoat and pocketwatch.

"This whole thing has gone too far," Butch said. "Your behavior has just gotten bizarre. You're not taking my liver!"

Tobey crossed the room to his desk and hit an icon, activating the Stationwide intercom.

———

Tepper looked up as Tobey's voice echoed through the Station. "Would you mind saying that again?"

Butch's voice replied, "I said you are not taking my liver. I think it goes way beyond your powers as Commander to order me to give up an organ that sustains my life."

"As an officer of Station Post One, you've always known that part of your duty may involve giving up your life to save the lives of civilians. Burt Kaisman is a civilian, and he will die unless he has a liver transplant."

"You cannot order *anyone* to give up a vital organ!"

"Do you have a better idea? This is the way it works, Butch. Burt Kaisman is a patriot and a true human who has stood up for our founding principles. You, on the other hand, are an alien-lover. You married an alien, you quit your job for an alien—your clear duty is to give your liver to this man."

"There are other alternatives. A new liver could be grown."

"You're advocating *cloning?!* Is there no end to your perversions? Why don't you go back to your privacy pod, have one last night with your alien wife, and—"

"No, it doesn't work that way. I'm not giving up my liver. I'm not giving up my life to Burt Kaisman."

"*Get the fuck out of my privacy pod!*" There came the sound of a scuffle.

Butch's "That was uncalled for!" sounded strained, as if in the middle of a physical altercation. Then came the sounds of scuffling across the floor, punctuated by grunts and *oof*s and shattering of fragile objects.

Tepper grabbed his sidearm and said aloud, "I'd better go see what's going on up there."

When he arrived at Tobey's privacy pod, he found four security officers clustered around with their sidearms drawn. The door was still closed, but Don Mendelsohn was reaching for the override key.

"Hey, guys, wait!" Tepper called. "Wait, let me go in." He pushed past them as Mendelsohn turned the key.

The room was less of a shambles than he had expected, but there was Butch, his nineteenth century overcoat torn and his Sherlock Holmes hat on the floor—next to the sprawled body of Tobey Dingell, head cracked against the bedframe.

"Butch!" Tepper gasped.

Butch was breathless, frantic. "Tepper—I didn't mean to hurt him, I swear to God I didn't mean to hurt him."

"Medical team!" Tepper shouted.

"I didn't mean to hurt him," Butch said again. "I swear to God it was self-defense."

"Calm down, calm down."

"He came at me, he was like a wild man, I had to do something, I—he fell against the bed—"

"It's all right, Butch, it's all right, Butch, but I am going to have to place you under arrest."

"I swear to God, Tepper, I swear to God I didn't mean to—"

"Butch!" Tepper grabbed Butch's shoulders and shook him. "Don't say anything more! All right? Please! Please."

"Tepper…"

"Now, you have the right to remain silent. Anything you say can be held against you. You have the right to legal representation. You have the right to challenge this arrest through the command section or through Civilian Security. You have the right to a supervised communication with anyone on the outside. Do you understand these rights?"

Pale, Butch whimpered through Tepper's recital, then snapped, "*Of course* I understand these rights—"

"Then please! Submit peacefully and don't make this look any worse than it already does."

Butch nodded. "All right, all right, all right. Okay."

———

DuBois heard the altercation over the PA system, as everyone on the Station had, and as soon as he received confirmation that Tobey had been moved, went down to the Infirmary.

Tobey lay in intensive care, his heart monitor beeping steadily.

Dr. Lazarev met him outside the room.

"Well?" DuBois asked.

"A severe concussion," Lazarev said. "He will be all right, but I must insist that he remain here for observation for three days."

"That means I'm in command, and as long as I am, there are going to be some changes around here."

"I hope so."

"Is there anything you need?"

Lazarev shrugged. "Time."

"Okay. I'll be in PHC if you need me."

He went up to PHC, expecting every face to stare at him as he entered. But life went on; everyone went about his or her duties and paid no mind to him as he entered and sat at the command desk.

"Jerry, I have PHC."

Flynn, sitting next to him, said, "Marked, Acting Commander has PHC."

On the way up, DuBois had mentally rehearsed what he was going to say. Now he took a few moments to finalize his thoughts, then stood and announced, "Could I have everyone's attention please?"

The Trench grew silent except for those who were communicating with other parts of the Station, and they quickly sent a hushed "Stand by," and turned to face DuBois.

"Mr. Flynn, make an entry in the log. As of right now, 1503 hours, I am assuming command of Station Post One due to Commander Dingell's injury. Please get me Civilian Security."

"Yes, sir," Flynn said. "Civilian Security, PHC."

"Civilian Security," the intercom crackled, "Pereira."

"This is Acting Commander Ebor DuBois. I am ordering immediate suspension of the house arrest of the Vron and Ophelia of the Etuknips."

"Yes, sir."

"Mr. Flynn, I'm lifting lockdown."

"Yes, sir."

"Inform the other worlds of the Unified Republic that Station Post One is open and delegations will be welcome."

"Yes, sir."

DuBois knew that Tobey would be furious—perhaps out of control—when he came back on duty, but nevertheless he was sure he was doing the right thing. If Tobey lost control in PHC, in front of witnesses, then DuBois would be within his right to relieve him of command on his own authority. He may well have to stand court-martial, but he would have plenty of evidence to aquit himself.

"Mr. Flynn, you're my new second-in-command."

"Yes, sir."

"Take over. I'll be in the Infirmary."

"Yes, sir."

Recalling that it was Flynn who had started the Galactic Civil War, DuBois left PHC with a feeling of unease, telling himself Flynn would not dare countermand him.

He found Dr. Lazarev in the intensive care ward, examining the unconscious Burt Kaisman.

"Dr. Lazarev."

"Dr. DuBois." Her tone was brusque; they never had gotten along, though they respected each other as colleagues.

"How's Tobey doing?"

"He will be fine. I'm giving him some cerebronol to speed up the healing process, but basically he just needs a few days bed rest. It's Kaisman I'm worried about."

"I see." DuBois couldn't summon up any sympathy for Kaisman, and he was ashamed of himself for it.

"Time is short," Lazarev said. "My facilities are limited. I need a new liver, and unless we find a donor, I will need to do something drastic."

"What do you mean?"

She lowered her voice and said, "Human cloning. I would like to clone him a new liver. It will take a week, based on the old records, and will require no surgery. It can be grown in his body."

"If you're asking my permission—"

"Cloning is a bit like nanotech. People fear it."

DuBois looked at the unconscious Kaisman. Funny; with his mouth closed he didn't look like a vitriolic extremist who devoted his life to riling up the most vile and hateful of human nature. He was just a patient. And for a moment, just a moment, DuBois did feel something akin to compassion for him. "Do what you need to do."

An orderly stuck her head in the door. "Dr. Du—I mean, *Commander* DuBois?"

"Yes?"

"The President is on the intercom for you."

DuBois went out into the reception area and leaned over the receptionist's console. "Mr. President? DuBois here."

"Dr. DuBois," Kramer's voice answered, "please come to my office."

"On my way."

On his way across the sprawling Station, DuBois wondered what the President wanted to see him for. He wondered if he had exceeded his authority by utilizing his three-day command to reverse Tobey's policies. Yet surely Kramer could not be in favor of those policies....

When he reached the Presidential Pod, a Secret Service officer conducted him in. Kramer stood next to his desk in a four-cummerband suit, gesturing for DuBois to sit. DuBois did so. Kramer sat across from him, regarded him for a moment, then spoke.

"You were concerned about Tobey's strange decisions."

"Yes. So were Butch and Tepper. So were a lot of people. It was just a complete one-eighty from all of his previous behavior patterns."

"Yes." The President was silent a moment, staring at his desk, before saying, "Did it occur to you that perhaps Commander Dingell was acting on information that you did not at the time possess?"

DuBois frowned. "Yes. That occurred to me. But in such circumstances, it's standard procedure for the commander to confide in his second."

"Yes, that is standard procedure. But perhaps in this instance there was valid reason not to confide in you."

DuBois was puzzled. "Are you saying that there's information that I'm not privy to?"

"Yes. Commander Dingell was acting under orders—my orders."

"*Your* orders?" DuBois stared at Kramer as though seeing him for the first time.

"Tobey and I discussed it together. The Station has a serious problem. Human Power is growing, becoming more militant, and they have a major mouthpiece in the form of Burt Kaisman. But how do we snuff them out without restraining their human rights? How do we handle security on this Station without confining a large percentage of the population to the brig indefinitely?"

"Well, that's why you went to the Congressional Council to approve capital punishment for minor offenses."

"Yes—not because I would like to impose that punishment, but in hopes of frightening people into behaving themselves—but discipline through coercion is not my preferred method. And it never works. What we have to do is try to change people's minds. So Tobey and I hit on the idea of embracing the most militant aspects of Human Power. By very publicly addressing all of Human Power's demands and going totally off the deep end with it, we were hoping to stir up widespread opposition to those policies that would stamp out Human Power's influence forever."

DuBois eyed the President, dubious of this plan. "And I noticed that *you* were not embracing Tobey's militant attitude."

Kramer nodded. "The people needed a more level-headed voice to turn to."

"And gain you re-election."

"That may have been a by-product, but..." Kramer chuckled. "I'd be just as happy to give up this job."

"Tobey was talking about forcing Butch to donate his liver to Burt Kaisman."

"Yes, and Tobey deliberately provoked Butch into attacking him. Now Tobey is a martyr to Human Power."

"And what becomes of Butch? What becomes of the aliens who are being targeted?"

"Polls indicate it's working. There's already widespread opposition against Human Power. Even many of Human Power's members are turning away, finding the whole thing to be too extreme to be palatable."

"May I speak candidly?" DuBois tried to keep the disgust out of his voice.

"Of course."

"I don't agree with this. I don't intend to shut out our Republic comrades. I don't intend to place innocent aliens under arrest. For as long as I'm in command—"

"That's fine. That's fine. I don't think anyone would believe you making a turnaround like that anyway. But hopefully, by the time Tobey returns to command, the situation will be over with."

DuBois squirmed. "I don't like lying to the people."

"Well, I don't either. But being President has forced me to learn a lot about politics. Leading by example—*bad* example. By showing people the worst way to be, I have faith that they will choose the best way to be."

"You have faith." DuBois stood. "I never was much of a man of faith. Are we done here?"

"We're done."

As DuBois turned to leave, Kramer called after him, "The only time you were a man of faith was when you were a Satan-worshiper."

DuBois turned and faced him. "That's right. And I still agree with the basic tenets of the Church of the Inverse: free inquiry and rationalism, the fundamentals of science."

Before going back to the Prime Hab Center, he stopped first at the brig and unlocked Butch's cell.

"Butch?"

Butch got up from the bunk, puzzled. "Dr. DuBois."

"You're free."

Butch's eyes widened. "I am?"

"Charges dropped. It's my determination that Commander Dingell attacked you and that you injured him in self-defense."

Butch exhaled, bordering on a giddy laugh. "Thanks—is—is he going to be okay?"

"Yes, he's going to be just fine. You're restored to full duty status."

Butch couldn't keep the silly smile off his face. "Thanks, Dr. DuBois. What a relief. Thanks."

———

Butch practically skipped all the way to his privacy pod. He burst in on Ophelia while she was dusting (having nothing else to do, she had been obsessively cleaning the chamber ever since her house arrest), surprising her with a big "*Ta-da!*"

"Butch!" She ran into his arms. "What doing you are out of the brig?"

"I'm free!" He lifted her off her feet and spun her round and kissed her. "I'm free. All charges dropped."

She hugged him. "Wonderful that is! And something on the intercom heard I all the aliens freed being on the Station."

"That's right, Ophelia, the lockdown is over and all house arrests are ended."

"Free I am?"

"You bet you are!"

She hugged him again. "Thank you, Butch. How do it did you?"

"Aw, I'd love to take the credit, but it wasn't me."

"Not does matter it. Always you for me there are. Always you count on I can."

"You bet. You bet!" He kissed her again, and soon had lowered her onto the bed.

Another two hours of house arrest wouldn't hurt her.

———

When Tobey awakened and saw the recovery room around him, he was confused. Then he remembered that this was exactly where he was supposed to be. The memories came back quickly and he pieced together what must have happened: Butch had defended himself and had injured him worse than expected. He had lost consciousness and been taken to the Infirmary. He wondered how badly hurt he was. He *felt* okay.

Then he heard a derisive chuckle and an aristocratic British voice said, "So you're awake."

He looked to his left and saw Burt Kaisman. Now the fog of sleep and medication cleared and he remembered. Dr. Lazarev had explained that he had a concussion. He had been recovering for three days and would be discharged soon. Kaisman had, meanwhile, been growing a new kidney.

Tobey closed his eyes. "Yep. Looks that way. How you feeling?"

"Well, there's some pain in my abdomen, but Dr. Lazarev says that's normal. You?"

"Oh, fine."

"So tell me…we've all been wondering about your miraculous turnaround. And of course, here we are, in private, no eavesdroppers. So tell me—if I promise not to say anything on the air…is your turnaround genuine or is this some sort of clever political move?"

Tobey didn't know what to say. He had hated all this lying. He had hated spouting ideas he detested. But he knew his duty. Or he thought he did. He let out a deep breath and said, "I'm going to tell you the truth, Kaisman: I don't even know anymore what sincerity is."

Kaisman closed his eyes and smiled, and Tobey knew that he had just provided a perfect quote.

WATCH FOR

THE SECOND COMING

THE NEXT ADVENTURE OF

**VOYAGE INTO THE UNKNOWN
STATION POST ONE**

VOYAGE INTO THE UNKNOWN
Collect the whole series!

SHORT STORY COLLECTIONS
Voyage Into the Unknown: Volume One
Voyage Into the Unknown: Volume Two
Voyage Into the Unknown: Volume Three
Voyage Into the Unknown: Volume Four
Voyage Into the Unknown: Volume Five
Voyage Into the Unknown: Volume Six

NOVELS
Voyage Into the Unknown
Voyage Into the Unknown 2: The Victory of Mordrax
Voyage Into the Unknown 3: Back From the Future
Voyage Into the Unknown 4: A Fond Farewell
Voyage Into the Unknown 5: The New Beginning
Voyage Into the Unknown 6: The Mind Machine
Voyage Into the Unknown 7: Passage to Hyron
Voyage Into the Unknown 8: The Reign of Edmonds
Voyage Into the Unknown 9: The Krotus Horror
Voyage Into the Unknown 10: The Thermian Menace
Voyage Into the Unknown 11: The Armageddon Strategy
Voyage Into the Unknown 12: Resurrection
Voyage Into the Unknown 13: Revelation

STATION POST ONE
The Priest Monster
Uneasy Alliance
"That's What They Want You to Believe"
Countdown to War
A Galaxy in Ruin
Loved and Lost
To Conquer the Dreb
Repercussions
A Station Divided
The Thermian Destiny
The Last of Zach Mortimer

View the series and buying options at
 https://www.deviantart.com/voyageintotheunknown/gallery/51355952/bookstore

www.ingramcontent.com/pod-product-compliance
Lightning Source LLC
Chambersburg PA
CBHW061505120726
48001CB00004B/1217